Surviving The Evacuation

Book 4: Unsafe Haven

Frank Tayell

Dedicated to my family (thanks for the title!)

ISBN-13: 978-1505408768
ISBN-10: 1505408768

The Lord of the Rings - Copyright J.R.R. Tolkein
To Serve Them All My Days - Copyright RF Delderfield

Other titles:

Strike A Match
1. Serious Crimes
2. Counterfeit Conspiracy

Work. Rest. Repeat.
A Post-Apocalyptic Detective Novel

Surviving The Evacuation
Zombies vs The Living Dead
Book 1: London
Book 2: Wasteland
Book 3: Family
Book 4: Unsafe Haven
Book 5: Reunion
Book 6: Harvest
Book 7: Home
Here We Stand 1: Infected

For more information, visit:
http://blog.franktayell.com
http://twitter.com/FrankTayell
www.facebook.com/TheEvacuation

Prologue: Fugitive
Kensington, London

22nd February

Chester ran. He knew the police were chasing him; he could hear their engines. In the hope of finding somewhere to hide, he dived into an alley. His foot slipped on a sodden newspaper. Off-balance he reached out, searching for something to catch his fall. He found a bin. It was empty, and toppled over under his weight. Falling face first onto the damp ground, he was about to curse when the alley was lit up by the red and blue lights of a police car. He lay very still, not even daring to breathe. Finally, the lights faded as the police car drove on. He allowed himself to exhale, but he couldn't relax. Not when he could still hear the vehicle patrolling a few streets away.

He got to his feet and took a moment to think. If they found him, they'd shoot him. It wouldn't matter if it was because he'd jumped out of the back of the van, or because he was now breaking curfew. They would shoot him and they wouldn't hesitate. He'd seen that at the supermarket. When they'd frogmarched him and a dozen others out of the cells, he'd had no idea what was going on. And he'd had no idea since they'd arrested him. Even when he'd asked to see his lawyer, they'd ignored him. He'd assumed it had something to do with the rumours he'd heard while he'd been in the cells. There was some talk about a viral outbreak in the U.S. The ports and airports had been closed. Martial law had been implemented along with a curfew. And there had been weird outlandish talk of zombies. He'd ignored those as too absurd to be true.

Along with a dozen others, he'd been bundled into the back of the van. Assuming they were being transferred, uncertain why they would do it in the middle of the night, he'd settled back in his seat and tried to get some sleep. But he'd barely closed his eyes before they'd arrived at a supermarket. Before he could open them again, the shooting began. He'd ducked down, so had all the others, assuming they were the ones being shot at. They weren't. A moment later, there had been a slap on the van's side and they were shouted out into the car park. Then he'd seen the bodies, and he'd seen a soldier walking up to one lying near a gate leading to a council tower block. The soldier had fired a single shot into the head of the supine figure. Chester was stunned. As he tried to work out what was going on, he spotted the desk sergeant he remembered from his arrest a couple of days before. The copper didn't say anything and didn't seem to be in charge. He just stood and watched as the soldier went from body to body, shooting the dead and injured alike.

Chester had done as they instructed and carried the bodies to a refuse truck. He'd kept his head down and said nothing, just tried to make himself invisible as he made his plans.

After they'd finished loading the bodies, they'd been told to get back into the van. He hadn't liked that. He couldn't be sure, but he doubted they wanted witnesses. Getting out of the van hadn't been difficult. It wasn't one of the prisoner transports with the double locks, wire, and handcuffs, but an ordinary van with doors that opened from the inside. They were barrelling along at twenty miles an hour when he threw the door open and jumped out. He'd hit the ground hard, friction tearing cloth and ripping skin. He'd ignored the pain and ran, and they had followed. He hadn't expected that. He kept running and they kept following. Or perhaps the police on his trail were just an ordinary patrol. It didn't matter. After what he'd seen, he knew they wouldn't hesitate to kill him on sight.

It was hours later, approaching midnight, and he was somewhere in the back streets of central London. He couldn't go home. He didn't know if they had the resources to actively search for him, but he couldn't risk it. That left only one place that he knew was safe. McInery's house in Kensington, about a mile from where he now stood.

More cautiously than before, he crept down the alley. He paused at the end and peered around the corner. The road was empty. There were lights on in almost every window, coupled with the streetlights, that made it almost as bright as day. There was a side road a hundred yards to the north. He knew it ended in a cul-de-sac that backed onto a construction site where they were halfway through turning an old department store into a hotel. McInery's place was just two streets beyond. He glanced up and down the road one last time. From the sound of the engines, the patrol was close, but he couldn't see them. He ran.

He made it to the cul-de-sac just as a police car turned into the road. Resisting the temptation to look behind, he sprinted along the narrow street. He leaped up and over the hoarding, and dropped down into the building site just as the car's lights stabbed through a gap in the wooden fence a few inches from his face. Unmoving, trying not to even think loudly, he listened. The car drove on. They hadn't spotted him. Finally, he allowed himself to relax and look around.

A multi-storey skeleton of concrete towered above him, dark and empty. He was alone. He should wait, he thought, until three a.m. The police should have forgotten about him by then. In fact, he thought, why not wait until morning when the curfew was over? With construction shut down there would be no workers coming in the next day. Even in this corner of London, filled with hotels and mansions, there would be enough odd-looking and oddly-dressed people wandering around that he could blend in. Except he was still wearing the jumpsuit they'd given him back at the cells. He knew they'd only taken his clothes in an attempt to intimidate him. It hadn't worked. It never did. But the jumpsuit would stick out. It would be easier if he could find a jacket or something to cover it.

He examined his surroundings more carefully. There were three pre-fabs stacked one on top of another at the other end of the site. He guessed those were the offices. There might be a jacket in there, he thought, perhaps even some—

The silence was shattered by the clattering rattle of something metallic toppling over. Chester peered into the darkness, trying to identify the sound. It came from somewhere behind the offices. It could be a cat or fox, but probably not. His gut told him that there was someone else on the site. Most likely it was one of London's homeless trying to find somewhere to bed down out of the way of the patrols. But that didn't mean he could ignore it. That was one of the first lessons his father had taught him. "Ignoring something doesn't make it go away, and ignoring someone is naught but a sure-fire way to end up in the slammer." It was sound advice that had kept him twice out of jail and once out of a life-sentence.

Tensed, expecting the worst, he moved towards where he thought the noise had come from. There. He heard it again. And there was something else, another sound that came with it, a wheezing cough. No, he thought, not a cough. It almost sounded like a snarl.

"Hello? You all right, mate? You need any help?" he called softly, as he peered into the gloom.

There was no answer, just the sound of something dragging along the ground, getting closer and closer and then, suddenly, a figure fell out of the shadows, almost on top of him. Chester batted the flailing arms away.

"What the hell?" he blurted, as he staggered backwards.

The man, and it was a man, wore a suit and tie. If Chester was any judge, it was an expensive suit. The man must be a guest in one of the hotels. Probably drunk. The man threw an arm out, not quite in a punch. It was as if the man wasn't aiming at all. Chester knocked the arm away and backed up another step. Drunk or not, the man was about the right height and build. The suit would fit perfectly.

"All right, mate. Just calm down," Chester said soothingly, as he raised his arms ready to grab the figure.

The man snarled, and as he turned, Chester saw his face. Its face. He knew what it was. The rumours had been true. The lifeless eyes, the veined yet bloodless visage, the gaping maw gnashing and chomping as it blindly sought for living flesh. It was a zombie.

Chester backed away. The creature followed. Its teeth snapped down, its hands clawed at the air between them, and its leg knocked against a wheelbarrow, tipping it over. The sound was loud. Too loud. Chester could run, but if the police were nearby they might hear this creature stumbling around. There was no way he would risk being caught. Not now.

Near the office was a haphazard stack of tools. They looked as if they were lying where they'd been dropped after the news from New York had first come in. Ducking under the creature's out-flung arm, Chester dived forwards and grabbed the first handle he could reach. It was a pickaxe. Turning and twisting, gripping the tool with both hands, he swung it sideways into the zombie. There was a splintering crack of bone as the metal point smashed into the creature's chest. The blow knocked it over, but it didn't stop moving.

Chester stared at the impossibly thrashing arms and legs for a moment. They'd said you had to destroy the brain. He'd thought they'd been exaggerating. Planting one foot on its chest, he grabbed the pickaxe, and with a wet sucking slurp, pulled it free. He swung it up and over his head and brought it down on the zombie's skull. It finally went still.

He slowed his breathing and tried to slow his heart. It was pounding so loud it drowned out every other sound. He looked down at the zombie. There was no way he was taking its clothes now, but he was curious as to who the creature had once been. He bent and searched through the corpse's pockets with a professional's thoroughness. He found a diplomatic passport. What remained of the face matched the picture, but it wasn't one that Chester recognised. Nor was the name in the passport. In another pocket was a folded sheet of paper with the address of a hotel in New York and the contact details of a private jet company. The man must have been infected when he boarded the flight. Or someone on that jet had been. That explained how the man got to London. What it didn't answer was how the zombie ended up in a building site at the fashionable end of the capital.

From the half-finished building came a clattering of metal, a rustling of plastic sheeting and an ominous rasping wheeze. He realised that this creature wasn't alone. Chester decided that how the zombies had found there way into the construction site was a question to which he didn't need an answer. He dropped the passport, stood up and ran over to the hoarding encircling the site. He climbed over and once more headed off through the streets of London.

Engines. He heard them again and they were close. There was no doubt it had to be a patrol. Doubling back and forwards and sideways, taking side roads and alleys, he kept running until he saw the bright-red door of McInery's house. He ran up the front path and smashed one fist on the bell, the other pounding on the doorknocker. The police cars were getting closer.

"Who's there?" It wasn't McInery. It was a man's voice. One that was vaguely familiar.

"It's Chester. Chester Carson."

"What do you want?"

"The cops are coming. They'll be here in a moment. Let me—"

The door opened, a hand came out, and Chester was tugged inside.

The hallway was dark. Chester hadn't noticed before, but the house's lights were off. McInery always kept them on. A fear of the dark was one of many fake neuroses that she employed as part of her cover. Ready to fight, he turned around and tried to identify the figure who'd pulled him through the door.

"Chester? Is that you? What on Earth happened?" And that was McInery's voice. She stood in the doorway to the cellar.

"Hey Mac. Everything okay?" he asked, imbuing each syllable with as much menace as he could force out of his exhausted and terrified soul.

"It's fine Chester. Really."

"Yeah, Chester," the man said. "We're all fine and cosy here. So, what did happen to you?"

And this time Chester recognised the voice. Though they had communicated many times by letter, dead-drop, and email, it had been years since he had last seen the man.

"Cannock," Chester stated. "What are you doing here?"

"I think we asked you first," he replied.

"I told Mr Cannock that you were locked up," McInery said.

"Actually," Cannock said, "you told me I had to go and get him released. But now I see I don't have to. So, how *did* you get out, Chester? I doubt it was good behaviour."

"I got drafted into a work detail. Clearing bodies from a supermarket. They were just people looking for food, and they shot them. All of them. I figured they would want to get rid of witnesses, so I ran."

"Which is about the dumbest thing I've heard this evening," Cannock replied, blithely. "No one's liquidating prisoners, not with so much work to be done. And speaking of work, we've got some that needs finishing."

Blue and red lights suddenly stabbed through the stained glass window above the front door.

"It's the police," Chester said. "Sorry, they were—"

"Oh, leave them to me," Cannock said testily. He opened the door and went outside. A moment later the police car drove off. A moment after that Cannock came back inside.

"Right," he said, "that's them dealt with. Now, as I said, there's some business to finish. And I'm not exaggerating when I say that I don't have all night."

McInery turned around and headed back down into the cellar. Chester followed, wondering, and not for the first time, exactly how his former childhood associate - even as children Cannock wasn't someone he'd call a friend - had gained such power that he could order the police away.

In the cellar, the other door, usually hidden behind the fuse boxes, was open. Chester stepped into the very secret office. The light was on and he saw that there was another figure inside. This one, though, was bound to a chair, a gag in his mouth, a blindfold over his eyes.

"What the hell *did* happen to you?" McInery asked, as Chester stepped into the pool of light cast by the room's solitary bulb.

"That building site, the one they're turning into a hotel, there was a zombie there. A real zombie. I had to kill it. I mean, I split its chest open, and it didn't die."

"You left it alive?" Cannock asked.

"What? No. I killed it."

"Really? That's a shame. It would have been useful. Still, what's done is done." Cannock glanced at his watch. "Now, I really do need to get going. You've heard my employer's terms," he said to McInery, "do you agree?"

She glanced at Chester, then at the bound man.

"Yes."

"Good. Then there's just this last matter to be dealt with." He drew a revolver from his pocket. "You sure this room's soundproof?"

"Very," McInery replied.

"Good, good. And it is good to see you again, Chester. Perhaps you'd like the honours?" He held out the revolver.

Chester examined the room. The solitary bulb, the wooden chair, the blindfold, but nothing to stop the victim from hearing what was being said. It was a set-up, a stage designed for an initiation. It was an act he'd been through himself, twice. On the first occasion, he had been the one sitting in the chair. That had been a few months after he'd first joined McInery. The second time, he'd been the one holding the gun. That was just after Cannock had given them their first assignment. Chester knew how the routine worked. It was always the same, always about fear and control. That was what bred loyalty.

"All right," he said, taking the revolver from Cannock. He stepped over to the bound man and pulled the blindfold down.

"Look at me," he said. "Look at me." He waited until the man looked up.

He raised the gun, pointing the barrel between the man's eyes, and pulled the trigger. It didn't click on an empty chamber, it roared as a bullet slammed into the man's head, blowing away the back of his skull and tipping the chair backwards.

"That was cold, Chester. Very cold," Cannock said with a grin. "Oh no. You keep the gun. It's an antique, but I've got far better."

"Who was he?" Chester asked, hoarsely.

"Does that matter?" Cannock asked. He turned to McInery. "Do we have a deal?"

"I think so," she said.

"Good." Cannock nodded to Chester, turned, and went back up the stairs. Chester followed a few steps behind, wanting to make sure the man really had left the house and was far out of earshot before he said anything more.

"What's he want us to do?" he asked McInery when he was sure they were alone.

"His employer wants to take over," she said with a sigh. "Cannock wants us to help."

"Take over what?"

"The country. The world," she said with a shrug.

"His employer? The same one who's been giving us those jobs these past few months."

"The same."

"I don't suppose you found out who that is."

"Oh yes, I did. It's Sir Michael Quigley. The Foreign Secretary."

Part 1: Outbreak
Penrith, Cumbria, Northern England

6th March

"I don't understand why we don't go on the evacuation," Jay said.

"Because I don't trust the government," Nilda replied.

"Yeah, Mum, you already said that. But you didn't say why."

She reached across the small table in the small kitchen of their small house and took her fifteen-year-old son's hands. "It doesn't feel right. I can't say what about it I don't like, but this plan of evacuating everywhere inland seems like it's beyond what the government would be able to do. Not just ours, but any government." She saw the frustrated confusion in her son's eyes and took a moment to marshal her thoughts. "You saw the police at the supermarket?" She refused to call it a Food Distribution Centre.

"Yeah. And?"

"And how they were dressed in military uniform? Carrying rifles?"

"Yeah, but that's what you'd expect, isn't it?"

"You've been watching too many bad TV shows," she said, although he hadn't been watching any these past few days. Since the phone networks went down, and the TV broadcast nothing but football and emergency government missives, Jay had actually been leaving the house. Due to the curfew, he hadn't gone much further than the backyard, but he had been going out. She'd been relieved at that. The teenage isolation into which he'd sunk as his grades had slipped over these past few months had begun to worry her.

"Do you know how long it takes to learn how to use an assault rifle?" she asked. "You can't just give someone a gun and call them a soldier."

"Maybe, maybe not. You don't know," he said, stubbornly.

"The police wouldn't choose to go armed. You see, that's the problem," she said, trying a different tack. "I mean, they actually had a ballot and voted against carrying guns."

"Yeah, but that was before, Mum. It's all changed."

Nilda closed her eyes, and took a breath. Her son was right. It had all changed, and just in the space of a few short days. But she knew she was right, too. He really didn't understand. It all stemmed from the lack of any solid information. When the radio broadcast that there were no reported outbreaks in the UK or Ireland, Jay believed it. Though she wanted to, Nilda couldn't. The last report she'd believed said the virus was sweeping through North America, Europe, and Africa. The way she saw it, that meant there would be billions of people trying to get away from those countries. They would all hear the same message stating that Britain was safe. It was inevitable they would head to the UK and bring the virus with them. There was no way of preventing it, and there was simply too much coastline to be protected.

"Okay, ask yourself this," she said. "Why are the police now dressed in Army uniforms? What good exactly is that camouflage pattern here in the streets of England?"

"I don't know, Mum, and the thing is, neither do you. I mean, unless you have some reason to think they're lying, then we should trust them, right?"

No, they shouldn't, but she couldn't quite explain why not to her son. There was nothing tangible behind her wariness. It was just a gut feeling that they were safer on their own. As she gathered her thoughts in preparation for another assault on his uncharacteristic reasonableness, there was a knock on the back door.

"Stay here," she hissed.

"It's only Mr Baker," Jay said. Ignoring his mother, he went to open the door.

They lived in a two-up, two-down terrace in a part of the small town that the council had tried to forget. The bedrooms upstairs were just that, with enough space left over for a small wardrobe. Most of Jay's clothes were in a dresser on the small landing. Nilda had only two well-laundered outfits for work, and had become used to ignoring the snide comments from her clotheshorse colleagues. Downstairs was the living room, the wall of which the previous owner had partially knocked down during an evening that was never explained to the court's satisfaction. It was this that had caused the council to put the house up for sale. Unable to afford a contractor, Nilda herself had completed the work that debauchery had begun, and had knocked through the living room into the kitchen. That had been the extent of the improvements she'd been allowed to make. Her house, with its eighteenth-century frontage and cobbled backyard, was under a preservation order. All the houses in the terrace were, including the one opposite belonging to Sebastian Baker.

"What do you want, Sebastian?" Nilda asked, as she went to stand in front of the now open back door.

"Look," he said, quietly, "I know you've got food—"

"We've just enough for the two of us," she said firmly.

"You've got more than that," Sebastian said. "You've enough for the two of you for three months. I helped you carry it in from the taxi, remember?" She did. Times had been tough since the recession began. Her hours had been cut, her wages frozen. For two winters in a row they'd had to forego heating in order to buy food. Their car had been sold, but even then she'd often gone hungry in order that her son had enough to eat. The moment that she found a second job, stacking shelves during the middle of the night, she'd decided they would never go hungry again. She'd kept three months' food in the house ever since. She'd have liked to have kept more, but there just wasn't room.

"But don't worry," Sebastian continued. "I'm not here to beg. I'm guessing you're going to stay put tomorrow."

"We haven't decided yet," she lied.

Sebastian looked past her to the small living room, as if taking in the complete lack of packing.

"Well, I'm going," he said. "Sooner or later you've got to trust someone. For good or ill, that time is now."

"That's what I've been telling her," Jay said.

"What," Nilda asked again, though this time more loudly, "do you want, Sebastian?"

13

"Since I can't take everything with me," he replied, "I thought I'd give you what I'm leaving behind. In the days to come, it might help."

"Like what?" Jay asked with excited curiosity.

"Well, it's nothing much. Just my spare camping kit, some tools. That sort of thing."

"Oh, cool!" Jay stepped forward. Nilda raised her arm to stop him from going outside.

"And what do you want in exchange, Mr Baker?" she asked, coolly.

"Nothing," he said.

"I don't believe that."

The older man tilted his head to one side, and sighed. "In a few days' time," he said, "when the silence descends and the power is cut, you'll start going from house to house looking for the things that you need. It's rather obvious that you'll begin with mine. You won't see it as such a great crime robbing from me as you would from an unknown neighbour. I thought I would pre-empt your descent into criminality and offer you what I had."

She eyed him with even more suspicion. He just smiled.

"Well, come on," he finally said. "I'm not carrying it over for you." He turned, walked across the small alley, opened the five-foot high wooden gate, and entered his back garden.

"Mum. He's being nice," Jay whispered.

Nilda closed her eyes. Sebastian was always being nice. That was the problem.

"Fine. Go on. I'll follow."

Jay pushed his way past his mother and walked quickly - at fifteen he was too cool to run - across the yard. Nilda took a moment to lock the back door and followed through their yard, across the narrow alley and into Sebastian's garden.

Where hers was very definitely a yard, used for very little except storage, his was a garden. Dotting the small space were pots, some filled with evergreens, and others with empty earth in readiness for a spring planting that now would never come. No windblown leaves ever found sanctuary there, nor moss a foothold. Even the chipped and worn cobbles had been dug up and replaced.

Walking through the back door, Nilda found her son picking through the items stacked neatly on Sebastian's kitchen table.

"I've brought down what I think would be most useful," Sebastian said without pre-amble as Nilda closed the door. "There are two stoves. They burn paraffin, or paraffin gel. That's the stuff in the toothpaste tube." He pointed. "I haven't used it since last summer, but it should be fine. You'll have to find some more fuel. I'd suggest the camping shop on Packard Street. They don't keep it out on display, but in a metal box out in a storage cabinet next to the bins behind the shop."

"Why do they keep it there?" Jay asked.

"Well, Jay, because it's incredibly flammable," Sebastian said with the patience of a man who'd been teaching for the past thirty years. "If they have it inside, then their insurance premiums go up. But they have to stock it because it's one of the things you can't send through the post, again because it's incredibly flammable."

"Oh. Right. Yeah."

"There's a good little camping kettle here, and a saucepan and frying pan."

"We've got utensils," Nilda said.

"These are compact. If you do decide to leave, you'll want to pack light. There are some boots here that should fit you, Jay. They're well-worn, but waterproof. There's a first aid kit, some waterproof matches." He pointed at the items on the table. "And… well, you can go through the rest yourselves."

"Don't you want to take any of that with you?" Nilda asked.

Sebastian pointed through the door to the front room where a packed bag leaned against an over-stuffed bookshelf.

"I'm taking all I can. But you heard what they said. Bring what you can carry, but you'll have to carry everything you want to bring. Speaking of which, you'll need bags." He picked up a black, drawstring bag.

"Amity Finacial," Jay read.

"They didn't notice the spelling mistake until after they'd printed twenty thousand of them," Sebastian explained. "They gave them out to all the sales reps, even us part-timers. There's a box of them up in the spare room. And there's some other things in there you might want. Help yourself to everything. My spare food is down here." He bent down to open a cupboard. Neatly lined up inside three wicker baskets were a few cans, packets, and jars.

"That's kind," Nilda said. "Thank you."

"It's not really," he said. "And it's really not very much, but it might help. If you stay."

"I'm not planning on leaving," Nilda finally admitted. "That's our house. Our home."

"Just remember that circumstances may change. A time may come when you have no choice but to leave. Prepare for the worst, hope for the best. That's what I've tried to do, although in recent years I've just hoped for things to stay the same. Speaking of which, there's this. I definitely can't take it with me." He pulled out one of the chairs tucked under the table. On the seat was a bundle tied up in cloth. He picked it up and unwrapped it.

"That's a sword!" Jay exclaimed.

"A gladius. The type the Romans used. It's a replica, but it's an old replica. An antique in its own way. I shouldn't really have it at all, but it was, broadly speaking, my retirement plan."

"I don't know what you think we're going to do with it," Nilda said.

"I think you do," Sebastian replied. "Let's just say that with what's coming, it's better you have it and not need it, than need it and not have it."

"Is that some old Roman saying?" she asked.

"No, Mum," Jay said. "That's from Lord of the Rings."

7th March - Evacuation Day

Jay was woken by the sound of people in the street outside. When he came down to the kitchen he found his mother sitting by the window, peering out through a gap in the curtains.

"What's for breakfast?" he asked, blearily.

"Porridge. It's on the stove."

"Again?"

"Enjoy it while you can. It won't last for ever, and when it's gone you'll look back and wish for nothing more."

"Yeah, I doubt that," he muttered, as he emptied the saucepan into a bowl. "Is everyone leaving?"

"It seems so," she said, her eyes glued to the procession of evacuees filling the street.

"It sounds like it. What about Mr Baker?"

"He left at half past five this morning."

"But that's before the curfew lifted."

"I don't think that matters today. Or after today."

"Are you sure about staying, Mum?" he asked.

"I am." She'd watched her neighbours leave, chivvying each other along. As far as she could tell, they were the only ones staying in the terrace.

Jay ate in silence. When he'd finished he looked up to find his mother watching him.

"So, what now, Mum?"

8th March

"We need to go out for supplies," she said, when Jay woke the next morning. On the kitchen table was a road map.

"You mean looting?"

"You can call it that if you want. But there's no law and order anymore, Jay. No crimes. No authorities."

"Yeah, alright," he said, uninterestedly. "So, what are we looking for? We don't really need food."

17

"Yes, we do. There's enough here to last us until the end of May, but we'll need more. At least enough to get us through until autumn."

"Why autumn?"

"Well, my dear," she said in a sweetly patronising tone she knew he hated, "that's when we can harvest anything that's been planted in the farms hereabouts. You see here?" She pointed at the map. "That's Crockett's farm. You know, the place we used to go to just after we moved in?"

"No. Not really."

"They had that old tractor for kids to climb on. You used to love sitting in that thing. Always said you were going to be a farmer when you grew up."

"Did I? I don't remember. Why did we stop going?"

"Because you got older. You decided you didn't like it after they got rid of the animals," she said with a wistful sigh. "But the fruit trees there should keep us going for a few months. Maybe."

"If the birds don't eat the fruit first."

"Yes," she said, "and that's another thing, we'll have to work out how to trap them."

"Trap birds?"

"Yes, if you want fresh meat. After autumn we've got to think about winter, and then there's next spring. But that's a problem for tomorrow, or next month. As is going out to the farms and seeing what's already been planted. Today we need to find all the food that's been left behind. I think, with the two of us, we need about four times what we've got at the moment."

"What about the things Mr Baker left us?"

"That was mostly carbohydrates and coffee. We need vitamins and fibre and protein." She saw his blank expression. "Fruit, vegetables, fish, and meat," she added.

"We could get some vitamin tablets," he suggested.

"We probably will, if we can find some. But food is better. Now, come here and look at the map. Where would you start?"

He glanced at the map but found it was an unfamiliar way of viewing the town. The glance turned into a glare.

"Why don't we start with the houses around here?" he asked.

"Because we know they're empty." As she'd watched people join the evacuation, she had crossed her neighbours' names off a list. "We can go through these houses in the evenings when it's too dark to go further afield. But today, we want to start with the places other people might go. Places we might find more than just the scraps left after the rationing."

"Like one of the supermarkets?" he guessed, then changed his mind when he saw his mother's expression. "No. Not after the rationing." He turned back to the map, as if willing it to reveal its secrets by concentration alone. Then he smiled and stabbed his finger down in triumph. "Packard Street! The camping shop that Mr Baker talked about."

Packard Street was off a side road at the unfashionable end of the town centre. The shops there sold the essentials, often in bulk, but without the profit margin to afford the higher rents of somewhere with greater foot traffic.

"Good. That's what I was thinking. They said they'd cut off the power when the evacuation began. I'm surprised they haven't done it already. Either it couldn't be that easy disconnecting the homes from the grid, or with no businesses or industries running, there's more than enough capacity. Whatever the reason, the power will be cut, or a transformer will blow, or a tree will fall on an overhead line. We'll be without electricity soon, and we need to be prepared."

"So we start by getting the fuel for cooking."

"And heating and boiling water," she said. "But fuel is just our starting point. They'll have other things in that shop. Maybe there's some energy bars or dehydrated meals. We need things that have a long shelf life. There's a cake supply shop next to it. Here." She pointed at the map.

"Won't the cakes have gone off?"

"They didn't sell cakes. Mostly they sold tins and moulds and utensils, but they also had a range of icing and decorations. That's just coloured sugar stamped into shapes. I don't think anyone would have thought to loot there. And if they have, it's only a short walk to the high street."

"But if the supermarkets are empty, won't the butchers and bakers be cleared out as well?" he asked.

"Yes, but think about all the other places you find food. Think about the offices above the shops. They have break rooms, and those always have biscuits. Then there's the cinema. There aren't many calories in popcorn, but some is better than none. It might be worth looking in the Salvation Army place. They were running a food-bank over the winter. I doubt they'll have much left, but it's worth trying."

"I dunno," Jay said sceptically.

"Well, we won't know until we check for ourselves. Now, listen. This is important. It's possible that we're the only people left in town, but there might be others and there might be people out in the countryside who come looking for food. And there's still the government. Perhaps they'll have patrols roaming around to deter looters."

"You think they might?"

"I don't know. They'll probably need every able body to keep order in those enclaves. But it's possible. So if we hear an engine, we hide. If we get into any trouble, we run. We definitely don't try to fight. Understand?"

"You think we might have to?" He spoke with blithe unconcern, but she could see the worry in his eyes.

"Not yet. But we should be prepared for it."

"Then we should take the sword Mr Baker left."

"Really? And you know how to use it, do you?"

"Yeah, sure. It's the pointy end first."

"It's not a joke, Jay. A sword's like a gun. You have to know how to use it, and more than that, be prepared to stick it in someone's gut, and turn and twist the blade, and—"

"Mum!"

"I'm serious. If you go around carrying a weapon like that, then you need to be ready to use it. Otherwise someone will take it from you and you'll end up on the other end of it. So, we'll leave the sword here, but…" She walked over to the small cupboard under the stairs and took out two cricket bats. One new, the other well-worn, both mementos of Jay's brief dalliance with the sport before she'd run out of money to pay the fees.

"These'll do. No one will want to steal them, but should give someone pause. Now, get your shoes on. And don't forget your scarf. It's cold out."

He grunted a pro-forma protest before pulling down the red and blue striped scarf from its peg.

The streets were empty, but they weren't clear. The instructions on the emergency broadcast had been explicit. Bring clothes, a blanket, and food. Beyond that, evacuees were allowed to bring whatever they could carry. Judging by the bric-a-brac of discarded electronics and clothing, prams and pushchairs, walking sticks and suitcases, people had left their homes carrying far more than they were able.

"What are you doing?" Nilda asked, when Jay dashed across the road and bent to pick something up.

Jay held up a smartphone, "Do you know how much this is worth?" he asked.

"Nothing," she said. "It's worth absolutely nothing. Try it. There's no signal. No Internet. I doubt even the GPS will work."

"I bet you're wrong," he said, flipping his fingers across the screen. "Oh," he added with disappointment. "It's locked."

"The pinnacle of human civilisation," she said. "More computing power in the palm of your hand than was used to land Neil Armstrong on the Moon, and it's just worthless junk."

"Yeah." Jay made to throw it away, but stopped. Instead, with care, he laid it down on a garden wall. Nilda sighed.

They walked slowly, Nilda listening carefully for any vehicles. All she heard was a low susurrus drifting across the street as the damp morning breeze rustled the refugees' discarded gear.

"Keep your eyes open," Nilda said, softly. "Look out for twitching curtains, or tidy lawns, or anything that might suggest someone else has stayed in the town."

They didn't see any such sign until, a quarter of a mile away from Packard Street, Nilda grabbed her son's arm.

"What?" he asked, affronted.

"Tell me what you see," she said, pointing ahead of them.

"Nothing. Someone's just cleared some of the road."

"Right. Someone. People. So keep your ears and eyes open."

Her heart sank with each step as she realised the cleared path led directly to the camping shop. A few dozen yards further on, as the road curved, she saw two cars that had been parked in a V-shape to block the street. At a junction a few hundred yards further down, she saw another similar barricade. She stopped. So did her son.

"What do we do now?" Jay asked.

"Now we go," Nilda said. "Come on."

Before they managed four steps, a man called out. "What d'you want?"

As Nilda turned around she saw it wasn't a man, not really. The speaker was only a few years older than Jay. Certainly he was far closer in age to him than to her.

"We were looking for supplies," she called back. "For our stove. We thought the shops might be open."

"Open?" he scoffed. "What? You think the shops would actually be open to sell stuff?"

"We just needed some fuel for our camping stove," she replied, keeping her tone light and airy as if, despite all evidence to the contrary, it was just another ordinary day.

"Camping?" Now he sounded confused.

"Hence why we came to a camping shop," she said, adding, "I've got cash."

As they'd spoken the young man had stepped closer, and she was able to see him properly. He was tall and thin, but neither wiry nor athletic, just skinny thanks to the fast metabolism of youth. He was dressed in a black leather jacket that looked suspiciously new, black jeans that she doubted had been washed since they'd been blasted with sand in some sweatshop, finished off with bright red trainers that hadn't been designed for running.

"What'd I want with cash?" he asked, as he climbed up onto the roof of the nearest car. "The shops are closed." First, he raised his arms above his head, then his voice to carry above the deserted streets. "The world's ended. It's all ours now. Ours!"

Nilda nodded slowly. She knew exactly which movie he'd copied that line from. It might even have been intimidating if he hadn't tried to copy the accent, too.

"This is yours, is it? Your territory? You're claiming it?" she asked.

"That's right," he said, pulling out a skinny black-papered roll-up from his shirt pocket. "It's all ours." He lit the cigarette.

Nilda nodded again, looking around. She'd thought he was too confident to be on his own.

"I don't think we've met before," she said, breaking the silence a few seconds after it had become uncomfortable. "My name's Nilda."

"What?" he asked, the fake accent slipping.

"Nilda. That's my name."

"Yeah? I thought you didn't look like you came from around here," he drawled in a tone she'd heard many times before, though usually from someone much older.

"What's your name?" she asked, keeping her tone friendly despite her growing unease.

"Why'd you want to know?"

"I'm just being polite since it seems we're going to be neighbours."

"Neighbours?" And again he sounded confused.

"Well, as you say, this is your territory. You've claimed it first. We've claimed everything west of the railway line. That's ours."

"Yours? Just the two of you?"

"Oh no. There's a lot more of us than that. I could go and get them, if you like."

The man eyed her for a moment, then half turned around.

"Oy! You lot! Get out here!" he yelled.

Five figures slouched out of a doorway behind him. They all seemed a similar age; all were male, strutting with that testosterone-fuelled invulnerability of the naive-young, and all were armed with a variety of blades that looked like they'd come from the butcher's shop down the road.

"Is there trouble, Rob?" asked one who was twice the width and at least a third taller than the rest.

"No," Nilda said. Looking at the men - though youths would be a better description. She guessed they'd been in the same class at school, or had dropped out of it together. "There's no trouble. We'll be seeing you, Rob."

She turned, nodded to Jay, and they walked away.

"That was seriously dangerous, Mum," Jay said, when they were two blocks away.

"No, not really," she said. "It would have been dangerous if we did that next week, maybe even tomorrow, but today they still remember the world before. They saw a mother with her son. Give it a few days and they'll see us as rivals."

"Is that why you said there were more of us?"

"Basically, yes. Disinformation. When you're weak, pretend you're strong."

"And when he comes looking for us?"

"He'll be looking over by the railway lines. But he won't come looking for a while. Not as long as they've got food. No, I've seen dangerous kids before. Believe me. You were too young. You don't remember what it was like on the estate back in London. Those kids, or men I suppose, they're not dangerous. Not yet. They'll stay safe behind their little barricade, probably stay there until the foods run out. Then they'll be a problem. For now, none of them want to get hurt."

"And what happens next week or next month?"

"That," she sighed, "is a good question. If you have any ideas let me know."

"Huh," he grunted. "So, what do we do now? Go home?"

"No. Not yet. It's a beautiful day and I've had another idea. We'll have to forget those stoves. When the power is cut, we'll go old-school and cook over a fire. But I don't want to leave any food lying around for that lot to steal. And I think I know somewhere they won't have thought of. Not yet. Not until they're really hungry."

"Where, Mum?"

"You'll see."

They kept walking, heading almost, but not quite, towards their house.

"There." Nilda pointed at a row of shops.

"The fish and chip shop?" Jay asked, peering at the signs.

"We can have a look in there, but I was thinking more of the veterinarian's."

"What for?"

"Oh, Jay," she sighed. "There'll be no more ambulances, no more doctors. If we get hurt, we've no one else to turn to. It's just us to take care of each other."

"So why don't we go try one of the pharmacies if we want medicine?" he asked, confused.

"Because we need food, too. Come on."

A window at the back had already been broken. Inside, they found that someone had come in and selectively emptied the pharmaceutical cabinet. Whoever had done it had known exactly what they were looking for. Nilda scanned through the remaining vials, packets, and jars. She didn't recognise any of the names, so she left them alone. The looters, however, had only been interested in the drugs. Inside a store cupboard, just behind the reception desk, was row upon row of pet food.

"Here." She opened her pack and pulled out a dozen of the drawstring bags. "You fill each of these."

"What with?"

"Pet food," she said.

"You can't be serious."

"Start with… this." She pulled a packet from the shelf. "Bird food. Nuts and seeds compressed into lard. It's high calorie."

"No way!"

"Calories are calories. And fat and nuts and seeds can be baked into a cake. Start filling up the bags. I'll see what else we might need."

She found sutures, needles and sterile bandages, scalpels and a dozen other assorted instruments, most of which she only recognised as the kind of props they had in late night horror films. There was an eye-wateringly large pair of forceps, the world's largest syringe, and what looked like a miniature pizza cutter. She took the ones she could think of a use for.

"Do you want me to fill all these bags?" Jay asked. "I mean there's a lot here."

"This is food, Jay. We're not leaving it," she said. "Pack it all. We'll make as many trips as it takes."

"But still, it's a lot to carry."

"You keep packing, I'll worry about that."

She went out into the street. It didn't take her long to find two pushchairs. She brought them back and showed him how to balance the bags on the handles, with more on the seat.

"It's why I always had to make sure you were strapped in when I went shopping," she said, "otherwise you were liable to jump out every time you saw a bird, then the pushchair would topple, and the shopping would end up scattered across the street." He grunted in embarrassed indifference.

At Jay's insistence they went inside the fish and chip shop. It was empty, but not looted. Everything from fat to potatoes to flour had gone. The freezers were unplugged and defrosted. Even the fridge by the cash register had been emptied of soft drinks.

"Satisfied?" she asked her son. He reluctantly agreed, and they headed home. Ten minutes later, they'd unloaded their bags. Before Jay had a chance to sit down, Nilda pushed him back out the door. They'd emptied the vet's by lunchtime.

"All right," Jay said, collapsing into a kitchen chair. "We've enough food now, surely?"

"Enough?" She picked up a can. "This says rabbit in gravy. With extra marrow-bone jelly. It sounds nice."

"Huh!" Jay grunted.

"One of these," Nilda went on, ignoring her son's muted protest, "plus one of the tins of tomatoes, and some pasta, and we've got ourselves a meal."

Jay took the can, suspiciously. "I dunno. Maybe. But is it going to be enough?"

"Work it out," Nilda said. "One tin of rabbit, one tin of tomatoes. Forget the pasta for a moment and that's two tins per meal. Since we want at least two meals each day, we need four cans per day, or one hundred and twenty per month. That's fourteen hundred until we hit spring."

Jay turned to look at the pile of cans on the living room floor. "I suppose we've got about... two hundred?"

"And counting what we've got in the cupboards, I'd say it was close to five hundred. We need at least three times that. At least. That's the bare minimum for survival, and we want to do more than just survive. I think we should aim for three thousand."

"You can't be serious! Where are we going to put it all?"

"Sebastian's house," she said. "Come on, there's a couple of hours left until dark. We'll go to the garden centre down near the railway station. They sell pet food."

9th March

"Come on. Get up," Nilda said.

"It's still dark," Jay grumbled.

"And it's started to rain. But if you want to eat more than bark and leaves in the winter, we need to go out and find more food. Today, tomorrow, and every day from now on."

Jay groaned. She pulled the duvet off him. After he dressed, they went out. They came back, and they went out again. And again.

11th March

"It's not a bad haul, Mum," Jay said loyally. It was mid-afternoon, their living room, kitchen, and hall were filled with cans and boxes. There were some packets of pasta, rice, sugar, and other familiarly human food, but most of what they'd found was intended for pets.

"It's not enough," she said.

"It'll get us through until December, won't it?"

"Ye-es," she said slowly, as she turned the pages in the notebook. Every tin and packet they'd found was listed, the inventory annotated with each item's relative nutritional value, calorie content, and any vitamins or minerals with which it had been fortified. "Probably into January. It's what happens afterwards that worries me." She sighed. "I just wish we'd gone to that pub yesterday."

When she'd thought to go there earlier that afternoon, they'd found Rob and his gang ensconced outside. Nilda had heard them long before they were in sight. She and Jay had broken into a house and watched the group through a gap in a garden fence. Four of them, including Rob, sat at one of the tables outside the front door. They had a barrel lying on the table, dozens of broken glasses littering the ground at their feet, and a fug of smoke above their heads.

"Of all the pubs in town," she said, bitterly, "why did they have to choose that one?"

It wasn't the beer Nilda was after, nor what little might have been left in the kitchens. The pub had its own microbrewery. They specialised in a barley beer, and she knew for a fact that the barley was stored in a building at the back.

"We could try tomorrow. Or later tonight?" Jay suggested.

"No. They looked like they were settling in."

"Well, what if we went back to Packard Street and see if we can get that fuel for the stoves."

"They weren't all at the pub," she said. "No, it's too much of a risk. They'll probably leave when the beer runs out. And I can't see them touching the barley. We'll go back in a week." And hope Rob didn't set fire to the place in the meantime.

It was frustrating. During their search for supplies, they'd come across quite a few places that had been looted. Those Rob had been to were easy enough to spot, even if it hadn't been for the ubiquitous black-papered roll-ups he'd left behind. Jay said it was Rob's calling card. Nilda thought it was more like a dog marking its territory. Those places had been turned over and trashed; windows broken, furniture slashed, electronics taken or smashed. But there had been other houses, ones she was sure had been looted by someone else, someone who knew what to look for. There the food and some other supplies would be missing but only from one or two select properties on a street. Who that was, she didn't know. Not that she wanted company, but she'd seen no women at the barricade, or at the pub. She knew with someone like Rob, it wouldn't be long before he decided to come looking for her.

She'd planned on going to the pub first thing that morning. Had she done so they would have been there when he and his gang arrived. That probably wouldn't have ended well. Instead, on Jay's insistence, they'd taken a trip to the two nearest farms. He'd been the one to realise that without anyone to take care of them, any livestock left behind after the evacuation would be dead in a few days' time. The animals had gone. So had the farmers, and they'd managed to take every scrap of food with them. All that remained was one half of a formal requisition order.

"We'll have some dinner, then we'll have another think about where we'll look tomorrow," she said. "Maybe we could try one of the other pubs. There's another microbrewery a few miles down the road, although I think they made their beer with hops. I'm not sure whether you can eat those. We'll have to find a book on it. We could go to some more farms on the way." Maybe. It had been over a week. She doubted any livestock left behind would still be alive, and she couldn't imagine many farmers would have just abandoned their animals to die of neglect. Of course, what they would do if they actually found some animals, she wasn't sure.

She turned back to the stove. In a saucepan, a mixture of tinned tomatoes, herbs, and stinging nettles bubbled away. The nettles had been another of Jay's ideas. He'd spotted them as they'd crept away from the pub. He'd seen some reality show about living off the land in which they'd been prominently featured. Perhaps his summer spent doing nothing but watching TV wasn't as big a waste of time as she'd thought. His satisfied superiority in knowing something his mother didn't had faded when she'd stopped to pick them, announcing that they would be eating them for dinner.

"Now," she asked. "Do you want rabbit or beef?"

"I get that we'll have to eat it sooner or later," he said, "but why can't it be later?"

"Later we might be eating it cold from the tin."

"You said, right, that when we're hungry we're not going to mind what we eat. So let's wait until we're hungry. Here. This one's a ham."

"I thought we'd keep that for your birthday," she said. "Let's try the beef. Look at the ingredients. There's nothing in it you wouldn't eat normally, not if it came in a curry. In fact, you've probably eaten something just like it from that take-away down on—" She was interrupted by a knock at the door. "Stay here," she hissed, as she grabbed the cricket bat and headed to the front of the house. Jay, ignoring her, grabbed the other bat and followed close behind.

"Who's there?" she called out.

"It's me, Nilda. Sebastian."

She glanced at her son, opened the door, and then took a step back in shock. Sebastian was almost unrecognisable. His hair was matted, his clothing was torn, and his face was coated in dirt except where it was covered in grey stubble.

"What happened to you?" she asked.

"There was no vaccine," he said. "It was all a lie. The muster points were just… It was a killing field. They murdered the evacuees."

She made Sebastian strip off in the hall, and sent Jay over to his house to collect some clothes. An hour later, they were sitting at the table, a pot of stew - containing no trace of dog food - between them. Jay's and Nilda's bowls were untouched. Sebastian was on his third before Nilda finally gave in to impatience.

"What do you mean murdered?" she asked.

"There was no vaccine," he said, and as he spoke, his tempo rose, so the words came out in a barely coherent slur. "Of course there wasn't. We should have known that from the start. We didn't, did we? No, we wanted to trust the government. We needed to believe that someone was in control. That *they* would sort it out. Well *they* were in control. *They* did sort it out. *They* found a way of neutralising the entire population."

"Slowly, Seb! Slowly. Tell us what happened. What did you see?" Seeing the usually composed man so disturbed was unsettling.

"I don't know. I can tell you what I saw, but I can only guess at what it might mean."

"Just start with when you left," she said. "It was half-five in the morning. The curfew was still in place."

"Oh, they didn't care about that. I passed a police car down by the station. Not that they were dressed like police. They wore the same Army uniform as everyone else. They just nodded to me and pointed out the way I should go. Not that I needed to worry about directions. They'd printed signs. Signs! Can you believe the cold-blooded ruthlessness of that? Not that the printers would have known, of course. Nor those who erected the fencing. Nor even the mis-uniformed police. They were probably as ignorant, as blind, as I was—"

"What about other people. Did you see other people?" she cut in.

"Oh, there were some. Not many to start with. Most waited in their homes, blithely obeying their instructions. Ha! Sleepwalking unto death, they go—"

"Seb! On the evacuation, what happened?"

"On the evacuation? Nothing." He took a breath, and gathered his thoughts. "It was just a long walk. And it has been a long time since I walked those types of distances. And I've never walked anywhere without knowing what my destination might be."

"I thought the muster point was about ten miles away," Jay said, speaking gently before his mother gave another abrupt interjection.

"And that they'd take us by train or bus up to an enclave in the far north of Scotland? Yes, so did I," Sebastian replied. "Well, that was a lie, too. I walked, and I kept walking, and I really put everything I had into it. I thought if I got there first I'd be on one of the first trains and so among the first to arrive at the enclave. I hoped I might be there early enough to volunteer for some easier work detail. But after two hours, I'd covered more than ten miles and hadn't arrived anywhere. By then, I was no longer alone. People were streaming up the side roads onto the motorway. I kept on. What else could I do? I asked a few people where we were going, but no one knew, and no one really wanted to talk. Having slowed when I thought I was nearing my destination, I found I couldn't speed up again.

My energy was gone. If I were a younger man… but if I was, then I would now be dead."

He raised the spoon, dropped it, and pushed the bowl away.

"I'd been near the front, or at least in front of anyone else from here. As weariness took its inexorable hold, those who'd opted for a more sensible pace, those who'd indulged in a proper last night's sleep, overtook me. Some were on bicycles and some were on foot. I even saw a few who were running. Didn't they use to say jogging was bad for your health? Ha!" He sniffed. "By mid-afternoon, I was nearer the back than the front and perhaps fifteen miles from here. Perhaps more. I'm not sure…" He trailed off. Nilda gave her son a look, prompting him to be the one to ask something to keep the older man talking.

"Did you see anyone you knew?" Jay asked.

"Knew? A handful. And some I recognised but couldn't name. Few spared me a second glance, and none spared me a word. Certainly no one came to my aid. And then there were too many people to spare the time to look around. For a while, it was all I could do just to avoid walking in to the back of someone or tripping over the feet of someone else. It was strange, not at all the way that I thought people would act. There was no camaraderie, just this nearly tangible focus on getting to the destination. There was a woman, an old woman, far older than I. She had a little shopping cart, a two-wheeled affair with a tartan pattern. One of the wheels had come off, but she was resolutely dragging it along. That scraping rasp cut through the noise of stamping feet and through my exhaustion. I helped her as best I could, and as much to have that noise cease than out of any sense of duty. And that slowed me even more. She'd been on the evacuation route for four hours and had only managed three miles. She just wouldn't give up that trolley. Nor would she tell me what was inside. It was heavy, mind you, and clinked a bit. Not as though metal was rubbing against metal, but that softer tinkle of delicate china."

"Why'd she bring that?" Jay asked.

"As I said, she wouldn't tell me. Not directly. But I think she, and others, they took what was important to them, not that which would be vital to their immediate survival. It was ever thus. Around four o'clock, an

Army half-track started making its way along the northbound lane, travelling in a direction opposite to us lambs. They were blaring out a message over their speakers, telling the slower people to get into the left-hand lane, the faster into the right. I waved to the vehicle, trying to get their attention. I thought they'd ignored me. Certainly they gave no indication they'd noticed our plight. Yet a few minutes later, perhaps ten, perhaps twenty, a string of lorries came up the road behind us. They were picking up the stragglers, you see, and one of them stopped for the old lady. They took her, but not me."

"Didn't you want to go with them?" Jay asked.

"I did. They asked if I could still walk. When I said yes, they said that that was what I had to do. I kept on. I didn't check the time. I didn't want to know how long I'd been walking, not when there was seemingly no end in sight. It must have been after six. I'd just gone through Carlisle, but there was hardly anyone behind, nor in front. I was almost alone, walking at a near crawl. I sat down by the roadside to rest. It wasn't long before another vehicle came up. Again, I asked for a ride, and again I was turned down. They told me, no, they *ordered* me to keep going. They said there was no room. I could see that there was. But you know, ultimately, it was their spite that saved me. And I did get the muster point's location out of them. It was five miles east of Gretna. On the border between England and Scotland," he added in response to Jay's blank expression. "The route left the motorway just a mile further on from where I'd stopped. So it was ten miles walking by road, or six if I went in a straight line. I continued walking, but only until the vehicle was out of sight. Then I left the road."

"I thought you said the road was walled in."

"It was, but there were gaps. Sometimes it was barricaded with concrete, cement, and double-thick chain-wire fence. But they clearly hadn't enough of it. Every few hundred yards the impregnable wall would stop and be replaced with riot-barriers or rolls of chicken wire. It was easy enough to get out. I'd passed a sign for a lay-by. It wasn't much more than a stretch of asphalt large enough for lorries to park up when they reached their daily maximum number of driveable hours. There were no trucks there, but there was a food van and a couple of portable toilets. I broke into the van, closed the door behind me, and sat on the floor. I'd only planned on staying there a few minutes, just long enough to boil up the last of my water and make some tea—"

"Seriously?" Jay blurted. "You were going to use the last of your water to make tea?"

"Of course. You wouldn't understand. It's the comfort of familiar ritual. But I didn't make the tea. I fell asleep. When I woke, it was half past ten. And, no, I didn't then bother with the tea. I just drank the water and headed back to the road. In my earlier exhaustion I'd not really thought about all those abandoned bicycles. There was at least one every four hundred yards, discarded when some part had broken. I found one with a punctured tyre near the gap in the fence. I dragged it along on one wheel for about three hundred yards until I came to another bike, this one with a broken chain. About five minutes after that, I had a working bicycle. I left the evacuation route and cycled down the country lanes. There was a shortcut I knew that would get me to the muster point and outside of a good meal before the hour was out."

"They didn't stop you?" Nilda asked.

"At that point there was no one to even try. There were no police cars. No military vehicles. No evacuees. I didn't pass a single soul nor did I see a solitary light, not until I was about a mile from my destination. I was on one of those single-lane farm-tracks, and I'd thought I'd become lost. It's been a few years since I was able to spend my summers doing nothing but hiking around the border, but those old roads have been there for centuries. I wasn't lost. I ended up exactly where I wanted to be. Through a gap in the hedgerow, and across the fields, I saw the lights. I knew it was the muster point, but that knowledge wasn't reassuring. I left the bicycle there, and tramped across the corrugated earth. It wasn't easy. The only light was coming from ahead of me. Perhaps because of that, because I was concentrating so much on where to put my feet, I didn't become aware of the noise until I was clambering over a fence about a quarter of a mile from it."

"It was loud?" Jay asked.

"No. That was the point. It should have been loud, but it wasn't. There was just the gentle hum of generators mixed with the harsh growl of heavy-duty engines. There should have been the crying and groaning and growling of thousands of frustrated refugees. I couldn't hear a single voice. I grew cautious. I continued on more slowly, keeping my head down, my shoulders hunched, following the fences and hedges until I was close enough to see. It was a camp. Searchlights mounted on towers of scaffolding picked out the road they'd used as the evacuation route. They must have been funnelling people in from both directions onto a slip road that led down into farmland. This slip road was split into two lanes, and each of those split again and again. Each time, the pathway down which the evacuees could walk became narrower and narrower. The fenced-in paths snaked up and down and back on themselves forming a horrific maze until, when the paths were so narrow that the people would be walking in single file, they reached the front, and a row of desks. There was no one sitting behind them. I think that must have been where the evacuees were sorted and given the vaccine because a few dozen yards further on there was another row of barriers. These were far less intimidating, just the kind they used for crowd control at sports matches. You know the sort? About five feet high with a wide base, but designed to be knocked over if the weight behind them became too great. It looked like they'd been moved around so that the evacuees could be directed into different walled-off enclosures. When one was full, the barriers would be moved so the next enclosure could be filled. And those walled-off enclosures, there were dozens of those still standing, but I couldn't see inside from where I stood. Their walls were too high. I crept closer, to an old spreading oak jutting out at the edge of a field. I had to climb it to see inside." He coughed. "I mean that I had to see. I had to know. To do that, I had to climb a tree. Inside those walls were bodies. Hundreds upon hundreds. All the evacuees..." He trailed off.

"Seb, it's all right. If you don't want to—"

"No, it is important you know. The evacuees weren't shot. Either it was the vaccine itself or some biological weapon. I don't suppose it matters which. Those people had gone seeking safety. They had trusted

35

the government, and they'd been betrayed. And there was nothing I could do. I just stayed up that tree watching and trying to understand how it all came to pass. How the soldiers and the police could have let it happen."

"Does that mean they knew?" Jay asked. "That the government planned all this?"

"Wait, I haven't finished. But, yes, someone had planned for something. Those signs, the fences, and all those spare military uniforms, it all suggests that they were preparing for some truly terrible act. Whether it was for this exact eventuality or not is immaterial. They saw the danger and came up with an elegantly savage solution. The ranks of the undead grow when people are infected. The undead are hard to kill. People are not. The easiest way of reducing the number of zombies on our island is to kill the population before it turns. It is elegant, and simple, and the purest evil. The noise I'd heard was the sound of bulldozers toppling the walls down onto the bodies. I watched as this pair of uniformed thugs sprayed something onto them. It was some type of incendiary. They lit it. By the light of the pyre, I saw how many people were there. Including those in the vehicles and the two in the towers, there were less than two-dozen personnel. I won't call them soldiers, because that's a disservice to those who... but I'm getting to that part. My world was in ruins. Everything I knew and believed had been torn from me. I was still in that tree, frozen with shock. I saw some people, more refugees, approaching along the road. Perhaps they'd left later in the day so as to avoid the crowds. It was the person in the watchtower who spotted them first. He shouted a warning. An officer on the ground called out an order. The man in the watchtower started arguing with him, while four others broke off from their clean-up duties and ran towards the evacuees. They stopped about twenty yards from the refugees, unslung their rifles, and opened fire. They killed them all, and there were children in that group. Children! The oldest couldn't have been more than eight. Before the firing had stopped, the soldier in the watchtower had started climbing down. The moment his feet touched the ground, the officer in charge shot him in the head."

Nilda glanced at Jay. He was staring at the older man with horrified disbelief. She gripped her son's hand, tightly.

"I stayed up in that tree all night," Sebastian said. "I suppose it was shock, but I was concealed well enough. When dawn came, the thugs left, leaving nothing but smouldering ashes. I climbed down and again felt compelled to see. I walked in to the killing field. I'm glad I did. Mixed in with the bodies of the old and young and civilian were uniforms. Dozens of them. Who exactly they were, I don't know. Nor who gave the orders for them to be shot. But whoever it was, not everyone blindly followed them. I found some strength in that. I wandered there for a while, trying to burn those images into my soul. But the body is weak. Thirst forced me to leave. I went back to the bicycle and began looking for some stream or brook. I was so filled with anger I made no effort to conceal myself, but I saw no one for the remainder of the day. That anger was my undoing, however. I should have been back here that night. Instead, I ended up lost. By nightfall, I was at least thirty miles north of the border. Ah!" He raised his hand to forestall a comment from Jay. "There's one more thing. Perhaps the most important part. Yesterday, was it yesterday or was it the day before? The reason it took me so long to come back; I saw the undead. There were three of them walking along the road towards me. I turned around. They followed. I lost them, but I had to detour three more times. The closest of these creatures was twenty miles away, but that's still too close. They will come. There is nothing to stop them."

12th March

"Mum! I think the fuses have gone. The shower's running cold," Jay yelled furiously from the bathroom. That morning they'd limited their scavenging to the houses in their immediate neighbourhood. It was at one of those, a few hours after midday, that Jay had fallen into a fishpond, ending up coated in slime. They'd cut short the expedition, and returned home.

"It's not the fuses," Sebastian said. He was in the living room, peering through a small gap in the closed curtains. "There was a light left on in that house over there. It's gone out."

Nilda was sitting at the kitchen table sorting the tins by calorie content. She stood up, tried the electric stove, then the kettle, and then the microwave.

"The power's been cut," she said.

"Seems like it," Sebastian agreed, walking into the kitchen.

"You mean I have to shower in cold water?" Jay groaned.

"No," Nilda said. "I mean, no more showers. No more baths. We can't waste the water."

"But the water's still running," Jay protested.

"Then turn it off! The reservoir is on higher ground than the town. Gravity will keep it flowing. Probably," she added. "But there's the water treatment plant between us and it. That definitely required electricity. If some sluice gate or valve is closed, then there'll be no more water." Or if the pipes burst or there was some mechanism to automatically shut down the system in the event of a power cut. She didn't think there was. There had been a blackout two years before, and the water had kept flowing then. But for all she knew, they had a backup generator at the treatment plant. She'd thought about going there to see, but she wouldn't know what it looked like, let alone how to turn it on. The only preparation she'd been able to make had been to check that all the hot-water tanks in the terrace and in the larger houses in the road opposite were full, and the taps were closed.

"But I'm covered in soap!" Jay protested self-pityingly.

"Alright," she relented. "You can rinse yourself off. Two minutes. No more."

There was a grumbled growl from behind the bathroom door as Jay went back into the shower to rinse off.

"How long before we have to boil the water before we drink it?" Nilda asked Sebastian.

"I couldn't say. A week? Less? I don't know so I suggest we start doing it from tomorrow."

"That's what I thought. We'll need fuel for the stoves then," Nilda said.

"I don't know where else you'd find it except the camping shop," Sebastian said. "And if that's not going to be an option—"

"It isn't."

Sebastian had suggested they traded for it. She'd tried to explain that they didn't have anything to trade - not anything she was willing to, at least. Sebastian hadn't understood, and she hadn't wanted to spell it out to him.

"Well, it doesn't really matter," Sebastian said. "Even with all the paraffin they had in stock, we'd run out in a month. No, we need a more permanent solution."

"You mean fire?"

"There's enough furniture in these houses to spare."

"But we're not going to burn anything in that," she said, gesturing at the fireplace in the front room." Like all the houses in the terraces, the chimney had been removed when the indoor plumbing was put in. In its stead stood a now useless electric heater.

"We could rip this up," Sebastian said, stamping on the lino. "There's stone underneath. Start a fire in a tray with a grill over the top."

"Why not just use a barbecue outside?"

"No. It would be too dangerous," he said. "Too great a chance of being seen by the undead. It's not just about gathering food, finding freshwater, and all those other basics of survival. We have to be ready for that ever-present threat. We have to be prepared in case they come."

Nilda looked at the floor, and then at the low ceiling. "It's not a permanent solution. I mean, it'll do for a few days, but not much longer than that. And we can't burn furniture. Not inside. Not if we don't want to be poisoned by the fumes from the varnish."

"No. That's a good point. I forgot. I… I find it's hard to get my mind into the right gear. I can't stop thinking about the coming siege."

"Let's start with the immediate," Nilda said. Her thoughts had been turning in that direction herself, but she wasn't ready to embrace them. Not yet. "We need heat to cook on. And we need batteries to see at night because I'm not sitting in the dark with only my thoughts for company."

39

"We can find batteries in most houses," Sebastian said. "Coal, on the other hand, will be far more scarce. The only place I can think of that definitely had some was the petrol station up near the industrial estate. They used to have it stacked on the forecourt. It might still be there."

It wasn't. The forecourt was empty. The shop's windows had been smashed. A rope had been hung across both the entrance and exits, but it had pulled down. It now lay discarded in the road, a handwritten sign, blotted and blotched by rainwater, lay next to it. Nilda picked it up.

"Supplies seized by order. No petrol here," she read. "That's pretty much the same as we found on the requisition note left at the farms."

"But whose order?" Sebastian asked. "That's the question. And it didn't stop someone from checking for themselves."

The pumps lay loose on the cement forecourt, discarded where each in turn had been tried and found not to work.

"Perhaps there's something around the back," Jay said, as he started walking towards the building.

"Careful of the glass," Nilda warned half-heartedly as she followed her son towards the building. She didn't think he would find anything. This time she was right. Standing in the doorway, they could see that the shelves had been pulled down.

"I think," she said, "that the owners must have emptied it out. There's no wrappers, no boxes. It's all gone. Then someone, perhaps Rob, perhaps someone else, came along and trashed it when they found it empty."

"You know," Sebastian said slowly, "if they did take all that food, and the coal, then perhaps they didn't go on the evacuation either."

"Meaning?"

"Well, their address will be around here somewhere. We could find it, and go and find them."

"And then what?" she asked. "Beg for a hand out?"

"Why don't we, you know, join forces?" Jay suggested. "Work together. That'd be safer. Or maybe they'd be willing to trade."

"Right, but what did this place sell? Chocolate. Snacks. Cigarettes. We've got tins of vitamin and mineral enriched meat. Do we want to trade with them?"

"I don't know," Jay said, in a tone that suggested he wouldn't mind trading half of their tins for a single bar of chocolate.

"Then look at it this way," she said. "How many people do you think worked here? How many families? How many parents of hungry children who are prepared to do anything to keep them fed? What if they just decided to take everything we have? No. We shouldn't go looking for them. It won't be safe."

"What do you think?" Jay asked, turning to Sebastian. Nilda's jaw tightened at that small act of rebellion.

"I think," Sebastian said slowly, "that sooner or later we will have to trust someone, but if we're to trade, we need to do it from a far stronger position than we have at the moment."

"But what about the coal?" Jay asked.

"Well, since we're here, we could try one of these farms. We did want to have another look for livestock," she suggested uncertainly.

"I'm not sure that..." Sebastian began, but he trailed off. He was staring out across the forecourt at the field over the road. "I think our discussion just became moot." He pointed at a distant figure walking towards them across the ploughed earth.

"Do we go?" Nilda asked.

"We'd have to talk to others who stayed behind sooner or later," Sebastian said. "And there's three of us and only one of... him? Or her? I can't tell."

Jay began walking back across the forecourt.

"Wait!" Nilda snapped. Jay ignored her. "Oh come on, then," she added to Sebastian, and followed her son.

By the time she reached the road, Jay was on the other side. He leaned against the fence, and stared out across the field. Nilda thought there was something odd about the now not-so-distant figure.

"Hey! Hi! Hello!" Jay yelled, waving. "We're..." But he didn't finish. He started backing away from the fence and the figure shambling through

41

the muddy soil towards them. Its movement was erratic. Its arms flailed in front, its legs moved spasmodically. As it got closer, Nilda could see its teeth snapping up and down.

"Zombie," Nilda murmured as she ran across the road and grabbed her son's arm. "Come on!" she barked, pushing him in front, "Quickly, now. We need to get out of here."

He didn't need much encouragement.

"What now?" Jay asked, when they were sitting around the kitchen table, the doors firmly closed, and the curtains pulled tight.

"We need bikes," Nilda said. "It wasn't moving that quickly. I don't think they can. I mean, did you see any of them run on your way back from the muster point?"

"No," Sebastian said. "They just have that slouching shambling gait, as if each limb is operating independently of the others. I don't think they can move quickly, but they don't need to rest."

"We run and we hide," Nilda said. "On bikes we can outpace them."

"And then what?" Jay asked. "What if we see one and it follows us back here?"

"We'll be careful. We won't come back here, not directly. And we should block up the alleyway. Maybe…" She hesitated. "Maybe we've got enough food. For now, at least."

"That's not what you said yesterday," Jay said.

"It's what you were saying, though, wasn't it?" she replied.

"Well, what about the coal?" he asked.

"We knew this would happen," Sebastian said. "We just didn't want to believe it. However you look at it, the numbers just don't add up."

"What do you mean?" Nilda asked.

"Take water. Within a few weeks, if not a few hours, the water will stop flowing out of the taps. That will leave us with the water in the tanks in these houses. For three people that will keep us going until August, but we'll need to boil it. So we start by burning the furniture we can find in the terrace and then in the houses nearby. What do we do when we've burned it all? We'll spend our time going out, further and further, just to find firewood. We'll run out of water during the height of summer, and then we'll spend our time searching for that and carrying it back. When autumn arrives we'll need a fire for heat as well as cooking. Every day we'll be searching for water and fuel, and in all that time we won't have gone looking for food. Any that we don't gather now will have spoiled, been taken by others, or eaten by vermin. No, if we stay here, stay safe behind our meagre walls, we are only delaying our inevitable demise."

"Unless the zombies stop," Nilda said. "If they do, then we can go out and—"

"And only have other scavengers and the harsh weather to worry about," Sebastian cut in. "But why should they ever stop when there's no reason in their being alive?"

"You're saying we need to move?" Nilda asked flatly.

"What was it you said about Rob?" Jay asked. "About how he was scared, and that was the reason he was staying where he was? Sebastian's right. We need a better house than this."

The words stung. It was the best house that she could afford. When her salary was frozen and her hours cut while the prices kept going up, it was better than she could afford. She'd kept the roof over their heads because a house was important to her. Jay was too young to remember their life in London. Far too young to remember that brief happy time when there were three of them, and thankfully too young to remember the miserable months when it was just her and him. He didn't remember that dismal flat in the middle of an estate. A grim apartment in a block that would have been condemned if the council hadn't owned it, with neighbours above, below, and to either side. A place where there was no point owning anything of value because, locked door or not, they would be broken into on a weekly basis. When the settlement came through, she'd decided they would leave London. She'd applied for dozens of jobs, but only received one interview. After she'd explained why she'd brought a bawling infant with her - there was nobody left to whom she would entrust his care - the manager had been too riddled with guilt not to offer her the job. She'd bought the house because she didn't want to owe anything to anyone, not a bank and certainly not a landlord. It was a second chance for them both. She'd had such high hopes. Most had come to nought, but the house was theirs. It was their home. Except…

"I know," she said reluctantly. "We'll find a house with a working chimney. And a high fence. Maybe with a proper garden in which we can plant something."

"No. Not a house," Sebastian said. "We might have a bit more space, but we'd have the same problems."

"What about one of the castles?" Jay suggested. "Lowther or Penrith or… what's the other one?"

"Brougham," Sebastian said. "They're just ruins. Broken shells standing in manicured grounds. Wonderful backdrops for wedding photographs, but of no use to us."

"What about one of the ones further away?" Jay asked. "There are plenty of proper ones, aren't there? Like the ones you took me too when I was young."

"There are some, I suppose," Nilda said, pleased that her son remembered those trips. "But they're really just large houses. They have strong walls, but you can't eat stone. They would have wells or streams nearby, but those would be away from the main buildings. If the undead came then how would we get to the water? And there's another problem. Castles are the obvious place to go. Other people will have thought of going there first."

"Then we trade for a place," Jay said, waving his arms at the piles of tins on the counters and in the living room. "This is all worth more than money now."

"We'd have to cycle," she said. "So all we'd have to trade is three bags of pet food per trip. Let's say that they believed we had more. We'd have to leave our food with them and come back again and again and again. And then, when we'd made our last trip and almost all our food was inside, we'd have to hope they would let us back in." She didn't mention the risk posed by the undead that they were surely to meet travelling back and forth through the British countryside.

"Then we drive," Jay said. "We find a van, fill it up, and take it all in one go."

"No, we can't," Sebastian said. "I think zombies are attracted by noise. They would follow the sound of the engine and no one would welcome us for bringing the undead to their refuge. Even if we were to find the place empty, we would still be under siege. Assuming, of course, that we found enough petrol to get us there, and that brings us back to the problem we started with."

"Okay, fine," Jay said. "So what's your idea?"

"We need somewhere close," Nilda said. "Somewhere we can reach by bike and where it won't take more than a few days to move all of our things. The best I can think of is one of the farms. Perhaps we could find one with crops already planted."

"Perhaps," Sebastian said, "but we need water more than we need food. And we need strong walls more than we need either of those."

"Yeah, okay," Jay said with growing impatience. "But where?"

"St Lucian's," Sebastian said.

"The school?" Nilda asked.

"Exactly."

"The big private one up on the hill?" Jay asked.

"The same. The boarding houses were evacuated a week before—" He stopped. "God, I wonder what happened to all those children?"

"Well," Nilda said after a moment's silence. "The schools were closed, so there might be some food there. What about water?"

"They had their playing fields dug over and a flood prevention system put in," Sebastian said. "It's essentially a large underground reservoir to collect the rainwater. It was plumbed into the wastewater system. They were going to use it to flush toilets, irrigate the cricket pitches, that sort of thing."

"So there's water," she said. "What else?"

"The playing fields themselves. There's more than enough space to turn into a farm, and not much more effort than would be required in working already ploughed fields. You know what they say about farming, that it's ninety-percent pulling weeds and only ten-percent planting seeds; well, the pitches there are weed free."

"Ploughing up playing fields? I don't know. We'd have to do it by hand. There'll be no tractors, no horses. That's going to be a lot of work for just the three of us."

"We'll need more than three," Sebastian replied, looking at Nilda. "A lot more. The school has a wall, but it only goes around the older part of the school. The newer part just has a chest-high fence. We'll need to reinforce it, and that means work, and that means people. And once our walls are built, we'll need to keep them patrolled. But we need to be selective. We need to invite people to join us, not the other way around."

They waited for Nilda to speak.

"Fine," she said, standing up. "It's agreed. Well, come on then. There's no point putting it off."

"Should we take some of the food with us?" Jay asked.

"No," she said, "We'll pack light, in case there are people there or… or in case we need to turn and run."

Sebastian stood up and went over to his pack, one he'd kept ready by the door since he'd returned. He hefted it onto his shoulder. It was clearly still half full.

"Well, what are you taking, then?" Jay asked.

"Call it a precaution. I'm not being caught unprepared again."

"And you should take this," Nilda said, taking the replica gladius out of the cupboard under the stairs. She held it out to the older man.

He took it, nodding. "For now," he said.

It took them an hour to get to the school. It was only a twenty-five minute walk from the terrace, but they stopped to find bicycles. Even that wouldn't have taken quite so long if Jay didn't refuse the first one they found on the grounds that he "wouldn't be seen undead on a girl's bike."

"It's big," Jay said, as they dismounted outside the closed school gates. "But I was expecting… I don't know. Something grander."

Beyond the gate of ten-foot-high wrought iron embedded in faded red brick, they could see a car park. Beyond that was a solitary 1970s block of concrete and glass.

"The school was built long before cars were invented. The main entrance used to be over on the other side. Ah, that's a good sign," Sebastian said, lifting the chain running through the gate. "The padlock's intact."

"You want me to try to break it?" Jay offered.

"No," Nilda said, suppressing a smile. "We'll climb over."

They left their bikes against the railing and broke into the school.

"Whoa!" Jay exclaimed, as they walked up the drive into the car park, and the school opened up before them. "That's impressive. Is this really all a school?"

"Oh, yes," Sebastian said. "The cricket pavilion's over there. Behind it, you see the trees? Well, behind those is the sport's centre."

"You see that building, that one there?" Jay said, pointing at a monstrous redbrick and sandstone building on the far side of the car park. "That's bigger than my entire school."

"That's the Lord Henry block," Sebastian said. "Big school, they called it. Traditionally it's where they taught the older children."

"It's like something out of a movie," Jay said.

"A television series would be more accurate," Sebastian replied. "Did you see that version of *To Serve Them All My Days* they broadcast at Christmas? They filmed it here. The exterior scenes, at least. No? Well, it doesn't matter. That two-storey redbrick, that's the staff room and offices. That newer building is the Lower School. The science block is just behind it, behind that are the Scrub Fields. Those are the sports pitches for the younger children. Art was taught across the road. You can't see it from here. Of course, they call it Architecture and Engineering. The boarding houses are next to it."

"And this is actually a school?" Jay asked with frank disbelief.

"You must have seen the pupils, surely?" Sebastian replied.

"In their uniforms. Sure. Wearing those straw hats and crimson blazers."

"Oh, yes. Those. The imperial purple. Only worn by prefects. A mark of authority, you see."

"Oh. Yeah. Right." Jay nodded, though from his tone he didn't get the reference. "And you taught here?"

"Not really. Not anymore. Thirty years ago, they hired me to teach full time. That's why I bought the house. I thought it was a job for life. Five years ago, they decided that classics were too… difficult for the pupils. Unnecessary for their future lives. You see, this school wasn't for the academically gifted, more for the… financially endowed."

"It was a place for rich parents to send their stupid sons," Nilda summarised. "Right?"

"I wouldn't put it so crudely, but yes. The kind not expected to work, but who were expected to be able to read and count and—"

"And know which fork to use with the salmon," Nilda finished.

"Not quite, but examinations and academic success were not as important as the whole child."

"I don't know why you're defending the place," Nilda said. "They sacked you."

"That wasn't the children's fault. It was the staff. Or the governors. Generation after generation, they took care of princes and future oligarchs. That they didn't instil some sense of purpose was not the fault of youth."

"But you were sacked?" Jay asked.

"They cut my hours down to a few months in the summer and a few in the autumn. That was all they thought sufficient to teach the children enough phrases that it would appear they'd had a deeper education than was the case. That was why I spent most of the year selling life insurance. Which, in one of those deliciously ironic quirks of fate, I discovered I preferred. It certainly paid more."

"And thus were world leaders made," Nilda finished.

"I think it was mostly the children of pop stars and other celebrities," Sebastian corrected her.

"Who cares?" Jay asked. "I mean, seriously. So, okay, we're here, but can we live here? Where's the water?"

"The pump is over in The Backs."

"Where?"

"The groundskeeper's shed." Sebastian pointed to the trees beyond the cricket pitch.

"Does everything have another name?" Jay asked.

"It's an old school. Three hundred years of history. Of course, they claimed a far older pedigree than that. There was a monastery on this site back in the fourteenth century."

He stopped talking. Two figures were approaching in the distance.

"Are they...?" Jay began.

"No," Nilda said. "They're human."

The two figures had noticed them, and stopped.

"Smile, then," Sebastian said. He raised his arms and waved.

"Do you recognise them?" Nilda asked, as the two people got closer.

"No. Just keep smiling."

Warily, the two small groups approached one another. The pair, a man and a woman, stopped ten paces away.

"I'm sorry, I don't believe we've met. I'm Sebastian Baker." He spoke warmly, as if this was a chance meeting on some remote island holiday. "This is Nilda and Jay."

"I'm Tracy. This is Mark," the woman said.

"We came here because of the water," Sebastian said.

"The flood defences. We're the same," Mark said. "But we can't figure out where to access it."

"The pump's over there. In The Backs," Jay said.

"The where?" Tracy asked.

"The groundskeeper's shed." Jay pointed.

"You went to school here?" Mark asked.

Jay gave a snort of laughter.

"I used to teach here," Sebastian explained.

"Ah." Mark nodded.

They looked around at one another, each waiting for someone else to make the next move.

Jay broke the silence. "Shouldn't we go and have a look at this pump then?" he asked.

Cautiously, uncertain of each other's intentions, they headed towards the smattering of small buildings on the edge of the school grounds.

"That's it?" Nilda asked, staring at the mechanism. A large cylinder, eight feet in diameter, jutted out of recently laid cement. She'd been expecting something more recognisable.

"That's the pump," Tracy said, pointing at the mechanical box at the side.

"Why's it so large?" Jay asked.

"It didn't need to be," Tracy replied. "It could be about half the size and still do twice the work needed. It looks like they've prepped it to go into their plumbing system. I think," she added as she opened the box and peered at the mechanism, "that they were planning on adding a water filtration plant to this, to use it for their drinking water. They didn't, but that's not going to be a problem."

"So, what do you think? Is it a goer?" Mark asked her.

"Maybe," she said. "With a car battery and, let's see…" She peered at the pipes. They tracked across the floor, disappearing into the concrete floor just before reaching the shed walls. "Yes. I think there's a reservoir tank in, or underneath, one of the buildings. The tank feeds the toilet cisterns. As the toilets are flushed, the tank empties. You see here?" She pointed to a dial. "When the level drops below a predetermined point, the pump kicks in and tops it up. We're what? Twenty feet higher than the school?"

"Yes, that's about right," Sebastian said.

"Right," she said. "So it's all gravity feed. What's that building we passed, the large one with the white paint and red tile roof?"

"The cricket pavilion," Sebastian said.

"Jeez, Tracy, didn't you see the scoreboard?" Mark asked with a shake of his head.

"I think," she said, giving him a friendly glare, "the storage tank is under there."

"Are you an engineer?" Nilda asked.

"Close. I'm a plumber."

"Oh."

"Yeah, people always react like that. I was an engineer. Astronautical. I dreamed of building space ships. It turned out that there wasn't much call for that kind of thing, but people always need their toilets unblocked."

"But how do we get the water out?" Jay asked.

"That's simple enough," she replied, standing up. "We just need a power supply. A car battery will do it. Do you think the pavilion has toilets?"

"Yes, in the changing rooms," Sebastian said.

"That's something. I think, with a bit of work, we can isolate that block. The water's not going to be clean, but I can get it coming out of the tap."

"What about the noise?" Jay asked.

"Noise?"

"Because of the undead," he added.

"I don't think that's going to be a problem, but" she added, "we can insulate the walls here easily enough."

"And what if the pump breaks?" Nilda asked.

"Well…" Tracy blew air out through her teeth. Nilda almost smiled. "It's not a complicated system. We can easily replace the electric motor with a hand pump."

"So we've got water," Mark said.

"And since I've got a stove, perhaps now would be a good time to have a cup of tea," Sebastian suggested, "and get to know one another."

"What is it with you and tea?" Jay asked.

"I'm an Englishman," Sebastian said. "It's hardly an apocalypse while you still have tea and the wherewithal to brew it. Perhaps we should go back outside so we can see anything that approaches."

"I doubt anyone will," Mark said. "It's unlikely the government will come back any time soon. It'll be months before those enclaves are anything but chaos and disorder."

"I didn't mean the government," Sebastian said. They went back outside, and while they waited for the water to boil, he told them what he'd seen at the muster point.

"Murdered? I can't believe it," Mark said.

"It's true," Sebastian said. "There'll be no one coming. Or we have to hope there won't."

"So we're on our own," Tracy said.

The conversation stalled until the tea had been poured.

"We've been cooking on an old barbecue," Mark said. "It works well enough, but everything tastes of smoke."

"He was never very good at outdoor cooking," Tracy said, stretching her legs. "Or indoor cooking, come to that."

Mark shrugged affably. Their good-natured bickering tugged at Nilda's memory, bringing up memories she'd long tried to bury.

"You think we can redirect the water to the pitches?" Jay asked, pointing at the green field interspersed with mud.

"Probably," Tracy said. "Why?"

"Because that's where we're going to grow all the food," he replied.

"Well, we've uh…" Mark glanced at Tracy.

"We've got food," she said. "We've been raiding the houses I used to get emergency call-outs to, and which I remembered had a second freezer. I figured if they stocked up on frozen food, it was likely they'd have kept a store of cans and packets as well. Mostly I was right. We're happy to share. Split five ways it should still last us a couple weeks."

"Oh, no. We've got food for now," Jay said. Nilda gritted her teeth. "I meant for the autumn and winter. But," he added, "is yours human food?"

"What do you mean?" Tracy asked with genuine suspicion.

"All we've got—"

"We've been raiding the vet's and pet food stores. We've got cat food, dog food, bird food. Pet food, that's what he means," Nilda said quickly.

"Oh." Tracy nodded, relieved understanding clear on her face.

"I didn't think of that," Mark said. "But food's food, right? What does it matter what animal's on the tin?"

"So, we're alright for food and water," Jay said. "What else do we need?"

"We should check the Refectory. That's the dining hall," Sebastian added. "I doubt we'll find anything to eat, but there'll be pots and pans there. And we'll find clothes in the boarding houses. Men's and boys' clothes, but that would do in a pinch. It's the library that will be of most use. All those textbooks on how civilisations developed. On how our ancestors lived in the ages before electricity. Yes, those will be a real boon."

"So this might work, then," Mark said, slowly. "The five of us, here, ploughing up the fields, growing food. We'll work together. Agreed?"

Jay and Sebastian looked at Nilda.

"Yes," she said, trying not to show the doubt she felt.

"Then there's no point hanging around," Tracy said, standing up, "I'll need my tools if I'm going to get that pump working."

Nilda nodded. "And we better go back and start ferrying up the food. We'll... Well, I suppose we'll see you later."

"We won't bring all the food back with us," Nilda said when they were a mile away from the school.

"You don't trust them?" Sebastian asked.

"I wouldn't go so far as saying I distrusted them," she replied, "but I don't trust anyone right now. We'll leave a third of the tins upstairs under the floorboards. If this all goes wrong, then we'll still have a few months of supplies. We'll just say that we've cleared out all the houses around there, and there'll be no reason for them to investigate too hard."

"Others might," Jay said.

"They might," Nilda said, thinking about Rob. He was a problem that would have to be dealt with. "We can't plan for every eventuality, but we can try."

When they reached the house Nilda went upstairs, pulled up the floorboards and began hiding one third of the tins. Jay and Sebastian started packing the rest into bags.

"It'll take an entire day to move all of these," Sebastian said, when Nilda returned downstairs having finished hiding one third of the tinned food. All of the bags were now filled, but the kitchen and living room were still cluttered with cans and packets.

"Not if we get Mark and Tracy to help," Jay said. "And why shouldn't we? I mean, the rest of the food has been hidden, right? And if you're worried they'll find out where the house is, well, if we're just going back and forth tomorrow, they could easily follow us."

"He's got a point," Sebastian said. "The hidden food notwithstanding, you have to trust someone sooner or later."

"You said that the night before you went on the evacuation," she reminded him. "But, okay. Better to get it done quickly."

Their bikes heavily laden, they cycled slowly away from the terrace. Jay occasionally stopped to pick up a discarded phone. Nilda tried to stop him the first few times. He'd pointed out that if it was unlocked, he could watch whatever videos and listen to whatever music had been left on it, at least until the battery ran out.

"It's like when I was teaching him to ride," Nilda said. She and Sebastian had stopped at another junction, waiting for Jay to catch up.

"You taught him yourself?" Sebastian asked. "You never told me what happened to—" Sebastian was interrupted by a yell. They turned to look. Jay had nearly fallen off his bike. Both his feet were on the ground as he pushed, rather than pedalled, his way along the road. His frantic desperation was as clear as the reason for it.

A man had half fallen through the hedge just behind her son. No, not a man. It was a zombie. She threw off the bags hanging from her handlebars, and pedalled furiously back down the road. She'd made it twenty yards before Jay remembered the pedals. A scant few seconds later, he shot past her.

"Seb!" she barked over her shoulder, after a moment's frantic calculation. "Catch him!"

"What about you?" Sebastian called back.

"Just go!" she yelled. The man turned and followed her son.

Nilda stopped the bike in the middle of the road, two houses from the creature. It was caught in the hedge. As it thrashed, red-brown pus oozed out of great rips in its face where branches had torn through its skin. It was monstrous, yet had to have been human only a few days before. She dismounted, letting her bike fall to the ground, and pulled the cricket bat out from the bag over her shoulder. It seemed like a wholly inadequate weapon to her now.

Slowly, she walked down the street towards the zombie. As she approached, its writhing became more manic. When she was twenty feet away, there was a cracking of branches and a tearing of soil as the creature's violent flailing ripped the bush, roots and all, out of the ground. The zombie tumbled over the low wall and out onto the road. She gripped the bat, then re-gripped it, trying to find reassurance in its heft.

The creature tried to stand. No, she realised. Its legs kicked, and its hands clawed. It was trying to walk towards her, with no comprehension that it had to stand up first. She was ten feet away when, with an accidentally timed pivot of its arms and legs, the creature got to its knees. She was five feet away when it staggered upright. Never taking her eyes off the zombie, she brought the bat up and over her head, and swung it into the creature's face. Bone broke. Teeth flew. The zombie staggered backwards, but it didn't fall. She swung again. This time the creature's out-flung arm took the brunt of the blow. Its forearm snapped. White bone stabbed out through the remains of a woollen shirt. There was no pain to distract the creature as it swung its arm forward again. Nilda skipped backwards out of range of its clawing fingers. The broken arm sailed harmlessly past. Brown pus oozed out of skin pierced by jagged bone to splatter down onto the pavement.

Nilda backed away, changed her grip, and swung at the creature's legs. The bat smashed into its kneecap, and the creature fell forward. Nilda jumped to get out of the way, pivoted in mid-air, and brought the bat down on the zombie's spine. There was a sickening crunch of bone. She brought it down again on its neck, and then on its skull, again and again, until she was beating blood and brain into the asphalt.

Then she stopped and backed away from the twice-dead creature. Taking long slow breaths, trying to calm her racing heart, she looked around. She listened. Nothing. She was alone.

She looked at the bat. It was covered in gore. Splinters of wood stuck out from the side, and that brownish pus had seeped into the cracks. There would be no way of cleaning it. She tossed it aside.

Her hands were covered in spots of that same red-brown blood. So was her jacket. She ripped it off, wiped her hands clean on the lining, and threw it away. Cold air cut through her as she returned to the bike, and headed back to the school. She'd made it a street and a half before meeting Jay and Sebastian heading back towards her.

"Are you all right?" Jay asked, relief mixing with embarrassment.

"I'm fine," she said. "Running was the right thing to do. You just ran a bit too far, a bit too fast."

"And you?" Sebastian asked. "What happened?"

"It's dead. But when they said destroy the brain, they really meant it. You have to cave their skulls in. The creatures are impossible. They have no right, no reason to live. It's..." She saw the look on her son's face. "I had to," she said. "We couldn't leave it there. It's between the house and the school. It had to be done. And better it were done quickly. Now, let's get this stuff to the school."

There was no sign of Mark or Tracy when they arrived.

"You unpack those bags," Nilda said. "I want to find some bleach and clean my hands properly."

"What now?" Jay asked, when she'd returned and they had stacked the tins inside the pavilion.

"Now we go back. We have to get that food."

When they returned after the second trip, they found the other two walking along the road towards them. Each wore an overloaded backpack, with another bag in one hand, and a crowbar in the other.

"You didn't cycle?" Sebastian asked.

"I don't know how, okay?" Mark said testily. From his tone they guessed this was a topic the couple had discussed a lot that day. "And I didn't think this was the time to..." He finally noticed Nilda's expression "What happened?"

"Zombies," she said. "Or one of them. About a mile from here."

They looked around the school, at the vast buildings they had yet to ensure were empty, and then at the gates. They suddenly didn't seem as high as they had a few hours before.

Part 2: Fortification
Cumbria, and Dumfries & Galloway

13th March

"We need weapons," Nilda said.

The previous day, they'd spent a fraught two hours confirming the school was empty of the undead. They'd then spent a frantic three hours collecting food from the terrace. Even with the five of them working together - Mark pushing himself along as much as he was pedalling - they hadn't collected it all.

"Where do we look?" Mark asked. "A farm? I doubt there'll be any left in the police station. Though there might be, since the police were issued with Army rifles."

"No," Nilda said flatly. "Guns would be useless once we ran out of ammunition, and where would we find any more? That's not to mention the noise. I was thinking of spears and swords."

"Or bows," Jay suggested.

"They need as much skill as a rifle," Sebastian said. "Perhaps more as you'd have to be able to plant an arrow right through a creature's eye socket."

Jay nodded slowly. A small voice inside Nilda cried at how quickly her son had embraced the violence of their new world.

"Swords and spears, where do we find those?" Tracy asked. She looked at Sebastian. So did everyone else.

"Well," he said slowly, "museums and country houses are the two obvious places. But those would be antiques. They may be more rust than metal. We could spend a whole day searching and not find anything actually usable. I think we're better off sticking with what we know."

"Tools," Tracy said. "That's what we know. Axes and crowbars. And a manual pump would be useful for when the batteries die. Seems like the obvious place to try would be the fire station."

The fire engines were gone. The station appeared hurriedly abandoned.

"This coat," Nilda said, taking a jacket from the peg, "do you think it's bite proof?"

"Probably," Sebastian said. "If it's designed not to rip or tear when caught by jagged debris."

"Good enough. Here, Jay. Put this on." She threw it to her son. He did, without hesitation. She took one down for herself.

"Here. Found it," Mark said, after he'd levered off the bolts to a long metal cupboard. "This is what we want. Fire axes and crowbars. And not the kind you'd find in any old store."

They each took one, improvising slings and harnesses to carry them.

"Might as well have some spares," Nilda said, as she took down another axe and strapped it on to the back of the bike. "In fact," she added as she took down a third, "we might as well take them all."

"Did you find the pump?" Jay asked Tracy.

"No. I think they must keep them on the engines. Which, I guess, makes sense. It's not a problem for now, and honestly, we can just as easily make one. What about first aid kits?"

"There was only the one left," Sebastian said.

"We'll need more than that," Tracy said.

"We've got some supplies from the veterinarian's," Nilda said. "Though not much."

"Well, what about the hospital?" Mark asked. "Have you tried there?"

"Not yet," Nilda said. "I figured they'd have taken everything of use."

"Worth a look though, don't you think?"

It was only a short distance from the fire station to the town's small hospital. To appease Mark, they walked, pushing their bikes with them. They kept quiet, their eyes open. At each house they passed, Nilda couldn't help be aware that their owners were probably dead, and the homes would now be forever vacant. It wasn't the loss of life that was bothering her. The only thing that mattered was keeping Jay safe. Each empty house she saw represented another family of the undead that would have to be killed before her son could have a normal life. So lost was she in her thoughts, she didn't notice the noises until they'd rounded a corner.

"Oh no," she murmured, too softly for the others to hear. It didn't matter. They'd seen the danger. Up ahead, the road branched. At the junction was a detached house. Clawing at the doors, their arms already pushing through the broken window were nine of the undead.

"Back. Let's go," Sebastian whispered. "Quietly!"

They pushed their bicycles away and behind a wall.

"Did they see us?" Jay asked, too loudly.

"Shh!" Nilda said, gripping his shoulders.

"No," Tracy said, peering around the corner.

"Okay, so we find another way back to the school," Jay said.

"No," Sebastian said. "There's someone in that house. There has to be. Why else would those creatures be trying to get in?"

"You want to go and help them?" Mark asked.

"Do we have a choice?" Sebastian replied. "If you were trapped wouldn't you want us to help you?"

"No, we don't have a choice," Nilda said. "The undead won't go away. We deal with them now so we won't have to do it later. Listen, Jay, I want you to stay here."

"No way," he said, though his protest was half-hearted.

"Yes," she said firmly. "You stay here. We're going to try to kill them, but if we can't, we'll run back here and cycle away. You need to watch the bicycles for us. Understand?"

Leaving Jay with the bikes, she headed towards the house. The others followed. She tested her grip. The axe was well balanced but heavy. When she was fifty yards away she called out.

"Hey!"

One of the creatures turned. She yelled again. The others joined in. For a moment the zombies seemed uncertain, torn between the prey that was close but difficult to reach, and that which was out in the open but further away.

Nilda wondered, as the creatures stumbled away from the house, whether they really did think like that. Was there any spark of reason left in them, or were they acting on instinct alone?

And then there was no time for either thought or doubt. The first of the zombies was ten yards away. Its face was scarred, the nose flattened and broken. Its clothes were shredded as if it had fallen through glass. She stared at its forehead - she didn't want to look in its eyes. She swung the axe up and down. It crushed through the creature's skull, cleaving into its neck. She pulled it out, taking a step backwards. The zombie fell, but there was another just behind it. There wasn't time to swing. She punched the axe-head forward into the creature's face. It stumbled with the impact. She swung up and down. The blade chopped through the zombie's collarbone, deep into its chest, and stuck. The creature fell, but it kept moving. She grabbed the crowbar from her belt, took a step forward, and smashed it down on its skull.

Out of the corner of her eye, she saw Sebastian swing the sword. He mistimed the blow. The blade bounced across the zombie's head, neatly scalping it. Sebastian lost his grip. The sword flew out of his hand, skittering across the street. The old teacher's gaze automatically followed the weapon, and then the zombie was on him. Its flailing arms knocked him to the ground. Sebastian fell on his back, the snarling creature on top. Nilda started to run. She saw the creature snap at Sebastian's face. She could see him struggling, his arms trembling as he tried to push the zombie away, but he didn't have the strength.

Out of nowhere, Jay came running up the street. He grabbed the sword from the ground. One hand gripping the hilt, the other around the pommel, he took another two leaping strides and swung the blade into the creature's neck. It stuck. Momentum carried the creature off Sebastian, taking the sword with it. Jay didn't pause, he leaped over the older man, grabbed the sword, pulled and twisted, nearly decapitating the zombie. He changed his grip and stabbed the blade down through the creature's temple. Nilda had time to notice the brown red ooze dripping from the blade as he pulled it out, seconds before she saw another creature heading for her son. Still running, she took a skipping half step and dived forward, knocking the creature to the ground. It thrashed underneath her as she punched and pushed and tried to find the purchase to swing the crowbar.

And then, its edge still dripping brown blood, the sword plunged down into the zombie's eye, inches from her face. The creature stopped moving.

"Come on, Mum, get up! Quick!" Jay said, pulling her to her feet.

She spared a glance at him. He seemed fine but… different. She didn't have time to think about that. She looked towards the house, in time to see Tracy swing her axe into a zombie's legs, and then Mark stepped forward, bringing his down on its skull. Another creature, messily decapitated, lay a few yards from them. She looked around for the other three. They were still by the house.

A broad-shouldered man, with a flat stomach hidden under a potbelly, stood in the doorway. A poker was in one hand, a dead zombie at his feet, with two more trying to claw their way in. Nilda changed her grip as she sprinted towards the house. Holding the crowbar out in front, she speared it forwards, using her weight and momentum to smash through bone. The zombie's skull was crushed. The creature collapsed.

Now only facing one foe, the man swung his poker down. It narrowly missed Nilda before impacting against the zombie's shoulder with enough force to knock it to its knees. She ducked out the way at the same time as Mark barged past, swinging his axe down on the fallen creature's head. Nilda looked around again. Only the living were still moving.

"Jay, are you okay?" she asked, walking quickly over to him.

"Sure," he said with a shrug. The sword was still in his hands.

"Sebastian?"

"Fine. I'm fine. Just a little… I wasn't, uh… I'm fine," he wheezed.

She glanced at Mark and Tracy, then at the man with the poker.

"Thank you," the man said. "I knew someone would come along. I knew we'd made the right choice. Wasn't expecting firemen. I thought they'd send the Army."

Nilda glanced down at the firefighter's jacket she was wearing.

"We took these from the fire station half an hour ago," she said simply. "There's no help coming. We're on our own."

"You're not part of some relief column?" the man asked, disbelief battling despair.

"There won't be one," Sebastian said. "I went on the evacuation. The vaccine was a poison they used to cull the population. I think they thought if there were no people, there would be no zombies. It hasn't worked." He shrugged, and turned to follow Nilda.

"Wait. Where are you going?" the man called out.

"The hospital," Nilda said. "There might be supplies there."

"There isn't. That's where we went and we barely escaped. These creatures followed us. That's how we ended up here."

"We?" she asked.

The man nodded, then turned to the house.

"Sylvia!" he bellowed. A woman came out, pushing two children in front. Nilda guessed their ages somewhere between seven and nine. She didn't ask. She just turned and walked down the road. Jay followed.

"What's wrong, Mum?" he asked.

"There were two adults in that house, with eight undead outside the front door. The front door, Jay, not the back. They let themselves be trapped, and when it came to it, only that man came out to help in the fight. And now they're going to come with us. We can't stop them."

"But if everyone does their bit, if we work together, then it's four more people to share the work," Jay said.

"The two children will be nothing more than two extra mouths eating our food. And they'll need protecting, which means one less person doing something useful."

"So what are you saying?" he stormed. "You'd rather we'd just left those kids to die?"

"No, Jay, of course not," she replied, shaking her head. "But if it comes to a choice between you and anyone else, that's no choice at all."

It was Jay's turn to shake his head, and then he walked off, heading towards Sebastian. He held out the sword to the older man.

"Oh no, I think that's yours," Sebastian insisted. "You made far better use of it than I did. Here." He unbuckled the scabbard he'd improvised and handed it to Jay. "Now, what advice can I give you? The pointed end goes first, and remember that it is pointed. That's a stabbing blade not a hacking one. Twist when it goes in, you don't want it to become stuck

63

again. Keep it clean. Keep it sharp. More than that, learn from my mistake; try to keep a hold of it."

And another little part of Nilda's soul ached at her son's solemn expression as he sheathed the sword.

Without discussion, the plan of going to the hospital was put on hold, and they headed back to the school. This new family were the Harpers; Andrew, Sylvia, Chantelle aged eight, and Christof aged nine. They had driven from Kendal, heading north. Not to anywhere in particular, just with a vague idea that things would be better in Scotland. Nilda couldn't quite understand why they'd gone to the hospital, but that was where they'd run out of fuel. She found it telling that they'd left without either a set destination or the petrol to reach it. There was more to the story, something to do with neighbours and the days leading up to the evacuation. She tuned it out. Her mind was focused on the undead, on her son, and what she would need to do next to ensure he stayed alive.

"Drop off your gear, then we'll need to go out again to collect more supplies," Nilda said, unloading the axes and crowbars they had taken from the fire station.

"We've taken over the cricket pavilion," Jay said, in a far friendlier tone than his mother's. "There's plenty of room."

"That small building?" Mr Harper asked. "We'll probably take one of the rooms over in that block." He pointed to the main school building.

"Suit yourself," Nilda said. "The only working showers are in the pavilion."

That seemed to persuade Sylvia Harper, and the children were too scared to care, but not Mr Andrew Harper.

"Well, where are *we* meant to sleep?" he asked. And Nilda was amazed that there was no residual thanks from their rescue of his family.

"One of the changing rooms?" Tracy suggested.

There were two changing rooms downstairs, each with its own set of showers. One was for the home team. The other was for the visitors. These were on the ground floor, one on either side of a long corridor, bracketed by a plethora of storerooms. On the floor above were the offices, the box, a kitchen, and a long dining room with a working fireplace. According to the brochure they'd found, the dining room was rented out for fully catered functions. According to the same brochure, each meal cost more than Nilda made in three months. Tracy and Mark had claimed that room. Sebastian had claimed the glassed-in box overlooking the pitch, and Nilda and Jay had taken the largest office.

"No," Mr Harper said flatly. "We'll take one of the classrooms. Two of them I think."

Nilda thought of protesting, but decided she couldn't be bothered.

"Fine. Whatever." She grabbed her empty bag and headed back to the bike.

"Where are you going?" Jay asked.

"Same place as you. We need to get the rest of the supplies."

"I think," Tracy said, eyeing the newcomers, "that I'll stay here. I'll see if I can get some of the taps plumbed into the water system. You reckon you can fall off a bike if I'm not there to watch?"

"I've been getting a lot of practice," Mark said.

They went to Mark and Tracy's house. It was a semi-detached, nicely located near one of the better infant schools. It was the ideal home for a family with children, or one expecting them. As they were packing up the supplies, Nilda noticed a photograph. It was of the two of them building a snowman on the green opposite the house. The couple looked happy, almost serene. Nilda remembered the last time they'd had a snowfall that thick. It had been four years ago. She glanced around. There were a few other pictures, but none more recent than that one. Nor were there any signs of children, but upstairs there was one empty bedroom with a slight pink tinge underneath the white-painted walls. Nilda thought she understood.

It only took the four of them one trip to load everything from the house. Nilda noticed that Mark left the photographs behind.

"I'd like to go and see what's at the hospital," she said when they were all outside the house.

"What for?" Jay asked.

"If there are zombies there, it would be useful to know how many. And if there are only a few perhaps we can deal with them. If not… well, better we know now. You go on. I'll meet you back at the school."

"I'll go too," Jay said.

"We'll all go," Sebastian offered.

Nilda tried to protest. It did no good.

They saw no undead on the way to the small hospital.

"I doubt we'll find anything," Mark panted. "I saw them bring up vans and lorries to empty the place. That was back during the curfew."

"I can't believe they'd be efficient enough to take everything," Nilda replied.

But all plans for investigating the hospital were quickly abandoned when they saw the front entrance. There was a car, its doors left wide open, which had crashed into the main entrance. Around it, moving aimlessly, were two dozen of the undead.

"Let's get back. There's no point hanging around," Mark said.

"Wait," Nilda replied.

"What for?" Sebastian asked.

"I want to see if they're coming from inside or not."

"Impossible to tell," Sebastian said. "The doors are broken. They can roam freely inside and out. We've got to assume that the building's infested with them."

"Come on, Mum," Jay said.

Reluctantly, Nilda followed them back to the school. It wasn't that she expected to find anything useful in the hospital, but with each passing day there were more and more of the undead. She was starting to think they would need to prepare for a siege. And she was worried that was something none of them would survive.

"No!" They heard Tracy say to Mr Harper when they arrived at the school.

"I don't see why not. It can't be hard," he replied.

She was covered in dirt except for the parts soaked with water, and even those were coated in a thin layer of grease. She was sitting on the steps to the pavilion, Mr Harper standing just a few inches too close, towering over her.

"No, you're right," Tracy said. "It's not hard. It's impossible."

"What is?" Mark asked.

Harper turned, surprise on his face. Despite the noise of wheels and bags and feet, he'd not heard them approach. Nilda thought she now partly understood how he'd become trapped.

"I was just asking why she can't get the showers over in the boarding house to work."

"Because," Tracy said as she slowly stood up, "that building is over there, on the other side of the school. The pipes aren't connected. So I'd either have to lay new ones, or dig up the concrete to find the old ones. I don't have any pipes. I don't have any way of digging through concrete. You want showers? You use these ones. You want hot water? You boil it yourself. You want to eat, then you help find the food."

Mumbling something about 'getting the kids settled in,' he headed back to the boarding house.

"I don't like him," Tracy said, as they unloaded the bikes. "Since you left I haven't seen the kids or that woman. It's just him and there's something about him that I just don't like."

"He's here now," Mark said. "There's not much we can do about that."

Wishing she disagreed, Nilda finished unloading. She wanted to put her feet up. She was tired. Jay and the others were too, but there wasn't time for rest. They went out again, this time going back to the terrace to collect the food.

The problem was Mark. Had the roads not been covered in so much litter from the evacuation, he might have fallen off his bike less often. As it was, he stumbled to a halt every few hundred yards. He didn't always fall off, though he had a tendency to throw his feet out and let go of the handlebars, allowing the bike to drop to the ground with a clatter that echoed off the deserted buildings. At first it had been funny, then it had been frustrating, and then, when they reached the end of one particular road and saw four of the undead coming towards them, they realised how dangerous it was. They'd not fought, but turned, and found a different way around.

Jay, Sebastian, and Nilda made a second trip on their own. By the time they got back their exhaustion, caused as much by tension as exertion, was complete. They collapsed on the steps outside the pavilion next to Tracy and Mark. The Harpers appeared a few minutes later.

"What about sorting out some food then," Mr Harper half-asked, half-demanded.

"I don't cook," Nilda said firmly. Tracy said nothing.

"Oh? Right." There was that tone in Harper's voice, again.

"I do," Mark said. "And not as badly as Tracy makes out."

Despite what Tracy said, Mark was a good cook. Or good enough when the ingredients all came in tins.

After they'd eaten a meal in stilted silence, Nilda went outside to stare at the pitches. Sebastian followed her.

"Not quite the people one would wish to be stranded with at the end of the world," Sebastian said. "The timid wife, and the husband about to graduate from petty chauvinism to full blown misogyny."

"No. That I can deal with. There's something else about Andrew Harper I just don't trust."

"You think he's violent?" Seb asked.

"Towards Sylvia and the kids, you mean? No. He's not, I'm sure of it." And she was sure. She knew violent, but that was a long time ago, before Jay was born. "He's just not… I don't know. My gut says kick him out, but perhaps I'm being unfair. I was never that good at judging people."

"I had noticed that," he said.

She turned to glare at him, but saw he was smiling.

"I knew someone, once," Nilda said. "It was a long time ago. He would always watch groups and how they interacted. He'd look at the dynamic and explain why people acted the way they did. Like, he'd say that some of them were reverting to childhood, or trying to exert dominance or something."

"He was a psychologist?" Sebastian asked.

"Nothing like that. He was just fascinated by people. We used to go up to Westminster on Saturdays, and we'd sit on the bench outside the cathedral and watch all the tourists. I'd make up stories about the people, but he had a way of knowing what they were thinking. Like, if they were waiting for someone, and if it was a date or family. And he'd always get it right. Always. I mean, at first I thought he was guessing, but he actually went up to people to ask. And, once, there was this…" She shook her head, as if to banish a too raw memory. "Anyway, we don't have time for that. Not now. I don't care why they're acting the way they do. Either they pull their weight and help, or they go."

"Except they won't. I know you won't kick them out. Not the children."

"Yeah," she admitted. "Fine. That means we've got new mouths to feed and backs to protect, and out of the four of them only one is a provider, and at best he's going to only provide for them. Maybe we can change that. Maybe we can get the woman working. Maybe. But right now, they're a liability. We need more people. Or, one way or another, a lot fewer."

"But if they won't go… Wait, you're thinking of leaving?"

"Just you, me, and Jay. Perhaps. If I knew of somewhere safer than this, then I'd say we should leave right now. I'd even leave the food. Or some of it. But where can we go? We went through all that and ended up here."

"So we stay. And you're right. If that's going to work then we need more people. And it has to work. There's nowhere to run to. So how do we find others?"

14th March

They lit a bonfire. Wanting to separate the Harpers, Tracy and Mark enlisted Sylvia to help dig up the cricket pitch. The two children joined Jay feeding evergreen branches onto the bonfire to send up a pillar of smoke. Sebastian and Nilda took Mr Harper back to the terrace to gather the last of the food.

"This is your place is it?" Mr Harper said sniffily when he saw the small house. Nilda said nothing as they collected the last of the bags.

When they got back, they found a middle-aged woman Nilda vaguely recognised tearing away at the grass with a vengeful ferocity. She paused just long enough to introduce herself as Marjory Stowe, someone who'd worked at the fish counter at the supermarket, before ripping into the ground once more. Nilda didn't ask what demons she was exorcising.

Nilda headed over to the pavilion to unload the bags.

"Is that the lot?" Jay asked.

"More or less. How are things here?"

"This new woman's okay. The kids are… I dunno. Scared, I suppose."

"We all are." She looked around. She saw the activity. She heard the noise. "There's a few more things I want to get from the house. Will you be all right here?"

"You want me to come with you?" he asked, giving her a far too grown-up look.

"No. I'll go on my own. It'll be easier. If I see any of the undead, I'll just turn around and come back."

She headed straight to their house. She came across the undead only once. Two of them were shambling down the street towards the town. She doubled back and took a different road. When she arrived at the terrace, she checked that the street was empty and the alley clear. Only when she was sure she wouldn't be heard did she kick down the front door. Satisfied at the way the lock had splintered, she went inside and opened all the cupboards in the kitchen, pulling out the saucepans and crockery onto the floor. She stamped on a few mugs, kicking the shards out into the living room. She opened and emptied the drawers, then went upstairs and did

70

the same up in the bedroom. Taking one last look around her house she decided that, yes, if anyone came they would see a place that had already been looted.

She left the house to search for some more bicycles. After an hour, she'd found three. She hid them under a tarpaulin in the backyard of a house a little further down the terrace.

"Good, but is it good enough?" she murmured. Bikes were slow. She glanced towards the edge of town. The smoke from their bonfire was clearly visible above the rooftops. She thought about going straight back, but she wanted to check the police station, and wanted to do it without anyone else knowing. Sebastian had mentioned seeing a few police cars during his journey to the muster point, but he'd mostly seen Army vehicles. It had been the same in the days before the evacuation. There was a chance that the police vehicles would still be parked at the station, and have fuel in their tanks. Not a great chance, but one worth investigating. With so many undead nearby, if they were going to flee, she would prefer to drive.

She was nearing the town centre when she heard it. At first, she thought it was a car backfiring. Then she heard it again. It was a shot. Someone was shooting. She didn't know if she wanted to help. Anyone who was armed was probably a representative of the government and thus to be avoided. Whoever they were, they'd be able to see the smoke from the bonfire. She headed towards the sound.

The shooter was definitely not police. Though she was standing on the roof of an Army Armoured Personnel Carrier, the blue and silver streaks in her hair were definitely non-regulation. In the woman's hands was a pump-action shotgun with a folding stock that Nilda guessed was as military as the vehicle. Surrounding the vehicle were the undead. Nine were still standing. The remains of three lay on the ground. As Nilda watched from the shelter of an alley three hundred yards away, the woman fired again, messily decapitating a zombie in a blue and white ski jacket.

That left eight undead, but as she glanced down the street, Nilda saw four more heading towards them. And there would be more coming, she was sure of that. Each shot would be like a siren to them, but Nilda was

71

reluctant to help the woman. The undead were gathered around one side of the vehicle. The woman could easily jump down the other side and escape. Why hadn't she? The only explanation was that whatever was inside had to be something of value. These days that meant ammunition, fuel, or food.

The four zombies were getting closer. They were now only fifty yards from the alleyway. Whatever Nilda was going to do, she had to do it now.

Nilda got on the bike and cycled out into the road. She glanced back. The four undead behind had seen her and become more aggressively animated at her appearance. She glanced at the truck. The zombies were still pawing and clawing at the windows and frame of the vehicle. Pushing down on the pedals with all her strength, she sprinted towards the APC.

"I'll lure them away," Nilda called out to the woman standing on the vehicle's roof. "You see the smoke? Head towards it, okay?" The woman didn't respond.

Nilda cycled past, and stopped fifty yards further down the road. She turned in the saddle, checking that the undead were following. They were. She kicked off and, darting frequent glances behind, kept a slow and steady pace until a ragged creature in a tattered dress lurched out of a side road. The zombie tripped on the dress's torn hem and fell in a stumbling dive with its arms outstretched. Its clawing fingers brushed against the front spokes of Nilda's bicycle. She swerved, put on a burst of speed, and angled to the next side road. She headed down a narrow one-way street, pausing at the end until she was sure the undead were following. Then she cycled on, leading the zombies away from the truck. She took another turn, another side road, and decided that she was far enough away. Checking the undead were out of sight, she ducked down an alley, then another, doubling back towards the APC. More than ever, she wanted to know what was inside.

When she got there, she found the woman still there, filling a bag with something from the back of the vehicle. Judging from the broken glass scattered around a nearby shop front, the bag was a new acquisition.

Nilda came to a stop. The woman didn't turn.

"Hi," Nilda said.

The woman didn't reply, she just kept filling the bag. Nilda thought of just cycling away. She'd had enough of selfish ingratitude from those whom she'd rescued. Then she saw what was in the back of the truck. Box upon box of military rations. She dismounted, letting the bike fall to the ground. Grabbing the shotgun, the woman swung around, but relaxed when she saw it was Nilda.

"Hi," Nilda said softly, trying not to stare at the scars running up the woman's neck and across the left side of her face. The woman nodded back.

"Um…" Nilda was uncertain what to say. "That's a lot of food."

The woman nodded again.

"If you're coming to the school… I mean. We've water and shelter, and we've got food, though this would be a welcome addition to it. You can't carry it all. I mean…" She stopped. She realised she'd been babbling. It was the gun in the woman's hands coupled with the way her scar turned a bemused smile on one side of her face into a sneer on the other.

"I'm Nilda." She held out her hand.

"Tuck," the woman said taking the hand. Her grip was firm.

"Tuck?" Nilda said, trying to think of what to say next. "Um. Is that short for something?"

Tuck closed her eyes for a moment and took a breath. "Lu. Cy. Tuck. Er." The words came out slow, stilted as if each movement of her vocal chords had to be dragged out of some deep recess of memory.

Nilda took in the scars and the woman's obvious discomfort.

"You're deaf?" she asked.

Tuck nodded.

"But you can lip-read?"

Tuck gave her a look that seemed to say 'obviously'.

"O.K," Nilda said, over-enunciating each syllable. "There. Is. A. School. The Smoke. See?" She pointed.

Tuck rolled her eyes. Nilda flushed with sudden embarrassment, but then Tuck gave a crooked smile.

"Sorry," Nilda murmured.

Tuck shook her head, pointed at Nilda's bag, then at the vehicle, and then returned to grabbing at ration packs. Nilda joined her. The two bags were quickly filled.

"We'll come back with the others," Nilda said, "to collect the rest."

Tuck stopped filling her bag, took Nilda by the arm, and gently turned her so that she could see her lips.

"Sorry. We'll come back with more people to collect the rest," Nilda repeated. She looked back up the road. The zombies were gone, but they might return.

"Did you drive here?" she asked.

The woman nodded, then pointed at the fuel cap, then shook her head.

"Ran out of petrol?"

Tuck nodded.

"Where did it come from? I mean, I can see it's military, but you don't…" She stopped, and once again took in in the scars only partially hidden by the blue and white streaked hair and buttoned-up coat. "You were a soldier?"

Tuck nodded, and gave a shrug accompanied by a quick movement of her hands, before returning to finish filling her bag. Nilda took that to mean that there was a time and a place, and that wasn't here and now.

The bike laden with bags, they headed back towards St Lucian's. Even though she was cycling, Nilda had difficulty keeping up with Tuck running briskly by her side.

"Nilda, I see you've found someone," Sebastian called out, when they reached the school. "And another three arrived here while you were gone. All from out of town. They saw the smoke and were heading to the Lake District. I—"

"There's no time for that," Nilda said. "I want everyone." And she looked around and saw that they were all standing there watching. "Except Sylvia and the kids and… Mark, you stay here too. Everyone else grab a bike, grab a bag, and get a weapon."

"Why? What's going on?" Mr Harper asked.

"This is Tuck," Nilda said. "She drove here in an Army truck and ran out of fuel in the middle of town. It's laden with food." She emptied one of the bags onto the ground. "Enough to keep us going for a couple of months." She looked around at Tuck and the other three new faces. "Maybe six weeks. No more questions. Come on."

And they did. The only delay came when she had to tell some people to put down the cricket bats they'd taken from the pavilion and take an axe or crowbar instead.

Half an hour later, having only seen one zombie, and that one in the distance, they arrived back at the APC. They found it empty.

"Who did this?" one of the newcomers asked. Nilda didn't know his name. She didn't bother to ask. She thought there would be plenty of time to find out later. But she knew the answer to his question. On the ground, near the rear tyre was the stub of a black-papered roll-up.

"Rob," she said.

"Are you sure?" Sebastian asked.

She pointed at the roll up. "It's not evidence, but how many other people can there be left in this town?"

"And what do you want to do?" Tracy asked. Nilda looked from her to Sebastian, to Jay, and then to Tuck. Only the former soldier didn't seem nervous.

"There's no point hanging around—" she began.

"Zombies!" one of the newcomers whose name she didn't know, called out. Nilda turned to look. Seven of them were coming up the road towards them. Nilda wasn't sure, but thought that at least one had been part of the group she'd led away from the APC barely an hour before.

Before Nilda could open her mouth, Jay had drawn his sword and started running towards them. She was stunned, unable to move for a long moment. Tuck didn't hesitate. She sprinted after the boy, Nilda following close behind. Tuck reached him first, barrelling into him, grabbing the back of his jacket. He turned, the sword in his hand swinging in a glittering arc. Tuck jerked back out of the blade's reach, grabbed him again, and pushed him back along the road. Then Nilda was there.

"What the hell are you doing?" she yelled.

"I was…" he began, but stumbled to a halt uncertain how to finish the sentence.

Nilda shoved him back towards the increasingly nervous group by the Army vehicle, Tuck walking slowly behind them, shotgun in hands, eyes on the undead. After that, they headed straight back to the school.

When they arrived, she scolded Jay. That hadn't helped. She'd been treating him like an adult, and he'd been acting like one. Even his foolhardy dash towards danger had been a very grown-up response to the insane world they found themselves in. Sebastian had suggested he go and talk to him, but Tuck had reached out a hand and stopped the old teacher and indicated she'd go.

"What can you say to him?" Nilda asked, and regretted the ill-chosen remark.

Tuck took out her notepad.

"That there's a time to fight and a time to run, and the trick is to know which is which," she'd scrawled.

Now Nilda stood at the front gate, axe in hand, Sebastian next to her, watching her son and the soldier. They seemed to be getting along. Whatever had caused Tuck to lose her hearing - something she resolutely refused to discuss beyond that it had happened some years before - had also damaged her vocal chords. She could talk. She just didn't like to. Jay, it turned out, knew some sign language. Judging from the expression on Tuck's face, the phrases he knew weren't ones he would dare use around his mother.

Nilda turned her attention back to their small settlement. Sylvia Harper, with her two children, was working on digging up the playing fields under the direction of Marjory Stowe. Two of the newcomers went to join them. One, a lanky man who seemed all elbows and knees, didn't seem to know which end of the shovel went in the ground. Nilda made a mental note to ask him his name. And then she looked around properly and wondered whether there was much point.

"How long will the food last, Seb?" she asked.

76

"Until July. Perhaps we can stretch it into August, just in time for harvest. If there is anything to harvest. At least those two children seem to be getting on well. They're helping a fair bit."

"Opening cans and stirring pots," she said.

"They do anything they're asked and don't need to be told twice. Sylvia's the same, just as long as her husband isn't around."

"Hmm," she grunted. "But they'll need protecting. So will she. That means we'll need one person always doing that, and another always keeping an eye on the food. That'll have to be you, me, Tracy, or Mark. I don't trust the others. So half of us will stay here, while the other half goes out to gather food. That won't be enough. It's not sustainable."

"Be patient. That new chap, Clive," Sebastian nodded towards the beanpole-thin man in the field. "He saw the smoke from twenty miles away. More people will come."

"And they'll be coming in on foot. They won't bring anything with them."

"You think we should stop lighting the bonfire? You don't want any more people here?" he asked.

"No, I'm thinking the opposite," Nilda replied. "Whether the food lasts until July, or August, or even September, it doesn't matter because there won't be a harvest. Not this year. All we'll manage to grow is enough food to add some variety to our diet. No, unless we have enough food to last through winter we might as well give up now. One person, or three, can survive better than this group. We've got too many people for the food, but not enough to go out and find more. And then there's the other problem."

"The undead?"

"No, I meant Rob. He'll see the smoke. He'll come and investigate. We can probably scare him off at first. But he'll get hungry. And then what's he more likely to do, go out scavenging for himself or just come and take what we have?"

"There's enough of us to see him off," Sebastian said confidently.

"If we're all here, and if we're prepared to fight," she said. "But we're not ready for a fight. Tuck's the only professional among us. I think Harper can handle himself, but he's likely to run as stand his ground. Jay…" She didn't want to think what might happen to her son. "You, Tracy, Mark, and me, if we have numbers on our side, we're fine, but Rob's not going to come when we're all here. He'll sit and watch and wait until we go out, then he'll attack. And then people will die, and we'll lose the food. You see the problem? We go out, we risk losing the food we have. We stay, and we'll end up starving. There's just so much to do and too few of us to do it."

"One thing at a time, Nilda. You know what they say about building Rome?"

"Yes, but we don't have time to be patient. That's the trouble. We have to do it all now. We're going to end up trapped here, with the undead outside. Then what? If our walls aren't strong enough, our supplies not sufficient, we'll fight among ourselves and we'll die for scraps that'll do no more than keep us alive a few more days."

"You have to accept what we're able to do. We're limited by the people we have. More will come, I'm sure."

"And we can't wait. Like I said, there's still Rob. That threat has to be neutralised."

"I… see. Well, I suppose Tuck has that gun," Sebastian said slowly. "Perhaps if they were all out in the open… but it's a shotgun isn't it? She'd need to be close, and we'd be relying on them still being unarmed."

"I didn't mean kill them Sebastian," Nilda said. "We'll ask them to join us."

Most of the group, not having any clue who Rob was, had no opinion when, after dinner, she informed them of her plan. There had been more grumbling when she'd told them they would have to stand in watches. It had died away when she said she was sitting the first watch. Jay and Tuck followed her outside.

"Where did you get the truck and that food from?" Nilda asked the soldier.

Tuck took out the pad and pen, and scrawled a brief note. "The enclaves are gone. There was a battle. A mutiny. Too much fighting. The undead came. The walls were breached. All that food came from there," she wrote.

"And…" Nilda tried to find a non-intrusive way to ask a question that was nothing but personal. "The scars. How did that happen?"

Tuck's hands moved rapidly. Nilda glanced at her son.

"Don't look at me," Jay said. "I've no idea what that means."

Tuck scrawled another note. "When you understand, then I'll tell you."

"Figures," Nilda muttered. "Tomorrow I'll ask Rob nicely if he'd like to come here, but I'd like you and your shotgun to be standing behind me when I do."

Tuck nodded, and again put pen to paper. "What if he doesn't want to join us?" she wrote.

"He will," Nilda said.

15ᵗʰ March

He didn't.

"I'm not surprised to see you back here," Rob said. "Thought it was only a matter of time. But, no, we don't want to join you. You could join us, if you want. I reckon you've something you can trade. Just you and her." He nodded up the street to where Tuck, shotgun held casually in one hand, stood next to Mark.

"It was her food in that truck," Nilda said.

"And now it's mine," Rob said, with a wolfish grin.

Nilda nodded, feeling a slight sense of relief that there wasn't some other group lurking in the town.

"How many zombies have you killed, Rob?" she asked loudly.

"There aren't any round here," one of his men said. Rob stayed quiet.

"Yes, they are," Nilda said. "And you saw them, Rob. You saw the dead zombies around that Army truck."

There was a sharing of looks among the group. Nilda nodded, she'd guessed right. There had been too much food for even the six of them to carry by hand. That meant they must have used a trolley or stock-cart, probably from one of the shops. At the same time, she doubted he would have left his stash unprotected. So only one or two of his followers had gone with him. That he hadn't told the others about the dead zombies meant there were only one or two he really trusted, and that was something that she might be able to use.

"I lured twelve of them away from the truck," she said. "When we got returned to collect our food, there were seven more zombies heading down the road. That's nineteen of them, and that was yesterday. The day before, we went to the hospital and there were dozens, maybe hundreds of them there. Tomorrow there will be more. And they will come here. You'll have to kill them. All of them. If you don't, you'll be trapped. Are you ready for that, Rob? Do you have enough food and water to last forever? No help is coming. The government's gone. The enclaves have collapsed. We're all that's left. But we've got water, shelter, and food. We're planting crops. We're going to survive." She met the eyes of each of the small group. "And we're offering you a place with us. We'll share the work, and we'll keep each other safe."

"I just told you, we're not interested. We've got food," Rob said.

"But you'll run out," she said. "You can't grow any here. I know what you're thinking, but you won't be able to take it from us."

"No?" he scoffed.

"No. You'll be surrounded by the undead. You'll be trapped. You probably won't starve to death. It's more likely you'll die of thirst. The water's stopped running, hasn't it?" There was another sly exchange of glances. "I thought so. Then this is your last chance. You can stay here and die, or come and join us." She looked around the faces and saw uncertainty and fear. She opened her mouth, but before she could say anything to further reinforce their doubts, Rob spoke.

"Like I said, if you're that scared, stay here," he leered. "We'll keep you safe."

She stared up at him for a moment, then turned and walked back up the road to Mark and Tuck.

"What now?" Mark asked. "Leave them to it?"

Tuck shook her head slowly.

"No. We can't," Nilda said. "You can't see it from here, but they're filthy. They've no water. Give it a couple of days and they will come looking for us. Perhaps this was a stupid idea, but it's too late now." She glanced at Tuck and her shotgun. "One way or another, this has to end."

Tuck nodded her agreement. Nilda didn't find that reassuring.

"You want to attack?" Mark asked.

"There's one last thing we can try. Come on."

She led them across town, stopping outside a corner shop.

"This'll do," she said, dismounting.

"It's been looted," Mark said. "Probably by Rob."

"He won't have taken what I'm after. Mark, keep watch. Tuck, have a look around. Find me some washing line or rope or something."

Nilda stepped over broken shelves, climbed over the counter, and went into the back of the store. Amidst the piles of magazines, toilet paper - she made a mental note to come back to collect some of that - and other household sundries, she found what she was looking for. A flat piece of wood, three feet square, with a wheel in each corner. She found an old pair of gloves next to it. Tuck couldn't find any rope or washing line, but she did find a five-metre long extension cable.

"That'll do," Nilda said.

"Now what?" Mark asked.

"Help me carry it. We need to keep quiet."

Awkwardly, with only Nilda knowing where they were going, they carried the cart another half mile, not quite towards her terrace, but to the road where she killed her first zombie.

"You're not... Oh no! You can't be serious!" Mark exclaimed.

"Just keep an eye out for the undead," she said, as she pulled the corpse up onto the cart. She tied it down with the cable.

"I can't believe you're going to do this," Mark said when she'd finished.

"The thing about first impressions is that sometimes they're not the ones that stick," she replied. Together, they pulled the creature back towards Rob and his barricade. The cart rattled all the way.

"It's noisy," Mark murmured. "It'll summon all the undead in the town."

"That's the plan. They can join us. Or they'll get surrounded. Either way they won't be a threat."

"What the hell are you doing?" Rob yelled when they got within shouting range. He and the other five youths were standing on the barricade, an assortment of weapons in hand.

Nilda kept pulling the cart closer, not stopping until she was ten feet away.

"This is a zombie. One of the undead. We killed it, just now, about five streets from here. How long were we gone, Rob? Thirty minutes? How long until there's one in this street? How long until there's scores of them? How long until you're trapped? We're at the school. Come and join us. Bring your food. Or stay here and die. It's your choice. All of you."

She turned and briskly walked away.

"How did it go?" Jay asked when they got back. He and Tracy had been waiting by the school gates.

"I don't know yet," she said. Tuck went to stand by the gate, shotgun in hand, an almost amused expression on her face.

"Four more people have arrived," Tracy said. "They came from the south. They said they were fleeing the undead."

"Right," Nilda murmured.

"There's been no one from the north," Tracy added. "It's odd really. Unless there's some haven up there where it's safe."

"Maybe," Nilda said, but she wasn't really listening. She had her eyes fixed on the road, waiting to see if her plan would work.

Just before sunset, Rob and his gang arrived at the school gates.

"Welcome," Nilda said, before Rob had a chance to say anything. "All the food is shared. You can leave it at the pavilion. There's dinner cooking and we've showers that work. The water's cold, but I doubt you'll mind that. Once you've eaten you can wash. And we've clean clothes."

Rob nodded, and opened his mouth.

"You're all welcome here," she said again, before he could speak. "Get some food, and then get some rest. There's work to be done tomorrow. Go on."

It was obvious that Rob wanted to make some attempt to exert his authority, but the lure of food was too much for his followers. They pushed past him towards the pavilion. Wanting to follow from the front, he went after them. Only the large man lingered.

"The zombies came," he said. "While we were… arguing. Seven of them."

Nilda nodded.

"My name's Nilda, This is Tuck."

"Charlie," he said. "The thing is, um… about Rob… um—"

"Go and get something to eat," Nilda cut in, forcing a smile. "It'll be a long day tomorrow."

She watched him head off to the pavilion. She didn't need his warning to know to keep an eye on the gangly youth, but perhaps they weren't all like their leader. There was some hope in that. She watched long enough to see Tracy pigeon-hole one of the youths, Mark another, Sebastian a third, leading them to separate spots on the pavilion steps.

Nilda let out a deep breath. "That's one problem solved," she said to Tuck. The woman gave a noncommittal shrug. "Right. Just another million to deal with. Come on then." She headed towards the pavilion.

"Listen up," she said loudly. "Tomorrow we start on the perimeter. We need high walls."

"It's got walls," Rob said.

"Not all the way around. A lot of it's just railings. In a few weeks, perhaps just in a few days, the undead will gather outside. That's inevitable, so we need to be prepared. We're going to reinforce those railings with fencing. We can collect it from the houses and back gardens —"

"And who put you in charge?" Rob cut in.

"You don't strike me as the kind of person who votes, Rob. But if you want, we'll do that now. Hands up who wants me to lead."

Fourteen hands, some instantly, others hesitantly, went up.

"Majority rule, Rob. Breakfast will be at five. At first light we'll go out. I want you and you and…" She started pointing and allocating tasks to each of the group. It was only when she'd finished, and turned around to talk to Jay, that she saw Tuck had been standing behind her, the shotgun held not quite casually in her hands.

17th March

"How much does it come to?" Nilda asked.

"There's forty kilos of barley," the girl said. "It was still at the back of the pub, just where you said it would be."

"And the vinegar," Jay added. "That was Deb's idea. You know, for preserving."

Nilda glanced at the girl standing next to her son. She was a year older than Jay and had arrived the previous evening, alone and two hours after the sun had set.

"But vinegar won't go off," Nilda said eyeing the catering sized jugs. "We could have got it later."

"Not if we get surrounded like you think might happen. And there's the flour too. Two sacks of it," Jay said. "And the rats would have gotten that. We think they might become a problem." He glanced at Deborah as if for confirmation.

"Good work," she said. "Both of you. It's been a good day."

Jay shrugged and the two of them went off. The moment she was sure her son wouldn't notice, Nilda allowed herself a small smile. It was good to see him doing something so normal as boasting on the behalf of a girl to improve his mother's opinion of her. And it had been a good day. The flour, the barley, and the odd assortment of condiments had more than made up for the newcomers. A group of four from Nottingham had arrived an hour before Deborah, and seven more had turned up that morning. They'd come from the south and had been heading toward the Lake District when they'd seen the smoke. They had been disappointed to find a group of survivors who were little more prepared than them. To a greater or lesser degree, however, they'd all buckled down to whatever jobs they'd been given.

A good day, then, despite the undead. All of the groups that had gone out had seen them. There had been some fights, some of the undead had been killed, and everyone had returned unhurt. Rob had claimed to have killed five though no one else had seen it happen. She thought he was bragging.

They had planted some seeds, and had even found a few seedlings at one of the garden centres. They had been wilting, the dirt in their pots bone dry, but there was a chance they might take. Yes, she thought, it had been a good day.

18th March

Nilda decided she'd take personal charge of gathering the rest of the materials to reinforce the school's walls. There was a park less than a mile away on to which scores of houses backed. Each of those had a fence. It was, she'd guessed and Sebastian had calculated, more than enough to ensure that there was a solid barrier around the school.

She had one team tearing down the fences, another ferrying the fencing from the park to the school, while everyone else worked at putting them back up. They'd found a trailer next to the park-keeper's shed. It was a heavy thing, designed to be pulled by a van or tractor. It required more effort to pull and push than it would to have carried the fencing by hand, but it was easier to drop a handle to grab a weapon when the undead appeared. And they did appear. Twice, when the group with the trailer returned to the park, they reported having been attacked by the undead. Partly because Tuck was with them, they had held their own.

Nilda would have preferred to be doing that task herself. The difficulty was one of trust. As they were pulling down the fencing, someone had to go into the houses to gather any food that might be left. While that was a task anyone could do, she didn't trust any of them not to keep some of it for themselves.

It was nearing lunchtime when she found her first occupied house. From the outside it appeared no different to any of the others. She checked the back door. It was locked. She levered it open with the crowbar.

She heard movement almost instantly. Something was upstairs. She knew what it was, what it had to be. She glanced over her shoulder. Of course, she could ask for help, but out of the people nearby, Rob was the closest. She neither thought she could rely on him, nor wished to appear weak in front of him. She went in alone.

Step by cautious step, she moved through the house. It wasn't a large property, and soon she found herself at the bottom of the stairs. The noise kept on, but no zombie appeared. She went up, fear manifesting as anger at the inconsideration of this unseen creature. She reached the top. The noise didn't stop, nor did it get any closer. It was coming from behind a door at the end of the landing. She took a step towards it. The creak of a shifting floorboard echoed through the house. The sound got louder, but she was convinced the noise wasn't coming from immediately behind the door. A door that, she now clearly saw, was held closed with a hastily installed padlock. There was no sign of a key.

She gripped the crowbar, braced herself, and broke the door open. The moment the wood splintered she leaped back, bringing the crowbar up, ready to strike. The door swung slowly inward. There was nothing behind it. She breathed out and stepped forward. On the bed, tied up by its ankles and feet, was the zombie.

Male, she thought, somewhere the right side of fifty. It thrashed and twisted. The ropes held tight, but with each convulsive spasm, they bit deeper into flesh, ripping through decaying skin, muscle, and fat. From those wounds, thick red-brown pus oozed down onto the soiled bed-sheets.

It was obvious what had happened. He'd been infected, and then tied up and left to die. That was cruelty personified. Better to kill the person, than let him turn into this type of creature. She walked over to the bed, gripped the crowbar two handed, and punched it down into the zombie's head.

She wiped the weapon clean on the edge of the bed, and then went back downstairs to check the kitchen for food. There was none. She went outside.

"What happened?" Rob asked, taking a step back when he saw her expression.

"Zombie," she said. She would have left it at that, but others had moved closer to hear. "He'd been tied to the bed and left to die. I did the merciful thing." She regretted the last words. They sounded trite, like some line from a bad movie.

"Merciful? They're zombies. Not people," Rob said.

She stared at him for a moment. There was nothing provocative in his words, nor even his tone, but his stance, his demeanour, it all spoke of a man waiting for his chance. She nodded towards the approaching trailer.

"Load it up, and go back with it," she said. Before he could argue, she turned and went into the next house.

After that, she tried to be more cautious, but she felt an increased sense of urgency. There was so much to do, so little time, and yet all their lives, and especially Jay's, relied on getting it all done.

Four houses, later she came out to find the small group sitting idly in the sun, next to the large stack of fencing.

"What's going on?" she asked, dropping the two food-filled bags she'd brought out from the house.

"That's it," a man said. Nilda thought his name was Terry, though it might have been Jerry. "We're done. That's all the fencing. Just got to wait for the cart."

Nilda nodded and dropped the bags. She was about to sit down herself, but then she stopped.

"How long has it been?" she asked.

"Since it was here?" Terry, or possibly Jerry, asked. "Half an hour. Forty minutes. Maybe a bit more."

Too long. Nilda started moving towards the school. After a few paces she began to run. She didn't check to see if the others followed.

When she got to the school, her worst fears were realised. A group of zombies lay dead around a section of the wall. She saw her son kneeling among them.

"Jay! What happened! Are you okay?" she yelled as she ran over to him.

"I'm fine but..." he trailed off.

"Were you bitten?"

"No. Not me. Deb."

She'd not even noticed the girl lying at his feet.

"Let me see," she said firmly, bending down to examine the wound. The girl's jeans were torn. Her hands were gripped tightly around them. A thin trickle of blood seeped slowly between the gaps in her fingers.

"We need to get her inside," Nilda said. "Clean the wound. Bandage it —"

"What for?" Rob asked. "What's the point? She's going to die, so do the merciful thing. Isn't that what you said?"

She'd not noticed him standing there, a crowbar in his hands, the end dripping with the red-brown pus of the undead. At his feet was the boy, Charlie. The one she'd thought was almost pleasant. And lying a few feet away from his body, her head caved in, was Marjory Stowe.

Nilda bent down and picked up the wounded girl, and without another word, carried her over to the pavilion. Jay, with Sebastian a few paces behind, followed her into the changing rooms.

"Get me something to bandage the wound," she snapped. "And get him out of here."

Sebastian led Jay away, returning alone a few moments later with a first aid kit. He handed it to her, then took a step to one side, and pulled a chisel from his belt. He placed it on a bench out of the girl's sight. Nilda stared at him for a moment before giving a brief, understanding nod. He left. She bandaged the wound as best she could. The bleeding slowed, but didn't stop.

"It's going to be okay," she said.

"It's not though, is it?" Deborah replied.

"You'll be fine," Nilda said. She didn't believe it. The cuts had bled too fast and too much for such a shallow wound.

The girl smiled. Her mouth twitched as if she was trying to speak. Then she coughed. Nilda raised her hand, stroking the girl's cheek. She felt hot. Too hot. The girl closed her eyes. Her breathing slowed. Then stopped.

Nilda breathed out, looked down at the body, then at the chisel. She reached out for it, but just couldn't bring herself to pick it up. Then she realised someone was behind her. She turned. It was Tuck. She stepped past Nilda, picked up the chisel, and knelt next to the girl. Tuck placed a hand on the girl's neck, feeling for a pulse. Then placed the chisel close to the girl's ear.

"No," Nilda murmured, half moving her hand to stop the former soldier. Tuck glanced across at her, shook her head, and plunged the chisel through the girl's ear, deep into her brain.

Nilda bit back a wracking sob. She wanted to scream. She wanted to bellow her rage, and rail against such a cruel and capricious world. She bit back the anger. There wasn't time. She glanced over at Tuck. The woman seemed lost in her own thoughts.

"Come on. There's work to be done," Nilda said. "There's always work to be done."

Night fell as they brought back the last load of fencing from the park. They used up the last of the car batteries to keep the lights on while they finished erecting it around the school. Only when it was done did Nilda think about the body. She went to look for a shovel, only to find Tuck had already dug a grave behind the groundskeeper's shed, out of sight of the pavilion.

"What happened?" she asked Sebastian that evening. She'd tried to talk to Jay, but he didn't want to talk to anyone. He'd thrown himself into the work with furious abandon. He was trying to lose himself in it, she knew.

"Someone came in on a bike. The fifth person today. Except this last one, he had the undead following him. There was a fight." He shrugged as if to say that was explanation enough.

"And four people are dead. Which guy is this?"

"He's one of the ones who died."

Nilda was relieved at that. It was one less complication to deal with.

19th March

Nilda didn't go out on the supply run. Around noon, the first of the groups looking for food came back. They'd found three tins and a packet of lentils. She tried not to let her disappointment show. It was made more difficult when a second group returned in late afternoon with only a dozen cartons of orange juice to show for their efforts. She looked over the maps she'd given them. They'd marked off the houses they had been to and made far larger marks against the streets now filled with the undead. There were more of those each day. Including the places Rob and his gang had looted before coming to the school, there were only a few streets they hadn't searched.

She turned the map over, examining the area around the town. Before she'd died, Marjory Stowe had been working with Sylvia Harper on identifying the places they might find wild fruit. Both women had grown up in the area. While Andrew Harper got miserably drunk with Rob, the two women had spent a surprisingly happy evening marking out the spots they'd picked blackberries and scrumped apples. There were a lot of circles and lines now on the map, but autumn was an impossibly long way off. In some of the farms there would be kitchen gardens in which there might be vegetables waiting to be picked. Probably. Possibly. It was hard to know until they looked, but how much time could they spend wandering the countryside? Would they ever find enough? Or would the undead pick them off one by one as they searched?

Nilda calculated the distance between the school and the farms. Would there be enough food to make up for the energy expended in a return trip? Perhaps at first, but then they would have to go to the farms further away. Their best bet would be to find crops that had already been planted and bring them back to the school, roots and all. Or they could go to the Lake District National Park. There would be fish there, and plenty of water, but they couldn't live on fish alone. They would have to come back to the towns and villages for other supplies. Then, whatever they did, wherever they went, they would have to get it back safely. That was the biggest problem of all.

She turned the map over again. The one place they hadn't searched was the industrial estate. She'd found the address of a unit there where they might find some food. Perhaps a lot of food. She looked around. People were working, and they seemed happy to do it, but there were so few of them. She thought back to what Sebastian had said about the numbers not adding up. She knew then, whether they stayed or went somewhere else, it just wasn't going to work.

She went to find Jay and Sebastian. They were in the hallway outside the teachers' common room looking up at a painting.

"Who's that?" she asked.

"Alfred, Lord Tennyson," Sebastian replied.

"The poet," Jay added with an air of indifference.

"Guns to the left of him, guns to the right?" Nilda asked.

"Cannon, but yes. That was him. The Charge of the Light Brigade. An exercise in futile bravery. I thought the lesson apt under the circumstances."

"Yeah," Jay muttered. "And I thought I wouldn't have to worry about lessons now that the world had come to an end."

"There's always time to learn," Sebastian said. "That's what life is about. Learning not to repeat the mistakes of the past. You see, I was trying to lead you towards an understanding. Most people see the world as a series of either-or decisions where one can either fight or retreat, but there's always another choice."

"Yeah. Well, I look at that and you know what I see?" Jay asked.

"What?" Nilda asked, curious.

"The last of his kind."

"There were poets after him," Sebastian said. "Some fine ones. In fact, in the library—"

"I didn't mean poets," Jay said. "And I didn't really mean him. I meant people like him. Lords and Ladies and all that stuff. It's all gone, hasn't it? This school, all those rich people who sent their kids here. All that money, all that fame, that's gone. We're all the same now. That's what I meant. It's a new beginning. A new world. It's just not the one we thought we'd get."

Nilda wondered whether that thought had come from Deborah's death, from their circumstances, or whether it had been there all along, hidden under a sullenly impenetrable teenage exterior.

"That's what I wanted to talk to you two about," she said.

"Oh?" Sebastian asked.

She glanced around, checking that they were alone.

"I don't know if this is going to work," she said.

"This?" Jay asked.

"Three people died yesterday. Today, ten people went out. They brought back less than they ate this morning. We're eating dog food, Jay, and we're grateful for it. Or most of us are," she added. "Look, we're just a group of strangers held together by fear. We've not had a chance to think about next week or next month or next year. Walls and water and shelter and firewood. That's as far as we've got, and it's not going to be enough. The undead will come. More of them, and they'll keep on coming. What do we do then?"

"We'll fight," Sebastian said. "Tracy and I had a look at the chemistry labs. It's not my subject of course, but we've come up with—"

"Weapons? Chemicals? Explosives, perhaps? And will they kill a million zombies? Ten million? Twenty? We don't know how many there will be. Look at what happened yesterday. Do you think we'll fare any better tomorrow? All we're doing out there is building the walls to our own prison. What was it you said, prepare for the worst and hope for the best? Well, if we stay here I can't see our 'best' being anything but a slow death."

"Then what are we meant to do instead?" Jay asked.

"You were right. We should have gone looking for a castle to start with," she replied. "Maybe it's not too late. I thought I was thinking ahead, thinking about the winter, but we've got to plan for all the winters to come. This is just a school, Sebastian. It's better than that terrace, but it's still just a school. If it wasn't for the undead… But they're here. Wooden fences won't hold them off for long. Maybe even a castle wouldn't have been good enough. The only place we might be safe is an island."

"I see," Sebastian said slowly. "You want to pack up and leave?"

"No matter how much food we bring in, we're still not building up a reserve. We'll run out before autumn arrives. If there's one or two, we can fight and kill them. If there's ten or twenty, we'll fight, and some of us will probably die. If there's a hundred, or more, then we become trapped. And then we will die."

"You didn't answer the question," Sebastian said. "What do you want to do?"

"I think we need to be prepared to go it alone," she said. "Just the three of us."

"What about Mark and Tracy?"

"And what about the children and everyone else? No, if we go, it's just the three of us. We've still got the food left in the house. That will help. But we'll need more."

"You mean take the stuff that's here?" Jay asked.

"No, that wouldn't be fair. I think we make one last attempt at finding supplies. We split it up and go our separate ways. Everyone gets the same chance. But we don't go on foot. I say we drive to the coast and get out to sea. We stayed here because of the government, because of the enclaves and the muster points. But if Tuck's correct and all the enclaves have collapsed, then there's no reason why we shouldn't head for the coast. We'll find an island where there may be undead, but once we've killed them, we'll know we're safe. And then we can really start again."

"And that's how you really feel?" Sebastian asked.

"Yes."

"I agree," Jay said. "Look at Deborah. If she'd kept going, kept on heading into Scotland, she might be alive. You know all the people here, they all came from the south. There's got to be a reason for that. So maybe we go to one of the Scottish islands."

"Perhaps," Sebastian said. "But wherever we go, if it's somewhere that was sparsely populated, then we would really be relying on what little food we brought with us."

"Which is why," Nilda said, "we make one last attempt at finding supplies. I think I've an idea where we can look."

20th March

"Listen up," Nilda said. Except for the sentry on the roof, everyone was gathered at the tables in the pavilion's dining room, breakfasting on the last of the porridge flavoured with the last of the jam.

"We're doing well here," she began. "I think we can make it work. But we need more food, enough to get us through until spring. And there's something else. We need to plan for the worst."

"Worse than this?" Rob asked, pushing his bowl away.

"If too many of the undead come, then we should run," she said, ignoring him. "We're not ready to fight."

"Then why are we bothering with these walls?" Rob demanded, looking around for support, and Nilda noticed he had some, and not just among the men who'd come to the school with him.

"We need to be prepared, Rob. Retreat is better than death. If it looks like we'll be surrounded, if there are too many to fight, then we should fall back, regroup, and retreat."

"To where? You said this place would be safe."

"We head east, to the coast, or north into Scotland. Exactly where, we won't be able to decide until the time comes. We'll look for a boat and then for an island. I'm going out today. I've an idea where we might find some food. One big haul, more than we've found anywhere so far. I want another group to go and check out the bus depot."

"The bus depot? You won't find food there," Andrew Harper said.

"But there might be buses. One bus will need less fuel than half a dozen cars. That can become our fall-back. We'll move half the food there, just in case."

"It won't be safe," Rob said.

"Who's going to steal it?" Nilda asked. "You?"

94

"And while we're doing that, where are you going?" Mr Harper cut in.

Nilda took out an empty sack of dog biscuits. "The address on this packet is in the industrial estate."

"Sorry, but when you said one big haul, I was thinking of steak and potatoes," Harper said.

"It's calories that count," Jay said. "And this has got those, and iron and calcium and all the rest."

"Sebastian and I will go," Nilda said. "We can work out how many people it will take to bring it all back here."

"I'll go, too," Mark volunteered.

"You can keep up?" she asked.

"I've been practicing," he said. "And I've not done my fair share of the labour so far."

He had, Nilda knew. He was making an unsubtle point to all the others. She would have preferred it if it was just her and Sebastian. Then they would be able to plan for the next stage, but she could hardly refuse him now.

"Fine. The three of us then."

"I'll come too," Jay said.

Nilda looked at him. She wanted him safe, and the school was still safer than outside.

"No, you stay here," she said, and before he could protest, added quietly, "and keep an eye on Rob."

The industrial estate was at the north of the town, the bus depot was to the west on the other side of the motorway. They tried to head through the side roads to the east of the town, but kept finding the streets so often full of the undead that they were forced to detour out into the countryside. That in itself made Nilda confidant that she'd made the right decision. In the end they travelled ten miles to cover the two between the school and the industrial estate.

"You see what I see?" Nilda asked. Across a scrubby patch of grass, the low metal roofs of the estate were laid out before them.

"Well, it's not what I was expecting," Mark said. "I thought there would be more steel chimneys. Something more industrial. Not car showrooms and warehouses"

"You've not been here before?" Nilda asked.

"Tracy has, but it's not exactly the kind of place you visit on a wet Sunday afternoon."

"No, right," Nilda murmured. "But do you see what I see?"

"You mean the car showrooms?" Sebastian asked.

"They probably kept a supply of petrol. Even if they didn't, just look at the vans and lorries. There's got to be hundreds of them. Come on."

"Why? Let's find the food first," Mark said.

"It won't take long," Nilda insisted, avoiding his question.

They headed across the scrubland to the nearest showroom. Even as they approached, she saw something was wrong.

"The petrol caps are off," Sebastian said.

"Yeah, I think someone else had this idea before us." They reached the first row of cars, parked along a verge in sight of the main road. It was clear that someone had already syphoned off the fuel. They pushed their bikes over to the next showroom. It was the same there. They were heading to the third when they heard a rattling crash coming from inside the garage itself.

"Perhaps now would be a good time to remember why we came here," Mark said pointedly.

They backed away slowly, eyes on the metal and glass building from which the noise had come.

They eventually found the unit they were looking for on the far edge of the estate. It wasn't an encouraging sight, and was far smaller than she'd been expecting, with more space given over to the car park than to the semi-permanent redbrick and metal clad building.

"Are you sure this is the right one?" Sebastian asked.

"The sign says so."

They went inside and stared at row upon row of silent machines.

"I don't think they made anything here," Mark said, looking at the machinery. "I think this was just for packaging. They brought the food in and sent it out, just in time."

Nilda pulled off a label from a roll next to a conveyor belt. She looked at it for a moment then dropped it. "There's nothing here. There never was. Come on." She walked back out the door.

"Wait," Mark said, hurrying after her. "We can find out where the supply trucks came from. There'll be a delivery note here somewhere. And then—"

"And go from place to place finding nothing?" she interrupted. "No. There's no point." She stopped in the roadway outside the building.

"Why don't we try some of the other units?" Sebastian suggested.

"They'll all be the same, won't they?" Nilda replied. "I mean, look at this place. It's not where food is made."

"So what do we do?" Mark asked. "I mean, if we're going back empty handed we at least need a plan."

Sebastian glanced at Nilda.

"What?" Mark asked. "You've already got a plan?"

"Go on," Sebastian said. "He'd find out soon enough, and we can trust him."

"You trust too many people, Sebastian," she said. "Look, Mark, the school's no good. I don't know if we can make it work, but there's not going to be enough food, not for everyone. I don't want to be there when it all falls apart. I don't want to be trapped there watching my son starve to death as the undead beat down the fences. We're going to leave. The three of us."

"That's why you were talking about a fall-back point at the bus depot, why you wanted to check the cars? You were planning to leave anyway?"

"There's no food, Mark. The rationing emptied the city. Each day there's less for us to find and fewer places to look. Before we met you, we had enough to last the three of us through winter. Now, we'll have run out by the end of the month. We all need to leave, before the undead come. In small groups, just one or two of us, we might stand a chance. If we stay together, we'll fight among ourselves for the privilege of being the last to starve to death."

"You should have said this was what you were planning," he said reproachfully.

"I didn't want anyone to panic. More than that, I didn't want anyone to run off with everything they could carry. I don't want people to die, Mark. None of them. It's why we need to find vehicles. We can split the food and drive away, each going our separate ways. I've got to think of Jay first. Our best chance, our only chance, is on our own."

"So that's it. You weren't going to tell me?"

"Honestly? I don't know. I was hoping we'd find something here. I was hoping that... I don't know." She sighed. "A few of us, living hand to mouth, maybe we can make it until summer. But not all of us, not all together in that school. You know it's the truth."

"I see."

Sebastian gave her a look. She stared at him for a moment, then relented.

"But," she added, "you can come with us. You and Tracy. If you want."

For a moment he seemed genuinely affronted.

"I'd like to say no," he said eventually. "I'd like to make a stubborn protest, but what's the point? If you go, others will leave. No, I don't know if there will be anywhere safer than this, but you're right. I'll speak to Tracy. Come on then. No point putting it off any longer."

They headed back to the school but ended up taking an even more circuitous route on the way back. There were far more undead on the streets and, because they were focused on the road in front, they didn't see the smoke overhead until they were just over a mile from St Lucian's. It was black and oily.

"That's not the bonfire," Sebastian said. "That's a building. The school's on fire."

They put on speed, heading up a slight incline, and as the road straightened once more, they saw the school. It was swarming with the undead.

"Where did they come from?" Sebastian murmured.

"What does it matter?" Nilda snapped. "We've got to go down there and—"

"No!" Mark said, grabbing her handlebars. "I don't think anyone's down there. I think they've gone. Look. It's the pavilion that's burning."

"Then maybe they're trapped in there and—"

"No," Mark interrupted again. "Look at the undead. They're all heading off towards the west."

"Why?"

"Because that was the plan, wasn't it? Go to the bus depot. That was what you said this morning, and that's where they're heading. The zombies are following them."

Nilda hesitated. "But what if they didn't all go? What if Jay's still down there?"

"If there's anyone hiding in the school, we can't do anything to help," Sebastian said. "In fact, since the undead seem to be leaving, then going down there now would just endanger them further."

"Then let's go to the depot. Maybe we can help them." Maybe it would be too late. She didn't give herself time to think of that as she pushed off, cycling away from the school.

They found zombies on every other road. Only in ones or twos, but they now seemed everywhere. They didn't stop and fight. They dodged around and past the undead, and when there were too many they doubled back and found a different route. After twenty minutes of back tracking, detours and long-cuts, they reached the motorway and found the streets on the other side as empty of the living dead as they'd been the day before.

"They're not heading west. They're going north," Sebastian said at about the same time that Nilda realised it. The layout of the roads was funnelling the undead, leading her to misjudge the direction of their passage.

"Should we follow them?" Mark asked, his voice tinged with uncertainty and fear.

"No, we'll go to the depot first. I'm sure that's where everyone's gone." She wasn't. But she hoped that if she sounded confident she might believe it herself.

They set off once more. Nilda put everything she had into coaxing a little more speed out of the bike, desperate to reach her destination and find her son.

When they got to the bus depot, she thought it was deserted until Tracy appeared in a doorway to the side of the main garage. She ran out to meet them.

"What happened?" Mark asked.

"A car," Tracy said, flatly. "A group of people in a car. They must have seen the bonfire and been heading towards it. The zombies followed. Hundreds of them. One minute the road was clear, then there was the sound of the engine, and then there were the undead. Hundreds of them, all heading towards us."

"Where is everyone?" Nilda asked.

"Inside," Tracy said. "Some are missing, but most of us made it this far."

"And the pavilion? What happened? Why is it on fire?" Mark asked as Nilda pushed her way past Tracy and into the building.

"Someone set it on fire. I don't know who. Maybe it was an accident," Tracy said, but Nilda was no longer listening.

"Where's Jay?" she demanded. "Where's my son?"

"He…" Tracy looked around, as if hoping to see the boy. "When it was clear the zombies were following us, he led them away. Him, Tuck, and Rob."

"You mean he's still out there?" Nilda pushed past them, heading across the empty car park, and back towards the town. She'd reached the gates when she saw Rob walking slowly down the street. He had a pack on his shoulder, the shotgun in his hands.

"What happened? Where's Jay?" she yelled.

"I'm sorry," Rob said. "We were surrounded. He's dead."

It felt as if a weight had slammed into her chest. She couldn't breathe. She collapsed and was caught by Sebastian. He, Mark, and Tracy had followed her across the car park.

"Tuck too," Rob added. "Your kid went to help her. They got swarmed. Sorry."

"No!" Nilda screamed, struggling against the hands gripping her. "No. No. No. I've got to go and find him. He can't be... He can't be..." She didn't want to say the word. That would make it all too real. And it couldn't be real. It couldn't be true.

"Nilda, no! You can't." Sebastian tried to hold her back, but a moment later she was free and running down the road, and towards the undead.

With no destination in mind, she ran blindly through the streets until, rounding a corner, she saw three zombies. Uncertain, she stopped, jogging on the spot for a moment before sprinting on, around one, past another, dodging the third, and she was past them and heading on into the town. She turned another corner. A pack of the undead were moving along it, away from her. She wanted to keep running, she wanted to run straight through them until she found her son. Self-preservation told her to stop. But she couldn't stop. She turned around and ran back down the road to an alley. She pushed her way through and over a cluster of half-rotten mattresses and out the other side, right in front of a pack of the monstrous creatures. They saw her. She darted across the road and down another alley. Halfway along a zombie lunged out of the lee of a doorway. With barely a pause, she grabbed its head and slammed it into the brick wall. She didn't stop to see if it was unmoving.

She reached the end of the alley, and found herself on another road. It looked familiar, but was full of the undead. This was no pack of ten or twenty, this was a small army of hundreds of walking corpses, pushing and shoving and milling their way down the street. They were heading towards her, the nearest only four hundred yards away. And there, just behind the front rank of snarling snapping monsters, she saw a red and blue scarf, caught by the wind, twist up over their heads. She stopped dead in her tracks. There it was again. The scarf. Jay's scarf. Jay was there. He was dead. No, he was one of the undead.

She tried to see his face, tried to find it among the snarling mass of death moving inexorably closer. There. Was it him? She couldn't be certain until she saw the firefighter's jacket the creature was wearing. It was just the same as the one she'd insisted her son wore. And then, as creatures pushed and shoved and tumbled against one another, the figure was lost from sight. All she clearly saw was that scarf, waving above them like some mocking flag.

She screamed. She bellowed with frustrated grief. Her fists balled as her muscles bunched, and someone tackled her from behind, knocking her to the ground. She turned expecting to see a zombie's snarling face. It wasn't. It was Sebastian.

"Nilda. Please. Come on, or we'll both die," he pleaded with her.

"Jay!" she growled.

"Please, Nilda, please."

"His scarf!" she wailed plaintively.

"There's nothing you can do," he said softly. "Come on."

Her growl turned into a sob as he helped her up. With one hand firmly gripping her arm, the other holding an axe, the head dripping with red-brown ooze, he led her away.

An hour later, Nilda sat in the corner of the bus depot, silent. Sebastian sat next to her. Everyone else was just as quiet.

"Alright, look, I am sorry," Rob said again. He didn't sound apologetic. "But we can't just sit here. We need a plan. I reckon—"

"Ireland," Tracy said, cutting him off. "That's our plan. Or one of the small islands in the Irish Sea. Somewhere with no zombies. That's the only place that's going to be safe. To get there we need boats. And we'll find those at the coast. That's where we'll head."

"And what about the government—" Rob began.

"No," Tracy interrupted. "Tuck was certain about that. The government's gone. We'll avoid the enclaves and go north until we reach Carlisle, then we can either go west or up into Scotland. Either way, we'll follow the coast until we find a boat."

"And how exactly are we going to do that? Unless you hadn't noticed, there aren't any buses here."

"Engines would be no good," Tracy said. "You saw what happened when the zombies followed that car to the school. No, we'll cycle. We've all got bikes."

"I haven't," Rob said.

"Then you better go and find one. There were a couple chained up on the street outside. Tomorrow, at first light, we're heading west. We'll follow the train line north and we'll see where that leads us. We'll get off the mainland. Then we'll be safe."

She said it with such certainty that most people, taking comfort in the words of someone who sounded like they had a plan, nodded their heads. Most people.

"That's got to be two hundred miles," Andrew Harper stated. "Let's just cut across the Lake District."

"Did you bring food with you? Did anyone? No? I thought not. Once we're clear of the town we'll need to find more. We'll only find it near civilisation. We have to stick to the roads and railways. At least for now."

"But it's too far," Mr Harper said. "We won't make it."

"We have to," Tracy said, "because we can't stay here."

21ˢᵗ March

"Everyone up. Hurry," Tracy called out softly, moving from person to person, pushing and pulling them to their feet. "Ten minutes, and we're moving out."

Nilda was awake. She hadn't slept.

It took a long time to get everyone ready and outside. Or it seemed that way to Nilda. She watched people, seemingly in slow motion, grab their gear and try to organise themselves. The Harpers were the slowest of all. The children looked scared, perched on bicycles too large for them.

Nilda watched their mother comfort them. She wanted to go over and explain that the problem with Jay's saddle was that it was too high. No, that wasn't Jay. What was the boy's name? She tried to remember. She couldn't. She turned away. Her eyes fell on the road leading into town. Should she go back? She was still considering it when a steady hand fell on her shoulder.

"Come on." It was Sebastian. He moved her over to the bike. A moment later she found that she was sitting on it, with Sebastian on one side, Mark on the other. They pushed and dragged and cajoled until she began to pedal.

Cycling was easy. It was mechanical. She found it required no thought and gave her no time to think. She pedalled harder and faster. Feet turned to yards, road turned to rail, and they were cycling two abreast along the embankment. Not long after that, she was at the front. Rob put on speed to keep up. Tracy did the same. Yards turned to a mile, and then two. Soon, the ragged group was strung out on the railway line. Sebastian and Mark were at the back with the Harpers and a few others. Nilda was at the front, Tracy at her side, Rob and his gang trying to keep up.

"We need to slow down," Tracy said.

Nilda heard the words, but she didn't want to stop. She wasn't sure she knew how.

"Nilda?" Tracy called again, a few minutes and a hundred yards later. "We need to slow down. Let the others catch up."

"If they can't keep up, they're not trying hard enough," Rob panted.

"Nilda," Tracy began again, but was interrupted by a child's scream coming from behind them. The sound cut through Nilda's veil of grief. She stopped and looked behind. The rear half of their group was out of sight. There it was again, a pitiful wail of pain and fear. She glanced over at Tracy and saw on her face the fear that she too had lost someone she loved.

"We have to help them," Nilda said to Tracy, to Rob, to herself, and to no one as she began cycling back along the tracks. There was a third, more guttural scream, and a moment later it was Tracy's turn to put on a manic burst of speed. She shot past, overtaking Nilda.

The tracks curved, and Nilda saw the other half of the group. They were half a mile away and they were surrounded. A dozen undead were on the tracks in front, another dozen behind and more than she could easily count spilling up the embankment on either side.

Tracy was two hundred yards ahead and getting further away with each second. Nilda followed, trying to catch up, but found she couldn't match the other woman's desperate acceleration.

She kept her eyes fixed on the group. They'd formed a rough circle. The two children were in the centre, the adults ringed around them, fending off the undead. The zombies were too numerous to be defeated, but if she and Tracy and Rob and the others could just get there in time, maybe they would still be able to escape.

She was four hundred yards away when she saw a pitifully small creature claw its way onto Andrew Harper's back. She imagined the small teeth biting at cloth and scoring at flesh as the undead child pulled itself up to his neck. Mr Harper stiffened and screamed. He tore the creature off, throwing it back into the pack.

"Not my children! Not my children!" he bellowed, swinging left and right, an axe in one hand, a crowbar in the other. But his berserk blows left him without any defence. Two creatures came at him simultaneously from either side, tearing and clawing and biting at his legs and arms and chest. He collapsed to the ground, three more zombies piling on top of this now easy prey. Sylvia Harper jumped forward, beating ineffectually at the creatures with a cricket bat, but then she too was knocked from her feet and disappeared under the snarling mass of the undead.

Nilda searched for some last reserve of energy, propelled by a burning need to reach the children. She regretted the hasty way she'd judged the couple who'd died protecting their kids. She regretted not trying to get to know them. She regretted going to the school and everything in between. But she felt if they could just save those two children then not everything would be lost.

With only two hundred yards between her and the undead, she saw Mark try to clear a path through the zombies in front. He swung his axe up and down, cleaving limbs and cracking bone. Humans would have fled before the onslaught, but the undead felt no pain. Nilda wanted to shout at him, to remind him that he needed to kill them, that nothing else mattered. But she had no breath to spare for shouting.

A creature appeared behind Mark. Its left arm had been nearly sliced through and now hung from the merest scrap of skin. With its right, it clawed out, grasping at Mark's shoulder. He half turned, and almost as if it was waiting for that opening, a zombie lurched forward, its teeth chomping at his neck. He fell, and Tracy screamed as she leaped from her bike, sprinting towards her fallen man. She had the axe out and swung at a creature in front. She missed. Off balance, she didn't even have the chance to defend herself. She fell, her screams finally cut short.

Nilda kept going. She could see Sebastian, and he was still alive. So were the children. Both were huddling against his legs. The old teacher was timing his blows, swinging a crowbar methodically, left then right, then left again. With each blow he crushed a skull, and with each swing he took a step forwards, towards her, the children moving with him.

And then Nilda reached the undead. She fell off the bike. She reached behind her, unslinging the axe. Idly wondering who had put it on her back that morning, she swung it around in a long horizontal arc. It crashed through a zombie's face. The creature fell. She pivoted, turned, and swung again. She threw the axe up and down, splitting a zombie's skull in two. She pulled the axe out, swung again, and again.

There were only twenty yards separating them now. The others would arrive soon. She just had to keep swinging the axe and keep the undead focused on her. Sebastian would be able to protect the children. The others would arrive, and they would be safe, and then she could die. Perhaps then, she might see Jay again.

She swung, aiming at the legs, keeping the axe low, scything it around. They might still be in time, if only the others would hurry up and arrive. And she sliced the axe around again, this time twisting with it so that she could see how far away the others were. The tracks behind were empty. There was no one coming to help.

Rage overtook her. She hadn't saved her son, but she could save someone. If she managed to save just one person then, somehow, she would be redeemed. She cleaved and hewed, and the axe stuck. She dropped it, pulling out the crowbar from her belt. She swung and hacked, but there wasn't the weight to the blows of the heavier axe. She split skin, she cracked bones, but the zombies didn't fall so easily.

She vaguely registered passing Mark's body. She vaguely noticed Tracy, dead, her hand outstretched towards him. She vaguely noticed the fingers twitch.

"Sebastian!" she called. He heard her. He looked up.

"I'm coming!" she yelled.

But it was too late. Sebastian was surrounded. She knew she couldn't reach him in time.

"No! No! No!" she screamed, laying about her left and right. But Sebastian and the two children disappeared under the weight of the undead.

All reason gone, the crowbar fell from her hand as she tried to push past the undead to reach her fallen friend. She didn't notice the first bite. She noticed the second, and with it the rage disappeared to be replaced by a cold bitter fear. Acting on instinct, she pushed the creature away. Stumbling across the tracks, she backed away from the pack of zombies still tearing apart her friends. They were dead. She glanced at her arm. So was she. There was nothing she could do to help them. There was nothing she could do to help herself. But they could be avenged. Not by killing the undead. They were the weapon not the cause. It was Rob's fault. If he had followed her, then Sebastian and the children would still be alive. He would pay.

Her foot caught on one of the sleepers. Stumbling, she fell, grazing her hands on the gravel. She pushed herself upright and onward, back towards the bike. Glancing behind, she saw the creatures were getting closer. She may die, but she wasn't going to die like that. Not yet. She turned and ran back up the tracks to where she'd dropped the bike. She had to catch up with Rob and the others. Then she would let herself die, and in death she would become her own avenging spirit.

She pulled herself on the bike and began pumping at the pedals. She was tired. More than tired. Exhausted. Running on adrenaline, and that was running out.

"No. Not yet," she said. "Soon. Just a few miles more."

She felt weak. She felt tired. She tried to tell herself it was only the adrenaline wearing off, but perhaps it was blood loss. Perhaps it was something else.

She reached the point where she'd heard the first scream. There was no sign of Rob. But she knew which way he'd gone. He couldn't be far ahead. She forced herself to continue, heading north along the tracks. When she looked behind she saw no undead. She had outpaced them. She glanced ahead. There was no sign of the others. She cycled faster, pushing herself on, forcing her feet to pedal, not wanting to stop until she caught up with them.

"Just a few more miles. Just a few more."

But she knew she was slowing down. The last of her strength was finally beginning to ebb. She knew this was it. She was dying. And with that thought, the last of her energy was spent. She brought the bike to a stop next to an old brick signal box. The bushes to her right rustled. There was a snapping of branches followed by the low wheezing snarl of the undead. No, she thought, that wasn't fair.

She leaned the bike up against the signal box and used it as a step to climb up onto its low roof. It wasn't much of a last resting place, she thought, but she would die in peace and afterwards… afterwards didn't concern her. Not any more.

She lay down and stared up at the grey sky.

"I'm sorry," she said to no one and everyone.

She passed out.

And then she woke up.

Grey clouds scudded across a bruised sky, and she could see them. As that realisation seeped through her, she became aware of how bitterly cold it was. She raised her hands above her face. The movement sent a jarring pain through the back of her neck. If she felt pain, she wasn't dead. She hadn't turned. Or maybe she had. Maybe, she thought, she was undead but somehow... different. Slowly, painfully, she rolled onto her side. Another dagger of pain, this time from her arm, pierced her skull. She glanced at the bite wound. Red blood beaded up through the cracks in the scab. She bled. The blood was red. What did that mean? Maybe, she reasoned, she'd only been asleep for a few minutes, yet one glance at the long shadows told her that wasn't the case.

"Either I'll turn or I..." But she left the sentence unfinished, for as she spoke she had heard a sound from below. There it was again, louder this time. A slow scraping sound followed by a snarling wheeze. She remembered the zombie that had caused her to climb the signal box in the first place. She rolled and crawled to the roof's edge and looked down. The creature was there, but it was alone.

I'm alive, she thought. A treacherous voice at the back of her mind added 'for now'. But when throughout the scope of human history had anyone truly been able to say any more than that? She got to her knees and breathed deep, filling her lungs with the cold early evening air. If she was alive, then she could still have her revenge. And she would have it. More than anything, right then, that was what she wanted.

At some point she'd lost her bag. She checked her belt, then her pockets. Empty. She was unarmed. No matter. She spotted a broken cinder block lying discarded amidst the gravel. She walked around the edge of the roof. As she did, the creature moved, following her, its hands pawing against the brickwork. When she'd reached the opposite side, the creature slapping at the wall below her, she ran back across the roof and jumped down. She landed hard, breaking her fall with her hands. Her injured arm sent a spike of protest into her brain. She gritted her teeth, channelling the pain into furious rage as she grabbed the cinder block and stood up. As the creature rounded the corner, she swung the block into its face. The impact knocked the zombie backwards, she swung again and again, and the creature fell. She stepped forward and brought the cement brick down on its skull.

She took a moment to look at the creature she'd killed. She tried to see it as the man it had once been. He had dressed like most of the others, in a thick winter jacket, jeans and trainers. Comfortable clothes for the evacuation. No, not he, it. It was just a creature. Not a human. Not anymore. None of them were. Not even Jay. She let the cinder block fall to the ground, grabbed the bike and began cycling north once more. She found she was cycling much more slowly than before, barely faster than a brisk walk. She hadn't the energy to go any faster, but Rob would have to stop, she told herself. He would stop to rest and search for food. He would pick the most convenient house, the one closest to the railway line. She repeated the words to herself, kept her eyes scanning the tracks and overgrown embankments and tried not to think about being alive. It was hard.

She followed the tracks until she saw, with dusk's last light, a railway station up ahead. She didn't want to stop, but knew that if she didn't she would collapse.

The station was small, consisting of nothing more than two platforms connected by a pedestrian bridge, each with a small waiting room. The southbound platform had a customer toilet with a faded 'out of order' sign. Next to it were two vending machines. She thought that an oddly appropriate place for them. She pulled herself up onto the platform and checked the machines. The doors had been forced open, the contents taken. Probably by Rob, she thought. It had to have been him. The sight of that oh-so-familiar poster on the vending machine's side reminded her that she'd neither drunk nor eaten for hours, possibly not since the day before. She couldn't remember.

She turned her attention to a small door marked private. Like the machines, the lock had been levered off. The contents inside appeared untouched, probably because none of them had any obvious value. She rooted around and found mops, buckets, a few bottles of disinfectant, a stack of bright orange 'Warning! Wet Floor!' signs, and at the back, behind a pile of lurid, high-visibility yellow vests, she found a pallet of water. She pulled out a bottle and downed it in two gulps. Only half of the water went in her mouth, the rest spilled over her face. It felt wonderful. She took another bottle. Her stomach gurgled as it began to fill. She felt more human, though that feeling was almost immediately suppressed by a flash of doubt as to whether she really still was.

Looking for a distraction, she grabbed the bottles of bleach. She walked back out to the platform and emptied the bottle over her wound, scrubbing at her hands, then rinsed the disinfectant off with water. The bite on her arm burned, but it was growing to be a familiar pain. She went back for another bottle of water and saw there was a note stuck to the pallet. It dated back to the previous summer. The water was an emergency supply in case a train broke down between stations. She laughed. She couldn't help herself. She remembered the story well enough. Back in June, a train had broken down on a remote stretch of track up near Carlisle. The passengers had been stranded for six hours. In the end, it had been a local farmer who'd first ferried them water from a local shop, then into Carlisle itself on a tractor-trailer. That photograph had been on the front page of all the newspapers. The press had had a field day, and the train company's CEO had been forced to resign. New management was installed, and they publicly pledged to put in procedures to ensure it never happened again. And this was their response, twenty-four bottles of water gathering dust at the back of a store cupboard. She took another bottle.

Feeling restless and more awake, she thought about going on, but the light was now completely gone. She could still see the tracks in front, but not the fields and houses to either side. Rat that he was, she knew Rob would have found shelter. If she continued, she might miss him in the dark. She'd have to wait. And that meant… she looked down at her arm once more. She wasn't certain exactly how long it had been since she was bitten, but it was at least ten hours. That she hadn't turned didn't mean she wasn't going to. The Emergency Broadcast had said people turned almost immediately. That didn't fit with the footage she'd seen before the press was nationalised, or with her own brutal personal experience. They'd said everyone turned. Everyone. But those same broadcasts had said there was a vaccine. If they'd lied about one thing, she told herself, then why not about everything else? It was a slim hope to cling to, but it was all she had.

The train station was old-fashioned enough that there was a waiting room with a fireplace. There was a good chance no one had gone to the trouble of sealing it up. The idea of being warm again, even if only for a few hours, was enticing, but she had no matches. Besides, if she was inside when the undead came, she would be trapped. She couldn't allow that. Instead, she grabbed the fluorescent vests from the store-cupboard and took them up to the pedestrian walkway that linked the two platforms. It was partly enclosed with a roof and sides with unglazed windows. It offered a little protection against the wind, and if the undead did come, she could go down the stairs on either side, or climb out through one of the windows and drop down onto the track.

Better than nothing, she thought, and nestled down as best she could. With only the bottle of water for company, the thin jackets for warmth, she sat, and waited for dawn.

She fell asleep.

22nd March

And again, she woke up. It was around four a.m., going by the sharp glow on the horizon. Certainly, it was bright enough to see the train tracks and the hedgerows to either side. She pulled herself to her feet, walked stiffly down to the bike, and began to push it north. After a few hundred yards, her muscles warmed, she got on and began to cycle. She managed a few more miles, and was beginning to wonder why dawn hadn't arrived, when the rain began.

It started light, just a few drops that she found refreshing, but quickly turned into a steady torrent. Within a few minutes she was soaked to the skin. She needed to find shelter. About twenty minutes later, she spotted a spire jutting up above the trees. She guessed she must have passed farms and perhaps other buildings, but they'd been too far from the tracks to see in the rain-filled pre-dawn gloom. Leaving the bike by the tracks, she trudged through a morass of mud as she crossed a field, and approached the church.

It was a small affair, not really more than a chapel, and it was old, judging by the worn stone. But while the church might offer shelter, she needed more than that. She skirted the church to the vicarage, a twee, rambledown cottage with a fussily maintained garden. It looked unoccupied, but she knew appearances weren't to be trusted. Delineating the church-grounds from the vicar's small patch of garden was a low picket fence. She crossed to the gate and banged it open and closed a few times. Muffled by the rain she doubted the sound had carried far, but the weather was getting worse. She needed shelter.

The vicarage door was closed and locked. That, she thought, was a good sign. She walked around the cottage until she found a window large enough climb through. Picking up a fist-sized stone from the rockery, she smashed the glass. She listened. Nothing. She climbed inside.

She found herself in a small kitchen. Even in the pre-dawn gloom she could see it was clean. The floor was scrubbed, though now covered in glass. No crockery stood next to the sink. She opened the fridge. It was empty. So were the bins. It took only a few minutes to check the rest of the cottage. The appliances had all been unplugged with the depressing diligence of someone who thought that one day they would be coming back.

Overly conscious of the muddy trail she was leaving on the floor, she climbed the stairs. She rooted around the drawers in the main bedroom - it was far too poky to be called a 'master'. The clothes were absurdly large. So were the shoes. The vicar must have been at least seven feet tall. With the beams of the cottage at five feet six, she wondered whether the man had been sent there for punishment or chosen it as penance.

She went back down to the kitchen. The cupboards were empty. She tried the tap. No water came out. She checked the small living room, looking through the dresser in the hope of finding some forgotten box of biscuits. There were none. That meant she couldn't rest. Not yet. She took all of the saucepans from the kitchen outside to collect rainwater, and went looking for tools.

She found a screwdriver and hammer in a drawer next to the sink. They wouldn't be great as weapons, but she wasn't planning on fighting.

Grabbing a waterproof jacket from a peg by the front door, she went back outside, down the drive, and onto the road.

The rain was getting harder. Visibility was low. She couldn't tell if she was in a village, on the edge of a city, or in the middle of nowhere. She followed the road along until she saw another house.

With the hammer and screwdriver she levered the front door open. This house was different. It was permeated with the pervasive smell of death and decay. She stood in the doorway, listening. She heard nothing.

"Hey! I'm here!" she screamed, stopping herself from adding a perverse 'Come and get me.'

There was no response. Quickly, she moved from room to room. Downstairs was empty. She went upstairs. She found the occupants, a couple, lying next to one another in bed. There was an envelope on the floor addressed, she could see, to 'Whomsoever finds us'. She didn't open it. She knew what it would say. There would be a message to a loved one, with a request the reader seek them out. She had her own mission. She didn't want anyone else's.

Satisfied she was alone, she went back to the kitchen. The cupboards weren't full, and what they contained barely counted as food in her opinion. Water chestnuts, bamboo shoots, okra, and a dozen other tins that some cookery show had acclaimed as the new 'must-serve' ingredient. Calories were calories and at least these were sold for human consumption. She threw them into a bag. She went back upstairs and rooted around in the cupboards until she found some clothes. A few months ago they would have been baggy, now they were voluminous. They would do.

She returned to the vicarage, lit the fire, drank the rainwater from one saucepan, then emptied some rice into another and put it over the heat to cook. She sat back in a chair and watched the flames. Finally, she allowed herself to think of what she would do next.

Rob and the others wouldn't be able to travel as fast as she. They would have to stop more often, and for longer, to find food. They, too, would have to shelter from this rain. And she knew where they were going. She would either catch them on the railway, or somewhere along the coast. And then… what? That was the question. Their inaction had been criminal, but only in terms of old world morality, where the judicial system existed to overrule instinct. They'd acted in self-preservation. They weren't blameless, but there was only one punishment that she would be able to deliver. Did they deserve that? She brought to mind their faces. Was death a fitting punishment for… Terry? Or was it Jerry? And she realised that she'd never bothered to learn his name, or that of most of the others. She leaned back and closed her eyes. Guilt ran through her at the idea Sebastian, the children, and all the others might have lived if she had done that one small thing.

"No!" she said out loud. "No," she repeated it again more softly. They had acted instinctively, and their instinct had been to run. She wouldn't blame them, and while she wouldn't forgive them, she would leave them alone. Rob, though, would have to die. She'd thought he was just another small-town kid in a pond so small he didn't realise he was the only life in it. A wannabe-gangsta who, in the old world, would have amounted to nothing. No one would've noticed his existence long enough to ignore it. But here and now, as long as he lived, pain and suffering would follow in his wake. No one deserved to share the loss she felt. So she would kill him, and after it was done… Well, then she would return home. She would find her son and… and bury him. She refused to think of what she would have to do before that.

She looked at her arm. She wasn't going to turn. Either she was immune or she had already turned, just into something else. That was a possibility wasn't it? For Jay's birthday they'd rented a movie where that was the plot. She'd wanted to take him to the cinema, but he'd refused. He didn't want to be seen going there accompanied by his… She turned her mind away from that thought. It was too painful. Whatever she was, it didn't matter. She was alive and she had a plan. She just had to wait for the rain to stop.

The water boiled. Mechanically, she ate the rice. Then she slept.

She didn't know what time it was when she woke. The rain still fell. She thought about going to fetch the bike, but she was warm, she was comfortable. Except for her arm. She gathered more water, boiled it, and then did her best at cleaning the wound, bandaging it with a strip of clean linen she found upstairs. Weren't human bites often fatal? Hadn't she read that the mouth was the most bacteria ridden part of the body? Then again, if she hadn't turned, why should she worry about any other kinds of bacteria? It didn't matter. She went back to the fire and soon fell back to sleep.

23rd March

The next morning, she woke to find a light drizzle falling out of a dismal sky. She gathered the remains of the food and left the vicarage without a backward glance. She set herself a gruelling pace. With no accurate way of measuring distance, she relied on the stations' names to judge her location. But there was something wrong with those. It took her until lunchtime to realise what. She had long since passed Carlisle and was in Scotland.

She brought the bike to a stop. Either she could head north, further into Scotland, or head west and follow the coast back down into England and the Lake District. But which route had Rob taken? The plan had been Tracy's, not his. The skies opened and made the decision for her. She would have to find shelter again. When she did, she would find a map. She regretted not looking for one earlier.

Her eyes now open for a spot in which to shelter as much as for signs of her prey, she pushed herself on. She did spot a few distant figures, mostly in the fields and once by the tracks. By their shambling gait, she knew almost instantly that these were the undead. When she got closer to the one on the tracks, she didn't recognise the person it had been. She didn't stop. She couldn't see the point.

Her muscles were beginning to ache, her stomach twitched, and there was a dull thudding at the back of her head. She put it down to the constant looking left and right and straight ahead. But she should have looked where she was going. A fallen branch caught in the rear spokes, bringing her and the bike to a tumbling halt.

She fell onto the tracks, grazing her hands on the gravel. She cursed. Then she saw the bike. The rear wheel was twisted, the spokes torn off, and the frame was bent.

The sky was split by sudden lightning, with thunder following on too soon for comfort. She had to find somewhere to shelter. She picked herself up and looked around. A few hundred yards behind her the train tracks had crossed a road. On it were a string of detached houses with large gardens. She trudged towards the nearest. She broke in and managed to check the house was empty before she collapsed on the sofa in the front room.

She woke in the middle of the night with violent pains in her stomach. When she tried to stand, her legs collapsed almost immediately. As she fell to the floor, she threw up violently. She heaved and retched, coughing up nothing but acidic bile. Sweat dripped from every pore. It felt as if every drop of moisture was being rung out of her. She knew she would die unless she drank something.

On her hands and knees, she crawled out into the hallway. Fluids, she told herself, she had to find some. She tried the taps in the kitchen. Water came out, but only in a trickle. She stuck a mug under the tap. It filled halfway before the water stopped. She swallowed the water and threw it up almost immediately. She opened the tins she'd been carrying, sipping at the sickly sweet syrup and the salty brine, forcing herself to keep it down.

She felt so cold. She just wanted to curl up and sleep. If she did that, she knew she'd die. And she couldn't die, not yet, not until she'd had her revenge. There was a fireplace in the front room. It was laid, but ornamentally with fir cones and dried flowers. She fumbled with a match, sparking one after another until the rock-dry petals caught. Her vision swimming, her head nodding back and forth, she watched the flames. She coughed. Smoke. The chimney must be blocked. She pulled herself to her feet, stumbling to the windows. She fumbled with the latch. It wouldn't open. She slammed her fist against the glass. There was no force to the blow. She staggered into the hall and threw open the front door. The action was too much. She fell to her knees, coughing and retching. She began to sob at the unfairness of it all.

The air felt cool, almost refreshing and, after a time, she managed to crawl back through to the kitchen and open the back door. The draft quickly cleared the smoke. She went back to the cans of food and began to eat their contents cold, mechanically chewing each mouthful. She couldn't keep it down, but she kept trying. It kept her awake. When dawn came, she didn't feel any better, but she didn't feel much worse. She was down to her last tin. What she needed wasn't food. She needed water. The rain still fell, but she didn't trust it. She'd not been sick until she drank it. She pulled the cupboards open and found nothing. She had no choice. She would have to try one of the other houses.

A small shed stood in the garden. She managed to stagger over to it. It wasn't even locked. She wondered about that, about a place where people didn't have to worry about theft. She found a rake about the right height. Leaning on it, she limped down the road to the next home.

Unlike that first house which had an air of abandonment to it, this one had been lived in. Two cars were parked in the drive, half deflated footballs were scattered across the lawn. She ignored them. It took her three attempts to break down the door.

She stumbled into the house and found herself in the kitchen. Half of the table was covered with a neatly arranged stack of food, the other half with pallets of water. All except the top-most one were still wrapped in plastic. She pulled out a bottle and took a deep draught. She coughed, spluttered, and sprayed the contents over the room. Gritting her teeth, she forced herself to sip. By the time she finished the bottle she found herself covered in sweat, but otherwise felt marginally better.

She closed her eyes, breathing long and slow. Whatever was wrong with her, perhaps the worst was over. Her breathing sounded odd though, almost as if there was an echo to it.

She heard a creak, then a sigh. She turned. A zombie stood in the doorway three feet from her. Its arms outstretched, its mouth open, it staggered forward and swiped at her. Fingernails scraped down the side of Nilda's face. She shoved her hands up, knocking its arms away. The creature didn't notice. It swung again, this time its hand caught on Nilda's arm just above the still-fresh bite marks. It squeezed as its other arm swung at her neck. Nilda stepped backwards, pulling the creature with her. Its teeth snapped forwards to bite at her face. She screamed a mixture of fear and pain, and as she looked into those dead eyes, the scream turned into a bellow of rage. She grabbed the back of the zombie's head and slammed it down onto the kitchen table. There was a crack of bone, but the creature kept thrashing, kept squeezing. She smashed the head down onto the table again. The creature lost its grip. Nilda slammed its head down, again and again until the zombie stopped moving.

She collapsed onto the floor and began to cry.

Before it had been infected, before it had been a zombie, it had been a she. A girl of no more than sixteen. A great wracking sob exploded from her mouth as she thought of Deborah, of Chantelle and Christof Harper. She thought of the children Sebastian had seen gunned down at the muster point. She thought of all the children who had been willingly poisoned by the vaccine. And she thought of Jay, and she wept for all those promises she had made to him that would now be eternally unfulfilled.

Her treacherous, feeble, and oh-so-human body didn't allow her to wallow in despair for long. Thirst returned. She took another bottle and, wanting to get out of the kitchen, went to investigate the rest of the house. There was nothing remarkable about it. She found no other occupants, living or dead, until she went out into the garden. There she discovered three graves.

She stood by them for a moment, trying not to wonder whether one of their occupants had infected the girl, and whether, in her last moments of life, she had buried her family.

She took some food from the kitchen and went into the front room to eat it. She had no appetite, but knew she'd need her strength. When she'd finished, she went to the garage in search of a shovel. Then she dug a fourth grave.

119

It wasn't deep. Dragging the girl's body to it exhausted her. She managed to make it back inside before collapsing again. When she woke she found it was night.

She ate. She drank. She threw up. She ate and drank again. She slept.

24th March

She filled in the grave.

25th March

She felt marginally better. According to the map she'd found in a kitchen drawer, she discovered that, blinded either by the storm or rage or whatever illness had struck her down, she hadn't just cycled past Carlisle but straight through it. She tried to remember when that could have been. Then she tried to recall the stations she had cycled through, but found she couldn't name a single one. In fact, she found it hard to remember very much of those days except that last sight of Sebastian just before he had died. She turned quickly away from that memory and back to the map.

There were dozens of places where Rob might have left the train line. If he hadn't, if he had kept following it north, then there was little chance she would be able to catch him now. She stared at the map, trying to will it to reveal his location.

The only decision she came to was that Rob was lazy. If he could avoid effort, he would. So, he would have gone looking for a boat as soon as possible. Her decision was made, then. She would head due west until she reached the coast, then follow it south down through Scotland, and back into England if necessary. And if she didn't find him? Then she would look in Ireland, and she would keep looking until she found him. Then she would kill him. She was determined of that.

She glanced out at the sky. It was only mid-afternoon. Suddenly there was no urgency. Revenge could wait, at least until morning. Once more, she fell asleep.

27ᵗʰ March

She could smell the sea. She thought she heard waves crashing against the cliffs. It was nearing noon five days after she'd found the house with the graves. She'd wanted to leave the house the previous day. She had the desire burning deep within her, but not the strength. All she had managed to do was find a bicycle at the back of the garage.

When she woke, she'd loaded all the supplies she could carry, though most had to be left behind, then followed a branch line to the west. She'd travelled slowly as the tracks curved in and around villages and hills, only picking up speed when she needed to outpace the undead. She saw them differently now. Dangerous, yes, but they were to be neither pitied nor feared, they were just people who'd not had her luck.

She'd left the railway line when it began to curve to the north heading, she supposed, to Glasgow. She had taken a road, then a footpath, and finally switched to farmer's tracks that snaked up and around the low hills.

She knew she would have to backtrack, but she wanted to see the waves. Every year on April 1ˢᵗ she and Jay had gone to the seaside. Regardless of the weather, they would battle the seagulls to eat fish and chips by the seawall, and then try to find somewhere that would sell them an ice cream. Always.

Clouds were gathering to the north. She guessed it would rain soon, but if she at least saw the waves, she felt she would be marking the anniversary. Though this year there would be two members of her family to remember. She pushed herself harder, forcing a way through the thick heather, propelled by the need for absolution.

Just before she reached the hill's crest, she saw the waves. It was a pleasing though painful sight. With her eyes fixed on the dark green-blue expanse, she wheeled her bike up to the crest of the hill.

Then she saw it. A boat. It wasn't far out to sea. It wasn't even powered. It seemed to be drifting. It looked like a lifeboat, emblazoned with the orange and white colours of the RNLI. She thought she saw some people moving about on board. Could it be Rob? The boat seemed to be drifting with the sea from the north. Perhaps they'd run out of fuel, and the current was now pulling them back south. It was possible, wasn't it?

If she signalled, would they stop? Would they see her? Would they guess who she was? Perhaps they would wait. But could she reach it? The grass-covered hill curved gently down to steep cliffs and a precipitous drop. If the boat was drifting she doubted it would be able to reach the shore. She had to try. She turned her attention to the cliffs. There had to be a path down them. Again she heard the crashing of the waves, except... except that wasn't the sound of waves. The noise came from inland.

She turned. Heading towards her, trampling walls, crushing trees, was a horde of the undead, tens of thousands strong. They were spread out across the countryside, this slow moving band of death, a mile wide and she couldn't guess how deep. The front rank was barely five hundred yards away. Above them, what she'd taken for clouds was a plume of dust and dirt thrown up by their incessant march. She glanced down the hill, at the way she'd come, looking for an escape. Then she looked back at the horde, and she realised she had waited too long. The creatures had gotten closer. Some at the front had seen her. They were moving faster, and the ones behind, though ignorant of the prey ahead, copied the pace. She gave up on thinking, pushed the bike out in front, and began to ride it down the hill.

Get ahead. Get ahead of them, she thought. Get ahead, and find a path down the cliffs. There had to be one. She scanned the ground ahead, but the grassy slope ended abruptly wherever she looked. She glanced behind. The creatures had crested the hill and were now stumbling and tumbling down after her. She threw off the bags hanging from the handlebars. The bike wobbled as she pulled off her backpack. She pushed her feet down on the pedals trying to pick up some speed, but then she realised that she was veering towards the cliff's edge. Stamping on the brakes, she skidded to a halt just in time. She glanced behind. The undead were getting closer.

She cycled on, following the cliff, trying to find some method of escape, trying to see the obvious solution she had overlooked, but she knew she hadn't. There were no options left. Ahead, the path sloped down before coming to an abrupt end at a lookout point overhanging the rocks below.

Without stopping, she glanced back one last time. The horde came on. One near the front fell, to be crushed by the multitude shambling on behind. There was no going back. That left only a slim chance. How high were the cliffs? Twenty feet? Thirty? Forty? If they were much higher it would be like hitting concrete. She would probably die. But she would die if she stayed where she was. A quick death was preferable to an agonisingly slow one at the hands of the horde. But there was no point reasoning. Her feet still pedalled. She'd already made up her mind. The cliff's edge was only three feet away. She was going too fast to stop.

Not out of design, but from an instinctive desire to hold onto life for just one more second, she leaned back as the front tyre spun on empty air. Momentum carried her and the bike forward. She let go of the handlebars. The bike fell. So did she.

It took seconds that stretched for years. Her mind filled with images of Olympic divers. She tried to twist and turn, and to get her hands in front and her legs straight as she plunged down. The bike hit the water first. A fraction of a second later so did she. The impact knocked the air from her lungs.

It was dark.

It was cold.

Panic gripped her. Which way was up? Which way was down? She couldn't tell. She struck out with her hands and feet. She was surprised to find they worked. She was thinking. She looked forward. There was only darkness. She stopped thrashing, and twisted around. The water clung to her clothes. They were dragging her down. Down. And she wanted to go up, and now she knew which way that was. She floundered and kicked, and then the water above seemed brighter. Her lungs were burning. It *was* brighter. Her hands touched something strange. Not something, but nothing, she realised, as with a final burst of strength she pulled her head above water.

She gasped for air. Coughed. Spat out a mixture of blood and water. Breathed. Coughed. Breathed, and sank below the waves once more. This time her lungs were full. A stroke and a half, and she was back above the surface. She breathed, and this time she didn't cough.

She began to feel pain. She remembered the blood. That didn't matter, she told herself. Not now. Not yet. Her legs worked. Her arms worked. Each stroke and kick was pain, yet she only experienced it abstractly. She looked about for the shore and saw the boat instead.

A wave struck her, and spun her around. She saw the cliffs. No, she thought. She had to reach the boat. It was important. She moved her arms, turning herself around. It took an age. She couldn't see the boat. The waves were too high. Then one caught her and carried her up, and when she reached the crest she saw it. The boat wasn't far away. There were figures on the side. They had oars. They were paddling towards her. Stroke by stroke, she swam towards it.

Now, with salvation so close, the pain really began. She screamed and swallowed a mouth full of water. She sobbed with frustrated agony. The screams seemed to echo around her. No. It was voices. Voices from the boat. They were calling to her. The words were unintelligible, but the tone was of concern. It was human. It touched something inside her, kindling a flame she thought had died a week before.

She forced herself to swim on. One stroke at a time. The boat grew closer. They were bringing it closer, she realised. One more stroke, just one more.

And then there was another noise. The sound of something hitting the water. And then there was another. And another. She turned. The cliff top was full of the undead. One by one they were continuing over the cliff and falling into the sea a few dozen yards behind her. She turned back to the boat, drew on her last reserves of strength, and swam. Behind her the zombies continued to fall.

"Grab the oar. Grab it! Quick, girl. Quick!"

Nilda heard the words. She didn't recognise the voice. She couldn't see the oar, or the speaker, or even the boat, but she could sense the waves churned by its passage. Something hit her arm.

"There. Take the oar!"

She grabbed and held on as it was pulled back. Her shoulders were lifted out above the waves. Her hand slipped. She fell back into the water.

"Hold it. Grab it!"

This time she did, and she didn't let go. The oar was tugged back towards the boat. When it was close, an arm reached down and grabbed the back of her shirt. Another arm came down and grabbed her wrist. She was pulled on board.

"You're safe. You're safe," the voice said.

She stayed on her hands and knees for a full minute, retching, her head swimming, unsure whether she was going to pass out. She didn't. Her vision began to clear. She looked up at her rescuer. He was in late middle age, with the build of someone who'd spent his life outdoors, working with his hands.

"Can you stand? Here, let me help you up." He held out his hand. "Odhran, Abbot of Brazely, or I was."

Nilda let him pull her to her feet. She looked over at the other rescuer. He was still on his knees, coughing and retching. He looked worse than she did. Her gaze moved to the rest of the small boat. It was packed with at least two-dozen people. All of them looked sick. She froze, suddenly afraid.

"Are they…?" she began.

"No, no. They're not infected. They're not even contagious, but they are sick," the Abbot said, his smile gone. "But, please. We need your help, now. We're drifting back to the shore, towards…" He didn't finish, just glanced at the cliffs. The undead were still streaming off over the side.

"Here." The man thrust an oar at her.

"I've never… I mean, what do I do with it?"

"One end goes in the water, the other stays in your hand," he said.

"Where are we going?" she asked.

"At the moment? Away."

Part 3: The Island
The Isle of Scaragh, The North Atlantic

30th March

The spade clinked against stone. Nilda scraped out one last shovel-full of dirt, then stood up and stretched. The hole was only four-feet deep, but that would have to do. Wearily, she climbed out. The cuts on her hands, which had been blisters the day before, were bleeding again. She walked down to the shore to rinse them in salt water, letting the sharp stinging pain do the job of coffee. There was none of that on the island.

There was no proper shovel, either. She had to make do with a folding spade from the lifeboat's emergency kit. It wasn't much bigger than the one Jay had had when he was still young enough to revel in the construction of sandcastles. Her soul wailed softly at the memory, but she was too tired to feel the full weight of grief.

She trudged back up the beach and grabbed the bottle she'd filled from the brook that morning. She was about to take a drink, but stopped. It seemed disrespectful to do it there by the open grave. She walked up towards the scrubby row of trees that separated the woodland from the stone and sand beach. Slumping down to rest against a scraggly pine, her back to the low prefab hut, she stared out at the waves.

At every moment, as they'd battled the current, she had expected to hear the sound of rock ripping through metal. Though it had seemed an uncounted age, it can't have been more than an hour before they had rounded the headland. Her last sight of the cliffs, from which she'd plummeted to such a bittersweet escape, had been of the undead, their numbers greatly reduced, still tumbling down into the water.

At first they'd tried to row towards the shore, then they had tried to steer a course close to land. The tide wouldn't allow it. They'd given up, and let the currents decide their destination. With the last light of day they had seen the ominous clouds gathering overhead. When night fell, the darkness was complete. There was no moon, nor even stars, to guide them. Not that Nilda knew one constellation from another, let alone how to navigate by them, but one of the passengers did. Callum McTavish had pulled cod out of the Atlantic for most of his youth. In middle age, economic necessity had forced him into selling it, battered, in a shop in Glasgow. But even he couldn't steer by the wind alone.

They hadn't seen the rocks until the waves broke white against them. By then it was too late. There'd barely been time to shout out a warning before the hull was pierced by a jagged shard of stone. The sound of metal being torn apart woke most of the passengers. A few, who by that stage nothing could rouse, slipped quietly beneath the waves before anyone was able to save them.

Terrified of what they might find in the dark, and with no notion of where they were, the remaining seventeen of them huddled together on the shore waiting for dawn. When it came, they found they were on a stone and sand beach twenty yards from the remains of the boat - now pinned to the rock that had pierced its hull - and forty yards from a one-storey building. It was made of prefabricated sections, with the front half on the beach, the other half suspended above the water on stilts. Next to it was a wooden jetty that ran out for fifty feet into the sea. There were no other boats and no other people, just a weather-worn sign that read 'Isle of Scaragh. Population: 19'. The sign was a joke. She realised that when she went inside and counted the nineteen bunk-beds and saw the other sign, the one pinned to the door that read 'Welcome to Pirate's Cove'.

The building itself was split in two. The larger half held the bunk beds, each screwed to the walls, with space for folding chairs and tables in the middle. There were no mattresses, no blankets, no pillows, just the metal frames, and they were quickly filled by the sick. The smaller half of the hut had a set of gas rings but no fuel-canisters, saucepans but no food, and cups but no coffee. No tea either, though she could live without that. She did find a brochure that said the island was uninhabited, and owned and operated by an outdoor pursuits company. It didn't say where the island was, only that bookings were available from April to September. On seeing it, the Abbot had said they'd arrived a few days too early. Surrounded by so much death, Nilda found no humour in the weak joke.

The discarded beer cans, and faded paint marks covering rocks and trees and one corner of the inappropriately jocular sign, spoke to what type of pursuits the island was used for. There were a few references to a centre somewhere in Wales and another in Aberdeenshire, and mention of sailing lessons. There was no boat on the island. Nilda had looked. There was no plumbing either, just a brick shelter a short way up the beach where a chemical toilet must have stood when the place was being used. At least, thanks to the brook, they had fresh water. She took another drink.

That first morning, Nilda had left the Abbot to tend to the sick and gone to make sure that the island really was uninhabited. That was what she had said. The truth was that she needed time away from the puking, bleeding, pitiful group that had saved her from death. But someone did need to explore, there was a small truth in that, and other than the Abbot, no one else was physically able.

She'd started by examining the boat. Most of what the group had brought with them from the Scottish mainland had been washed over the side when they ran aground. The only find of any substance was the emergency kit, bolted to the inside of the cockpit. In that, she found a few flares, a pack of twenty waterproof matches, the collapsible spade and a wholly inadequate first aid kit. There was nothing that would help the passengers. From what the Abbot said, there was nothing anywhere that could help them now.

Disappointed but unsurprised with how little she'd found, she had gone to survey the rest of their new home. That hadn't taken long. An estate agent would have described the island as having a desolate beauty. In truth it was an inhospitable rocky outcrop jutting out of the North Atlantic. Nearly sheer cliffs stood on the north, south and west. To the east, the slow trickle of the brook had worn down the cliffs, turning them into the gentle slope that led to the bay. There, the pebble beach was covered in driftwood and a plethora of plastic from that last golden age of humanity.

She'd followed the cliff-edge counter-clockwise around the island. There were trees, irregularly spaced but densely packed, and they were mostly pines. At their base, a thick carpet of needles was broken by an occasional cluster of nettles and weeds struggling to reach the sunlight. That, she discovered, was all there was to eat on the island. She did find two oaks and three other trees whose names she didn't know. None looked as if they would bear fruit.

She thought that whoever had optimistically built a house in the centre of the island in 1851 had planted those trees, perhaps hoping to sell them as timber. She knew the house, a one-and-a-half-storey hodgepodge of red brick and grey stone, was built in 1851 because that was the date inscribed on a plaque on the front wall. There had been some other writing on that plaque but it had been worn away by rain and wind. She'd spent half an hour trying to decipher it before deciding she never would. The house itself was a ruin. Three and a half walls, no roof, no floors, just the rotting stubs of a few timbers. The door had gone, as had the windows and their frames. The chimneystack had toppled down into the fireplace so long ago that a thick layer of springy moss covered the broken stone. The mortar between the bricks was rotten. The walls moved to the touch. She had decided it was unsafe to shelter there.

Just before she'd reached the northern most point of the island her foot had snagged against something. She tripped, fell, her outstretched hand brushing against air as it landed over the cliff's edge. Picking herself up, she looked down and saw a bramble snaking out between two large patches of stinging nettles. That meant there would be berries in the autumn. If any of them were still alive by then.

For the last two days her life had become digging and burying, tending the fire, and gathering nettles and roots. Somehow she'd escaped death only to find herself trapped in the final chapter of someone else's nightmare.

Her grim reverie was broken by the sound of the hut-door opening. She looked up and saw the Abbot step out onto the porch. He blinked a few times and turned his head up. The weather had settled. Since the storm had cleared there was rarely more than a stray wisp of cloud miring the blue sky.

The man looked tired. He always looked tired. He turned his head down and nodded to Nilda. Wearily, she got to her feet, walked over to the hut, and helped him carry the body out to the grave. They had no dignified way of lowering it in. She had to roll Callum McTavish's body down from the edge. It landed askew.

"No, I'll do it," Nilda said, as the Abbot bent down. She lowered herself into the grave and arranged the body so Callum's arms lay crossed on his chest. She climbed back out.

"I'd like to say a few words," the Abbot said.

She nodded, and waited as he uttered a prayer. When it finished, he began another, and then a third. He seemed unwilling to stop. Finally he came to a halt, murmuring an uncertain 'Amen'. They stood in silence for a moment, then Nilda put a hand on his shoulder and led him away from the grave.

"You need to sleep," she said.

"I can't. Not yet," he said. "Nor can you. We'll need another two graves before nightfall."

The Abbot went back into the hut. Nilda returned to the clearing and began filling the grave. Then she began to dig another.

31st March

"What do I put on the marker?" she asked.

"I… I don't know. Her first name was Glenys."

"You didn't know her?"

"No, I… I was just… there wasn't time to get to know one another."

"Glenys will do."

A few hours later as the sun was beginning to set, the Abbot came to join Nilda by the small driftwood fire she'd built above the high-tide mark. She had to keep the fire burning. There weren't enough matches to let it go out. She was cleaning dandelion roots, to be mixed with the nettles, which would make a change from the nettles mixed with roots they'd had for breakfast.

"How is it that you don't know these people?" Nilda asked. "I mean," she added, when she realised how accusatory the words had sounded, "did you join up with them recently?"

"Yes, I suppose," the Abbot replied, distractedly. "Recently. Yes. It seems a lifetime, yet it can't more than a few weeks."

"And you're sure it's radiation poisoning?"

"Positive. Their immune systems are shattered, their bodies are shutting down. There's absolutely nothing that can be done."

She'd asked the question before. She'd asked it in many different ways, and though he gave the same answer each time, she found it impossible to believe.

"Did you see the bombs yourself?" she asked.

"Yes. Well. No. I saw the mushroom clouds. That was fortunate. If I'd seen the explosions I would be blind or—" The sentence came to a spluttering halt as he was overcome by a wracking cough. She passed him a bottle of water. It was the only comfort she could offer.

"Do you think it was just Glasgow that was bombed?" she asked, when his coughing fit had subsided.

"No, I don't. I think it was everywhere. That's why there's been no sign of our government. Why there is no government anywhere. No planes. No rescue. If it wasn't... I didn't know about the muster points." She had told him the evening before. "I can understand the reasoning behind it. I don't agree with it. I don't condone it. But can you call something like that monstrously evil when the real monsters walk our streets? I suppose you can. And it was so unnecessary. I think the evacuation might have worked. If it had, and if it hadn't been for those bombs, then by now we would have defeated the undead in Britain and be preparing an army to take back the world. There would have been seventy million of us left to save the planet. But the bombs came. Glasgow was destroyed. Everywhere else too, I assume."

The Abbot sank back into his gloom. Nilda searched around for something to say; she didn't want to face another silent vigil, waiting for the next person to die.

"You don't sound Scottish," she tried.

"I'm not. I wasn't. I lived at an Abbey down in the south. In Hampshire. Brazely it's called. Brazely Abbey, though really it's nothing more than ruins. It was destroyed during the Reformation. We've been restoring it for decades. No, that's a vanity," he amended, with a wheeze that might have been a half-hearted laugh. "We had spent decades just trying to prevent the decay getting any worse."

"You weren't trying to re-open it?"

"Really, there was nothing left but stone walls and a few timbers. It would have taken millions to rebuild. I suppose the others are still there. Perhaps they are still building its walls. Working on it was…" He hesitated, "It was a penance. For all of us."

"You mean as in 'we're all sinners', or do you mean for something specific?"

"Does it matter?"

"I suppose not," she said. "So how did you come to be up in Scotland?"

"I was needed there. Not for anything glamorous. A soup kitchen was understaffed. Flu, of all things, had left them with only two people to cater for hundreds. A call went out for help. I heard it, and I went north. That was back in December."

"But you stayed in Scotland?"

"It's hard to get volunteers, especially these days. Those days. Even the most charitable have bills to pay. So that's why I was in Glasgow when the world came to an end. They were turning it into an enclave. I suppose geography and size made that the sensible option. Some of the buildings were cleared out, some of the tenements were so crammed with people that it was worse than in the darkest days of the city's bleak history. That makes it sound like a nightmare place. It wasn't. I don't know who was in

132

charge, but they knew what they were doing. The roadside verges, the parkland, the back gardens and schools, it was all being dug up. And the atmosphere. It was almost… cheerful. I think there was a feeling that finally they had found the independence they had so wanted."

"But you weren't there when the bombs fell."

"No. I was saved that because I was deemed to be trustworthy. What do you call looting when it's orchestrated by the government? Re-appropriation was the term they used. As I say, someone in charge knew what they were doing. They'd found the customs import notes and the tax records. They knew what had come in shipping containers, what had been brought up by road, and where it had been stored. They knew where it had been delivered, which warehouses to loot, and which shops to search. Everything was organised. It was slick. Efficient. I think it would have worked, in time. There was a spirit there, a sense of… camaraderie, I suppose…" He trailed off, disappearing back into his own thoughts.

"But you weren't in Glasgow when it happened," she prompted after the silence began to stretch once more.

"As I say, I was considered trustworthy. All of our group were. We were tasked with going to the nursing homes, the veterinarians, the doctors' surgeries, and the outlying pharmacies. We went to collect those drugs that might have been too great a temptation for others. We even had a police officer with us. When we found a place already looted, she would take fingerprints. It was kept quiet, but there was a plan to offer an amnesty. They still had their police databases and… Ah, it doesn't matter. But that was what I was doing when the bombs fell. There were eleven of us in the group. The police officer, two soldiers each driving a requisitioned minibus, and eight of us 'volunteers'. We'd done a sweep of outlying communities and found very little. Not wanting to return empty handed, one of the soldiers, a sergeant, decided we'd return via an Army training ground. There was a stock of boots kept there, and good footwear was in short supply. We all went in together, all traipsed down the stairs to the storeroom. We may have been trusted not to steal the drugs, but the sergeant didn't trust us not to slack off if we were out of his sight. The lights went out. That was the first thing we realised. There was no panic, just a lot of muffled cursing as we made our way back upstairs. When we did, when we got outside, we saw the mushroom clouds over the city. I counted four. Others said there were five. One would have been one too many."

"Over the city itself?"

"I couldn't say. Not really. I saw them, and of course I knew what they were. Who wouldn't? But there wasn't time to linger. The vehicles wouldn't start. But we were fortunate. The soldiers knew what to do. We took our supplies back down to the storeroom. There we waited. We managed to hold out for three days. We'd finished the food, we'd nearly run out of water, and tensions were sky high. There was little ventilation, no toilets, and no privacy when people got sick. When we were down to one bottle of water each, the sergeant announced he was leaving. That was the signal for all of us. He didn't say it would be safe. Nor did he say 'we were leaving'. But he seemed to know something, and that was more than the rest of us. We left our cellar. I don't know what I had expected to see when I got outside. I suppose I thought everything would be covered in ash. We had talked about it while we waited. But what did any of us know except what we'd seen in documentaries about Hiroshima and Nagasaki, two cities made mostly of wood? There was ash, but it wasn't thick like snow."

"And what about Glasgow? Did you see it?" Nilda asked.

"I did, but only briefly. It was a smouldering ruin. Thick coils of smoke tumbled up into the sky. Buildings were gone, replaced by rubble and glass. There were no lights, no people, and there was no sound. That was the most striking change. The hedgerows were still green, but no longer full of life. Beneath them... Oh, it was a miserable sight. Beneath them, the ground was littered with birds. They must have flown to the hedges seeking the only shelter they knew, and there they died. There were no planes, nor helicopters. Believe me, we looked. We thought that surely there must be some kind of rescue operation underway. There wasn't. So we turned our backs and walked. There were more dead birds, and after a few miles we saw them in the roads and fields. Whether they were killed by the shockwave or the radiation, I don't know. It was a grim omen, but

134

it galvanised us. We knew that to stop meant death. The soldiers set the pace. Everyone else had to keep up. We walked all day until we reached a farmhouse by a road sign that read 'Glasgow. Fifty miles'. We didn't want to stop, but we couldn't go on. I collapsed in a chair and fell asleep. When I woke, the sun was rising, and I was alone. They'd all gone, but they'd left me my water bottle, though it was nearly empty. There was water still coming out of the tap, but I didn't fill the bottle. How would I know if it was irradiated or not? I reasoned that I could go on for at least a few miles, and with each step I took, the safer the water would be. On my own, I made poorer progress. I wandered a dead countryside, trying to recite the lessons from St Paul." He gave a bitter laugh. "The trials of Job came to mind, and I repeated each of his ordeals and told myself that by comparison I was truly fortunate, but then I would remember the words from Revelations. The pit of the abyss had truly been opened. That was what I repeated to myself, though there was no comfort in the deceit." For the first time since he'd begun his tale, he looked up at Nilda. "You don't remember the Cold War. You're too young."

"I'm not that young," she said. "I watched the Berlin Wall come down, and the tanks rolling in the streets of Moscow."

"That was the end of it, when we knew that we'd won. What you don't remember is what it was that we'd won. You don't remember the fear that came before. The constant dread that, at any moment, everything could end. That we pitiful civilians, be we farmers in Minsk, shopkeepers in Newcastle, or executives in Los Angeles, that our lives were held in the palms of a handful of men in Washington and Moscow. When it ended, that fear left us. A golden age of prosperity and charity, of democracy and discovery, and of peace lay before us. It was a lie. Our destiny was in the hands of a few, and it was ever thus. At least the Soviets were an enemy we could understand. What they were replaced by, and now with the undead..." He started coughing again.

"But how did you come to meet them?" Nilda asked, gesturing to the hut. She wanted to keep the conversation going so she wouldn't be left with only the voices in her head to listen to.

135

"I was walking. I had no direction in mind, nothing but the road in front and my fear as motivation. I don't know how long I walked, nor how far. I stumbled out into the road, almost into the path of a coach. Morag was driving." He nodded towards one of the graves. "It was her coach."

"How did she get a coach working?"

"It was a museum piece. I mean that literally. She owned a transport museum, although that is a grand title for such a small place. Really, she made her money hiring the vehicles out for weddings and films. The one she was driving, her newest, was a 1940s affair. Post war, just. One of the first to come off the assembly line after peace broke out. Wooden seats, small windows, no seat belts, and no electronics. She hired it out as a prop for movies and TV shows. Even though it was built a few months too late, it looked the part. More importantly, it still ran. She was usually cast as the driver. She had seventy-three screen credits to her name. She was quite proud of that." He sighed. "Much like I'd done, she'd hidden in a cellar the moment that she saw the mushroom clouds. The passengers in the coach were just survivors she'd driven past. Some were sick, some got sick, a lot died, others seemed fine, and almost embarrassed because of it. I collapsed when they let me onto the bus. I didn't wake up until we'd reached the coast. We were at a small fishing village. Morag had provided the transport for a wedding there. Both the bride's grandfather and the groom's great uncle had worked in the factory that had made the bus. She was hired to take the wedding party to a church a few miles inland, then to the reception, then back to the village afterwards. That's where we went. She was hoping they'd be there, that the bus would be recognised, that we'd find help and refuge."

"But you didn't?"

"No. The village was empty. The boats were gone. We did our best for the sick, and for the people who came in over the next few days. It seemed as if everyone was heading for the coast. There was this constant stream of people. Some were tired, most were exhausted, some were close to death and a few died the moment they found themselves somewhere safe. I spent my time with the dying, offering them what comfort I could.

It was little enough. Two days, or three, or perhaps even a week later, I don't know, but I suddenly found there was no one to tend. At least, there was no one who would die in the immediate future. I left the improvised hospital we'd set up in one of the empty boatsheds and went outside. Around the outside of the village they had erected a barricade of cars and trucks, wood and stone, and anything else that was easily moved. There were no more refugees heading along that road towards us. There were only the undead."

"Did you try to fight?"

"Fight? Yes. Though not me personally. I swore off violence a long time ago. Not even these creatures could bring me to change that. But the others, they stood behind their walls, sharpened boathooks and garden tools in their hands. Morag had organised it, and she'd done it well. At first there were few enough zombies that the defenders could leave the protection of their wall and go up the road to meet them. But more came. There were always more. They had to retreat behind the walls, standing on improvised ramparts, plunging their makeshift weapons down, over and over again. They killed hundreds, but the ranks of the undead were legion. They set up a second ring and pulled back, letting the zombies swarm over that first barricade. And then there was a third ring, and each time the area they had to defend became smaller, and that meant fewer people were needed. That should have meant that everyone got more rest. But they didn't. People began to get sick once more. I should have realised what was happening, but as more people became ill, I became too busy to even think. Only when the walls were so thickly ringed with the bodies of the undead that the still-moving creatures couldn't be reached by their improvised spears did anyone realise how truly futile our efforts were. By that stage there were only a dozen left who could stand. Staying put was not an option. We had to leave, all of us. And the only way out was by sea."

"But you had no boats."

"Well, not quite. We had a rowing boat. Callum and two of the other, healthier survivors took it and headed up the coast to the lifeboat station. We thought they'd died, or worse, left us. But two days later Callum returned with the boat, alone. And that was how we got out. By the time we were out at sea, I realised that I was the only healthy one left. Some, like Callum and Morag had been hiding how sick they were. For others, pretence was impossible. The fuel soon ran out, so we drifted with the waves. I hoped we'd find a submarine or an aircraft carrier or even just another boat. We didn't. We found no one except you."

"And they're all sick now. All dying."

"Yes. In a few days they will all be dead."

"Who do you think was behind it?" she asked.

"The bombing? I think it was the same evil spirit that caused the outbreak and most of the world's evil."

Nilda looked at him askance. Dressed in tattered jeans and a patched sweater she found it easy to forget he was a monk. "You're saying you think this was the work of the Devil?" she asked.

He laughed. "No, I meant that evil spirit that lurks within us all. This was not the work of the Devil, nor of some vengeful God. I think this was merely the act of some foolish men blinded by the certainty of their own beliefs."

"Coming from a religious man that's—" she began, but was cut off by a loud moan from inside the hut.

"Excuse me," the Abbot said, wearily standing up.

Nilda watched him go back into the hut, then returned her attention to the dying embers of the fire.

1st April

Nilda stirred the contents of the saucepan. She tried not to think about the date and how, in past years, she and Jay had spent it at a beach watching waves identical to the ones beating against the shore. She looked down into the mess of stinging nettles and dandelions. It was a far cry from greasy fish and chips. A morning spent gathering leaves didn't amount to much food in the pot. She supposed she was fortunate that it didn't have to stretch that far. She regretted the thought almost immediately. She'd dug three graves first thing that morning and filled two of them soon after. The third would be occupied before noon. Her hands were blistered. Her arms had been stung. She barely noticed.

Fetch water, tend fire, collect roots and nettles, dig graves, and try not to think; that had become her day. As much and as often as she could bear, she had helped the Abbot keep the other survivors comfortable. There was no comfort, save water, and most of them could not hold it down. And as the only cloth they had was that which they were wearing, she was unable to even wipe their fevered brows.

In the afternoons, she helped carry those who asked outside. But even in the early summer air they complained the sea breeze felt like an arctic gale. She wanted to weep with the frustration, exhaustion, and bitter cruel irony of it all. They were good people. They were kind people. They didn't deserve this. No one did. But while they faced everything - except the weather - with such stoicism, she had to be strong when in their company. And when she was alone she found she couldn't cry. All she felt was burning fury at the evil humanity had created. The undead, the end of the world, it was all so utterly devoid of reason and yet, somehow, so inevitable.

She had stopped looking out to sea. No one was searching for them. No one knew they were alive. No one knew anyone was alive unless they could see them and touch them and... she shook her head, trying to think loudly of rescue to drown out those dangerously painful thoughts. But no rescue would come. She dared not admit it, but she was half-glad of that.

She dipped a spoon into the pot. It tasted bitter, almost entirely unlike spinach. She lifted the pan off the fire and left it to cool. The Abbot would distribute it to those among the sick who were still able to swallow. Nilda hated going into the hut and couldn't face it in her present mood.

Though she had stopped looking out to sea, she found her gaze inexorably drawn to the waves breaking on the shore. She'd seen a horror movie the summer before last. The film was appalling. The producers had blown their miniscule budget on the soundtrack, leaving nothing left over for effects, cast, or script. The plot, though she wouldn't call it that, was centred on an eighteenth-century Irish fishing village being terrorised by undead sailors walking up out of the waves. She'd thought it absurd. She'd seen enough of those Floridian cop shows to know that humans decompose in water. Now she wasn't so sure. She kept expecting that horde of the undead which had followed her over the cliffs to come slouching up the waves towards her. There was no reason she could think of why they wouldn't.

She didn't sleep much. Every time a piece of flotsam - or was it jetsam? She couldn't remember the difference. But every time some piece of sea-borne litter washed up against the shore, she would be startled out of sleep, convinced it was the horde, following her from where they had fallen off the cliff. If the undead did come, if whatever animated their bodies protected them from natural decay, then there was nothing she could do. There was nowhere to run, nowhere to hide, no way off the island. Her hand searched for the comfort of the short spade. One edge was serrated. She tested it with her thumb. It was sharp enough. If it came to it, she had her way out.

She'd seen that movie with Jay. It had been part of her strategy to treat him more like an adult in the hope he would stop shutting her out of his life. It hadn't worked. And it hadn't mattered. She bit back a sob, got up, and walked off into the woods.

There was no medicine, but if the others ate something nourishing, then maybe that would be enough to ensure that at least some of them survived. She had no basis for that reasoning but there was nothing else she could do, and she couldn't simply let them die. But roots and leaves weren't going to be enough.

A bird took off from a branch a short way off. Where there were birds, she thought, there was meat. There would be eggs too. She remembered that she'd said that to Jay a few weeks and a lifetime ago.

"Birds," she said out loud, in an attempt to dispel the memory. "They can be caught."

By the time she walked back to the beach, she hadn't worked out how. She found the Abbot sitting outside the hut. Next to him hunched Lorna Fraser, one of the older survivors. The Abbot looked tired, but following the old woman's instructions, he was busy at something. Propelled by guilt she walked across to them.

"Did you find anything edible?" Lorna asked kindly.

"A few more patches of dandelions. A lot more nettles," Nilda said.

"Ah well, that's something. But you know we need something more than that. I'm feeling a lot better today. I'm not the only one. I think a decent meal might do us all the world of good."

"I was thinking the same. Bacon and eggs for preference," Nilda murmured.

"Spoken like a townie. Spent your life in the city, I expect."

Nilda was about to snap back a retort, but the old woman began to cough. Nilda saw blood on the woman's raised hand.

"I was used to getting food from the supermarket, yes. But I watched enough documentaries to know what food looks like in the wild."

"And did any of these documentaries happen to mention fish at all?" the woman asked. There was a glint in her eye, an echo of a smile on her lined, wan face. She wasn't that old, Nilda realised, not that much older than her.

"I'd... no. I suppose I'd overlooked the obvious," Nilda said.

"Potatoes would be nice, but you can live on fish and nettles."

"We've no rod. No bait," Nilda said.

"You can dig can't you? There are plenty of insects in the ground. And we don't need a rod. We need traps. That's far easier."

"Traps for fish?"

"We'll try that. But we'll start with crabs. Good crabbing round here. Get some more branches. Thin ones that we can weave together." She pointed at the pile that the Abbot was inexpertly threading together. "And then I'll show you how to make a trap."

2nd April

There was meat to add to the pot.

3rd April

Nilda looked down at the body of Lorna Fraser. The woman had died in the night. The Abbot was still in the hut, offering comfort to those who would join her shortly. Nilda tried to think of something to say. Nothing seemed appropriate. She began to fill in the grave. There were more that needed to be dug.

5ᵗʰ April

"There's just four of us left now," Nilda said.

"Hmm," the Abbot murmured. He'd been quiet all afternoon. The last two survivors were asleep. That was how the Abbot described it. Nilda would have said they were unconscious.

"Is it Friday today?" she asked as brightly as she could manage.

"What? Oh, I don't know. Why?"

"Fried fish," she said, pointing at the saucepan lid she'd propped on top of the fire. On it two fish were sizzling away. "Maybe we should try to wake them," she added.

"There's no point," the Abbot said. "They'll be dead by morning."

"One last meal, then?" She regretted the words the moment she'd spoken them. She'd meant to be light-hearted, but they sounded callous.

"No. Let them sleep. Please let them die in their sleep. Please, God, let them have that last mercy."

She looked over at him. She'd not heard him pray before except over the dead.

"Are you okay?" she asked.

"I'm tired. Tired of all of this. Tired of just keeping going. One more day, just one more day, but there's always another day after that, all for what purpose? All to what end?"

Nilda didn't say anything. She'd had those thoughts herself. She had kept going because giving up was just too difficult.

"We should think about heading back to the mainland," she said, eventually. "We could build a raft. It's not far. It's only forty miles. Perhaps fifty."

"You know how to make a raft? You need rope and nails. We have none."

"We can't stay here. If we do, we'll die. We have to try to leave."

"But why?" he asked. "What is there for us over there but pain and death? Don't we have enough of that here?"

142

"We're alive aren't we?" she said angrily. "Doesn't your religion teach you not to give up?"

He gave a snort. She thought he was about to laugh, but it turned into a cough. He raised his hand to his mouth. When it came away, she saw the blood. Their eyes met.

"I thought…" she began.

"I was sick, wasn't I? We all got sick, down in that cellar. That's how it works. You get sick, then you seem to get better. For a few days or a few weeks, all depending on the dose. And then you get sick again, and this time there is no recovery."

"You didn't say. I… I thought…"

"I knew," he said. "I just didn't want to speak the words out loud. I hoped I was to be spared. I hoped I was different. That is the vanity of our race. We each think ourselves special."

6th April

"Now there are just the two of us. And soon it will just be you," the Abbot said. "And then what will you do? Will you return to the mainland? Will you still search for revenge? I know you think that is what drives you. It isn't. You are consumed with guilt. You desire to undo the mistakes of your past. None of us can do that. There are sins that can be atoned, others which cannot, and none which can be undone."

"What is it you did?" Nilda asked.

"Did?" he coughed. She raised the cloth to wipe his mouth.

"The reason why you were in the Abbey. You weren't always a monk. I've been thinking about it, about the way you care for the sick. There's a reason why you were still in the UK. A reason why you weren't out in some famine struck war zone. Why were you rebuilding old walls when you could have been out there doing some real good?"

"Why? Because I was caught."

"You mean arrested? You had your passport taken away?"

"I did. They gave me a choice. Disappear into a monastery or just disappear. That was the choice they gave me."

"Why? Who said that?"

"If I tell you, will you give me absolution? You can't. But telling you won't hurt. Not anymore. But once, the knowledge would have been fatal. I was only a young man, yet in a short space of time I managed some terrible things. Unforgivable things. All on the orders of others. On the orders of the government. But you want to know how I was caught. I was asked to set a fire. One of my… colleagues had killed his wife, and then himself. The couple had two children. An infant and a teenager. The teenager disappeared. The two bodies and the still living infant were discovered by our commanding officer. I was called in to set a fire and plant the evidence that would make their deaths look accidental. I never found out what happened to the infant, but afterwards I was tasked with finding the teenager. My instructions were simple. The entire family had died in that fire. That was what the press believed. I was to make that belief reality. It took years to find the boy. It wasn't the only task set for me. I committed many a terrible act, yet none was so great as my single-minded pursuit of a child who'd done no harm to anyone."

"And you found him?" she asked.

"Not exactly. I almost found him. The boy had fallen in with some very bad types. People as bad as me. Perhaps worse. An organised gang, exchanging passports and guns for heroin. I'd followed them to the exchange. I heard gunfire. I went inside. Something had gone wrong. Either one side didn't trust the other or, more likely, no one trusted anyone. Everyone there was dead, but the boy wasn't there. He had escaped. And that was where my pursuit ended. I wasn't the only one who'd heard the shots. The police arrived, and arrived too quickly. There had to be a trial and for that there needed to be a criminal. The whole affair was too complicated to be covered up. The passports had come via Ireland, the drugs thanks to the Soviets. A thorough investigation could not be allowed. I was told to plead guilty. I did. I thought I would be allowed to escape. I wasn't. I was left to rot in prison. But I knew my guilt. It crept up on me until I was consumed with a single question. What would I have done if I had found that boy? Would I have killed him? I didn't know. I still don't. And I hadn't been forgotten. They arranged for a retrial, then they arranged for the evidence to disappear. I was released. I wish they'd left me there, but they were always the cruellest of masters. They thought I would return to the fold. I would not, for I had peered deep into my own soul and seen the darkness staring back. They let me join the monastery. It was that or death, and I was not ready for it then. They told me the boy was dead, and my life became a prison. One from which I could never be freed, because the dead can't be asked for forgiveness."

"Don't you believe in eternal life and all of that?"

"Honestly?" He cracked a weak smile. "What I want, more than anything, is to find that in death there is nothing but an empty silence that will finally still the screams I hear every time I close my eyes. So, believe me when I say revenge will do you no good. Get off this island and find something good to do with your life. Find a purpose. Help others. Death will come soon enough."

Nilda murmured something non-committal. She had been thinking back to those first few days after the fight on the railway tracks. She thought of that cottage she'd taken refuge in, of the rainwater that had drenched her, and which she had drunk. She remembered how sick she had become. She looked over at the Abbot and wondered how long it would be before death came to her.

7th April

She looked down at the body. The Abbot would want words said over him. She looked up at the sky. What words could she say? None. She began to shovel earth over his corpse.

When it was done, she found two pieces of wood. She went to the fire and heated the small knife. Carefully, she branded his name onto one, then tied the two pieces into a cross, and planted it at the head of his grave. Then she returned to her fire and waited to die.

Interlude: Sam
Crystal Palace, Sydenham, London

6th April

The zombie momentarily forgotten, Chester Carson stared at the bite on his wrist, but the creature hadn't forgotten him. It snarled and bucked, and now that only one of Chester's hands was holding it at bay, it got free. He jerked backwards just as its teeth snapped down, bare inches from his face. He scanned the ground, looking for the billhook he'd dropped when the creature had dived out of the cover of the bushes. Though the moon was bright and the night-sky cloudless, he couldn't see it. The creature was coming at him again. He took a step back, and another. He couldn't get used to fighting the undead. He knew how to fight people. You hit them, and they usually backed down. If they didn't, you just kept on hitting them until they stopped trying to get up. But zombies were different. They never stopped, and this one was getting closer. Chester's back bumped against the low brick wall. There was nowhere left to retreat, so he did what he always did; he attacked. He punched his palm into the zombie's jaw. There was a satisfying crack of bone, and the blow twisted the creature around, but its arms didn't stop flailing. A claw-like hand scored down Chester's forearm, gouging out a deep track of skin.

"Won't you just die?" he bellowed. One hand around its throat, the other grabbing a fistful of damp soiled cloth, he picked the creature up and threw it across the path. Even in mid-air the zombie's limbs didn't cease their frenetic thrashing. It landed in a heap. Chester stalked towards it.

"Won't," he screamed, kicking its arms out of the way. "You." He kicked it in the head. "Just." He brought his foot up. "Die." He stamped his heel down on the creature's skull. Bone cracked, brain and brownish-blood oozed out.

He took a breath, and another, and turned away from the dead creature. He looked at his arm. He was going to die.

All thoughts and plans vanished as he looked around and saw the undead, hundreds of them, all heading towards him. He wanted to fight, but if he did he'd be torn apart. He didn't want to die like that. He turned and ran towards the edge of the park. When he reached the high railings, he glanced over his shoulder. They were following him, and there seemed to be more of them. He'd expected to run from hundreds, not thousands.

"Where'd they come from?" he murmured as he climbed up the fence and jumped down the other side. He gave the railings a shake. They seemed solid. But against that approaching horde he knew they wouldn't last long.

Leaving a bloody smear from his injured arm on his clothes, he searched his pockets for a weapon. His hand closed around the revolver. He'd forgotten it was there. It felt heavy in his hand and slick in his grip as blood dripped down from the wound on his arm. He switched it to his other hand. It was too loud to use effectively against the undead. He'd learned that lesson a week before. What did noise matter now? Ineffective or not, it was a reassuring weight and the only comfort he had. Eyes darting left and right, he began walking down the road.

He threw one last glance at the towering transmitter, that British parody of the Eiffel Tower that was nearly as tall, yet was just another iconic landmark in a city that had dozens on every street. The car was parked underneath it. In the back of the car, along with the diesel and the generator, were his spare weapons and the rest of his gear. There was no way of reaching it now. No, he'd find an empty house. There were plenty of those since the evacuation. And then he could die quietly without—

A snarling face lurched out from the gap between two parked cars. Automatically, he raised the gun and fired. The bullet hit the zombie in the chest. The force of the impact spun the creature sideways so it rolled across the car, but it didn't fall. He fired again, the shot entered just above its shoulder spraying out pus and bone. The zombie didn't notice. One arm now useless, the other swung out and around, almost as if it was trying to swim towards him.

Stilling his frustrated rage, he took aim before firing for a third time. The bullet entered between the creature's eyes, blowing the back of its head off. It collapsed to the ground, and for a brief moment Chester actually felt better. The feeling evaporated when he heard an ominous creak of metal from the park behind him. He started walking. Then came a sharp crack and a resounding gong as the railings broke under the weight of the undead. He ran.

He jogged down the dark road, across an alley, and climbed a low brick wall. On the other side was the car park of a large Victorian house some optimistic investor had converted into a hotel. He dropped down onto the asphalt just as a pair of creatures lurched out from behind a parked van. He didn't hesitate. He raised the revolver, paused, aimed, waited until those snapping mouths got closer, then fired. Once. Twice. The creatures collapsed. By sheer luck he'd hit both zombies in the head, but the second shot had only been a glancing blow, shattering the skull but not destroying the brain. The creature twitched on the ground. He ignored it and ran out of the car park and down a side road. It ended in a cul-de-sac. An alley ran left and right at the end. Judging by the painted lines it was meant to be a cycle-lane, though a plethora of industrial bins turned it into more of an assault course. But the bins belonged to shops, and one of those would do. All he needed was somewhere inside, and he'd only need it for a few hours.

He turned to the right and stopped at the first door. He recognised the type instantly. Underneath the bright paint was a thick metal security door. If he had time and his tools he'd have no trouble breaking in. But he didn't have time. He kept going. The next door was the same. The third one was just wood. He scanned the alley until he found a twisted metal bracket among a broken and dumped pile of self-assembly shelves.

He levered the door open. The wood splintered with a crack as nearly as loud as the gun's retort. Revolver ready, he kicked the door inward. It was dark inside, and as he stepped forward, a zombie tumbled out.

He screamed. He bellowed. He fell backwards. Despite the undead weight on top, he managed to get the revolver up and between them. He pulled the trigger. The gun exploded, spraying warm gobbets of necrotic flesh over his face. The zombie stopped moving.

Spitting and retching, Chester heaved the corpse off and pulled himself up. He wiped his eyes clean with his sleeve. There was another creature in the doorway and two more stumbling along the hallway behind. He raised the gun and pulled the trigger. It clicked empty. He turned and he ran, and kept on running until he was lost in the suburban side streets. He guessed an hour had passed since he was first bitten and even if by some miracle that bite hadn't infected him, getting sprayed with that zombie's brains would have done. He didn't know how long he had left, but death was inevitable. The only choice he had now was in the manner of his death, and he didn't want that to be in the streets, torn apart by the undead. That meant he had to find somewhere to hide, and he had to find it quickly because that incessant slouching shuffle was moving inexorably closer.

He crossed the road and climbed over a gate running between two semi-detached houses. As he walked down the path to the back garden, trying not to tread on discarded toys, he tripped on a coil of abandoned hose. He stumbled into the wall. His shoulder hit it with a dull thump. From inside the house he heard a noise. It came from something too large to be a pet. Quickly, he crossed to the fence and climbed over into the neighbouring garden, then into the next, and the next until he felt safely far away from that occupied house.

He looked at the garden he found himself in, then at the dark windows. He listened. He could hear nothing but the distant wheezing of the undead. There was a ceramic flowerpot standing on the patio. He kicked it over. He listened. Nothing. He stamped down on the flowerpot. It broke loudly, but not loudly enough to echo. He listened again. Still nothing. Good enough. He broke into the house.

It was dark, as every house was dark since the power had been cut. He took out his small flashlight and quickly checked the rooms downstairs, then upstairs. The house was empty. The light flickered and went out. He shook it and slapped it against his palm. It came back on. When did he change the batteries? He couldn't remember. There was no point finding new ones now. He looked at his hand. Blood still ran freely from the bite, and it flowed slowly down his hand to drip onto the floor. He thought of bandaging it, but what was the point?

He went into the kitchen. There were a few packets of microwaveable rice and those just-add-water noodles, but he didn't need food. He wouldn't need food ever again. He rummaged around, first in the kitchen, then in the living room, until he found a green bottle at the back of a cupboard. The label was printed in Cyrillic and it smelled vile, but he'd drunk worse. He took a long draft. He breathed out. And again.

"So this is it," he said to himself. "This is how it ends."

He collapsed onto the sofa. As he did, he knocked the flashlight, turning it off. As the room was enveloped in darkness, he was engulfed by a sudden wave of fear. He scrabbled for the light, searching for the button. He turned it back on.

"I don't want to die." The words sounded pitiful. Weak. He hated self-pity, but there was no one else who would feel sorry for him. There was no one who would miss him. Not even McInery. Theirs was a relationship borne of convenience and necessity.

"Have children. Have friends. Do something with your life. That's what you said, wasn't it, Dad?" He grunted. Shook his head. "Well, no chance for that now. So what'd you say about my life? Did I do something?" Had he ever done anything? He didn't need the judgemental silence to know the answer. He had spent his life as a crook, except for those brief periods he had spent as a con.

Wanting to slip quietly into death, he closed his eyes, but sleep eluded him. He opened his eyes and picked up the revolver. He was going to die. All that was left was choosing the manner of his death. He opened the revolver and spilled the cartridges onto the coffee table. They were all spent.

"Figures," he murmured. But he had one more round, the one given to him by Cannock. The man had said he should keep it separate because 'a time might come when you're grateful for that one last shot.'

"You were right about that, Cannock," he muttered, as he fished the cartridge out of his pocket and laid it down on the table. "Yes, one last shot. End it. End it quick." He stared at it for a moment, and then thought of Cannock. He wondered whether the man had betrayed them. When he had delivered that truck full of vaccine had he known it was

150

poison? Maybe not, but probably yes. And he knew why, too. He and McInery were loose ends. Cannock wanted them dead. Or his employer had. They should have guessed the moment Cannock had said who his employer was. Chester had guessed it was someone high up in that rarefied atmosphere where organised crime and politics met; where murders were committed by war, and thefts through the courts. He just hadn't expected it to be the Foreign Secretary who, the last they'd heard, had become the Prime Minister.

Chester thought back to their childhood. Cannock had never been someone you wanted as your friend, just someone you didn't want as your enemy. Chester, being twice the height of his peers, had fallen into the role of the more visible danger when the two of them went around bullying and robbing their neighbours. It was Cannock who was the real threat. He always had been. Right up until he disappeared.

Maybe Cannock was dead, too. That thought pleased Chester, and it made sense. He was another loose end. A politician like Quigley was unlikely to leave someone like Cannock around. The man was a thug, hired muscle, useful to navigate the slums of the underworld, but of no more use than he, Chester, was.

They'd done the jobs they were asked to because there was no real alternative, just as they'd done before the outbreak, before they had known who their employer was. Then the evacuation had been announced and Cannock had arrived with the vaccine. And he'd given Chester the box of ammunition, and the extra round and told him to keep it safe.

He took a swig from the green bottle. It was a stupid weapon, really. Cannock had been carrying a sniper's rifle that he'd said had been destined for the SAS until the outbreak, but all he'd left Chester was an ornate revolver. He loaded the gun, but then he hesitated. There was something missing. What if his body was found? It might be. Someone might come looking for food or shelter. They'd see his body and think him a man who'd given up. He'd done so many things in his life, but he'd never done that and wouldn't want it thought of him after his death. No, he'd leave a note.

"Not an apology," he said firmly to no one. "Just an explanation."

By the dim glow of the occasionally flickering flashlight he began searching the house. He found paper and pens in a bedroom at the front of the house. It was a kid's bedroom, judging by the posters and the Crystal Palace scarf pinned to the wall above the bed.

He sat down at the small desk by the window and propped the light so it shone on the paper. He glanced at the street outside. Were zombies attracted by lights? It didn't matter. He picked up a pen, and found he didn't know what to write.

"My name," he began, "is Chester Cars—" The light went out. He shook the torch. Nothing happened. With only a thin glimmer of moonlight coming through the window, he stumbled around the room until he found a clock by the bedside. He took out the batteries, put them in the flashlight, and turned it back on. He looked down at the words on the paper.

"N'ah. Who starts with their name? I mean, what's the point in that?"

What was the point in writing anything? There was plenty to say, but no one he would ever say it to. Then he looked deep into his own soul. There had been a few triumphs, but they were crowded out by oh-so-many regrets. There had been moments of joy. Some, but not enough. It was a better life than he'd expected to have, but he now saw that it had been a life utterly wasted. No one who found his body would know who he was and, he realised in a final blow to his soul, they wouldn't care.

He balled up the paper and dropped it in the bin. Carefully he put the paper and pens back in the desk. No one would mourn him. Not Cannock, not McInery, and he didn't want the pity of the likes of them. And then he realised that he knew no one else. A solitary tear rolled down his cheek.

He picked up the flashlight, went back downstairs, and returned to his perch on the sofa. There was no point putting it off. He took one last swig, picked up the loaded gun, and raised it to his temple. The barrel felt cold against his skin.

"If," he said loudly, "I could do it all over again, then I would do absolutely everything completely differently."

But he knew well enough that everyone invoked that particular deathbed wish, and knew just as well that it was never granted. He closed his eyes and pulled the trigger. It clicked.

He stayed motionless, thinking time, in its last moment, had slowed to a glacial crawl. He blinked. It hadn't. He opened the revolver, turned the cylinder so the live cartridge was in front of the hammer. He raised it to his temple and pulled the trigger again. Click. Again. Click. Again. Click. Click. Click. Click. Click. Click. Click.

"Cannock, you bastard!"

He dropped the revolver onto the sofa. He didn't need to take the cartridge apart to know what Cannock had done. He had given him a dud and done it deliberately so, in this last moment, in this exact eventuality, Chester would have that ultimate possible relief ripped from him. He wept. He cursed. He asked "why me?"

Frustrated with the silent walls, he stood up and paced the room. He could find a rope, of course. Or make one easily enough. But hanging wouldn't work. He'd still turn. Slitting his wrists wouldn't do any good either. He was trapped. He would die and then… He hoped he wouldn't know. Above all things, he hoped that he would truly be dead.

He slumped down against the wall and waited to die.

Hours past.

He fell asleep.

7th April

He woke up and wished he hadn't. Lost in despair, he finished the bottle. Then he found another. He drank it. He passed out.

8th April

His neck ached. He raised a hand to rub his eyes and realised his hand ached more. His wrist. The bite. He looked down at it. The bite marks had turned angry red. The gouged lines tracking down his arm looked inflamed. Perhaps it was infected.

Infected. The word echoed around his half-conscious brain. Infected. He'd been bitten. He was going to turn. Wishing he hadn't woken up, he looked around the room. In the clear light of dawn it seemed even smaller than it had before.

Dawn. Was it really morning? He stood up and walked over to the window. Moving the curtains carefully, he parted them and peeked through the gap. The undead were outside. A few were in that stationary half-crouch they adopted when they'd sighted no prey for a while. A few more moved down the road almost as slowly as the smoke drifting lazily from the chimney of a house opposite. He glanced up at the sky. It was morning. He didn't know what time, but it was early. He tried to work out how long it had been since he'd been bitten. A day? A day and a half? Longer? He wasn't sure. Not that knowing would help. His mouth was dry. He was thirsty. He was hungry. He raised his hand again, and as he did, blood beaded up through the broken scab.

He should do something about his arm, he thought. But why? He couldn't think of a reason, but self-preservation kicked in, and he found himself wandering through the house, rooting through cupboards and drawers, looking for a first-aid kit. He didn't find one, but found a stack of clean white sheets in the linen cupboard. He tore one into strips, and was about to start bandaging his arm, when he wondered whether he should clean it first. Again, he couldn't see a reason why.

"If you have to do a job, do it properly," he murmured. That was what his old man had said. And though the old man had been talking about dealing with witnesses during a bank robbery, the principle still applied.

He found a bottle of disinfectant in the bathroom. It was meant for toilets, but that was good enough for him. He emptied the bottle over his arm. It stung. Then it burned. He staggered over to the bath and turned on the taps. Nothing came out of the cold. He tried the hot. The water came out, draining from the house's tank.

He rinsed his arm clean. Then stuck his head under the tap. He left it there for a few minutes, revelling in the feeling of it, revelling that he could still feel something. Finally, he turned the water off and bandaged his arm.

"So what now? Go back?"

That was the plan. He would drive to the transmitter, lure the undead away, then go back and check that the area was clear. Only then was he meant to return to McInery. Then they'd lead the others there to wire it all up. But did he want to return? He'd thought of leaving. He'd been planning it. This was his opportunity. Except, what about the bite?

"Then I'll wait. Three days, that's how long I'll give it. If I don't…" He didn't want to say it out loud. "I'll wait three days."

And with that decision made he realised he was feeling hungry. He'd brought food with him, of course. It was in his bag, but that was still in the car. He went back to the kitchen and took out the packs of rice.

"Cooks in two minutes" he read. But a microwave needed power and that meant electricity, and there was none of that. He could eat it cold, but… no. He'd light a fire. Fire meant matches. It also meant smoke. Smoke. That jarred something in the back of his mind. Something important. Out of the window. The house down the street. There had been smoke coming out of the chimney. He ran over to the curtains. There was! There was smoke coming out of the chimney. He watched it for a moment until he was sure the house itself wasn't on fire. No, it wasn't. And that meant there was someone inside.

The hedge in the front garden was too high to properly see the house. He went back upstairs. Yes, there it was. The smoke came from a large house that had been turned into flats. Smoke meant a person. He looked up and down the street. There were too many undead for him to simply walk over to the other house, not unless the person in the house was ready to leave. Suddenly he found he wanted company but no, he had decided he'd wait for three days, so three days he would wait. But there was no reason he shouldn't try to communicate with the person. How? And then he saw something on the upstairs' windows. A message. He peered at it. There were letters, but he couldn't read them. However, that did solve the problem of how to communicate. He needed paper. That was it. He'd write a message and stick it to the windows.

He opened the drawer and took out a few sheets of paper. On one he wrote 'Hello'. He stuck it up to the window. But it didn't seem enough so, on another, he wrote 'Is there someone there?' and stuck that up. He still wasn't satisfied. He glared at the pen and paper. Then he realised the problem. The question wasn't what he should write, but what reply he was hoping for. What if there was someone there. What did he want to happen next? He mulled that over for a few minutes, and realised he'd already made that decision. He taped a third message to the glass: 'Do you want to get out of London?'

Then he sat back to wait. A few hours later a message came back, this one written one letter per sheet. 'E.S.C.A.P.E.?'

Chester smiled. That was a question he knew how to answer. He stuck up the letters 'Y.E.S.'

Letter by letter, they communicated. By early afternoon he'd gathered that the man - Chester assumed it was a man - had enough food and water for twenty days. Chester thought that must be the reason that he'd stayed in the house for so long. That assumption was shattered when the man laboriously spelled out 'B.R.O.K.E.N. L.E.G.'

Chester sat down in the chair and thought. A broken leg made things difficult. He'd assumed they would just be able to find some bikes and cycle away. Of course, thinking about it, if the man had been able to cycle away, he would already have done it. So what should he do? Leave him? Chester stared at his arm. He thought about that blank piece of paper, he remembered the words his father had said. And then he thought about the words his father hadn't said during that night in the hospital just before the old man had died. Chester had sat at the bedside and his father had wept. He'd seemed so strong, so confident so unrepentantly proud of all that he had done, right up until that night. And then he had wept, and it had all come pouring out. And he had told Chester to do something with his life, just one thing that he could look back on and be proud of. And Chester had looked at his father, held his hand, and tried to think of something to say, but all he'd been able to think was 'aren't you proud of me?'. He hadn't spoken out loud because his father had seen the question in his eyes, and Chester had known the answer the old man was too kind to give.

Here was his chance; the second chance that he'd wanted; the chance to do it all differently. Here was someone he could help. He would rescue the man and get him out of London and to somewhere safe. The broken leg was nothing but an obstacle to be overcome, and now that he thought about it, one that was easily dealt with. The station-wagon was just sitting there up at the transmitter. In the back was the generator and next to it were a half dozen fuel cans. Even if McInery sent someone up there to wire up the gear, they wouldn't take the fuel away. That was how they would get out of London. He'd forget about McInery and Radio Free England. He would start a new life. This was the second chance he wanted. He could start all over again.

He started putting together a message to tell the man that they would escape by car. It wasn't far to the transmitter. He thought he could get there and back in just a few hours. He glanced at the sun already heading towards the horizon. They should wait until tomorrow morning. And then he glanced at his arm. No, he'd said he was going to wait, he had to be sure he wasn't going to turn. Three days, then. In three days he'd rescue the man and drive him out of London.

10th April

There was a still a day to go and Chester was certain, as certain as he could be, that he wasn't going to turn. It was tempting to tell the man they should go sooner, but he didn't want to tempt fate. He felt a deal had been struck, and he had to stick to the terms. He'd gone through too many nights where only luck had saved him from finishing them in the cells, or worse, not to believe in superstition. But he was growing hungry. He'd finished the food the day before. There hadn't been much to start with.

He went back into the kitchen. He opened drawers and cupboards and came up with one stock cube, a pack of chilli flakes six years past their expiry-date, and a jar of economy herbs that looked like sawdust and smelled about the same. Fixing his mind on the tin of hotdogs in the station-wagon, and thinking about the feast they'd have just as soon as they got out of the city, he filled a saucepan with water.

There was a sudden bang from outside. Startled, Chester dropped the pan. It clattered loudly to the floor. The bang came again, and again. It was coming from the other side of the fence. Zombie, he thought.

How the creature knew he was here, or whether it did, didn't matter. The noise wasn't loud, but it would bring others. He pulled open the cutlery drawer and found a large carving knife. He went outside. There was a stack of white plastic chairs by the edge of the patio. He carried them over to the fence, dropping them opposite the part that shook with each blow. He climbed up and peered over and down into the next garden. Undead eyes stared back at him. The zombie's hands shot up and clawed at the air. He watched the movement carefully then, one hand on the trellis for balance, he stabbed the knife down. He'd mistimed it. Rather than punching through the creature's left eye, the blade hit the bone just above, tearing a line of flesh from eye-socket to lip. As it did, Chester's hand slid forward, slicing his palm on the edge of the blade.

Under his weight, the trellis cracked. Chester slipped and fell backwards, as the creature pushed forwards onto the fence. The wood split and the fence collapsed. Chester pulled himself up. The zombie was trying to do the same. He took a step towards it, ready to bring an end to the creature, but then looked beyond at the path running down the side of the house. There were four more of the undead pushing and snarling their way towards him, and more behind those. He backed away and darted through the kitchen door, slamming it behind him and throwing down the bolts. That, he knew, wouldn't be enough. He had to leave. The deal was that he would bring a car to rescue the man tomorrow. Well, he'd stick to that, but he couldn't stay in the house.

He grabbed a few more knives from the drawer, went back into the living room, grabbed his jacket, the bottle he'd kept filled with water and, after a moment's hesitation, the unloaded revolver. He went to the front door. He took a breath before opening it, then went out into the road. There were zombies in either direction. That didn't matter. He'd lead them away. It would make the job tomorrow easier. Briskly, he walked down the street. He looked up at the house. He thought he saw a figure in

158

the window. He thought of waving, but there was no point. He'd be back soon.

Occasionally, he glanced behind to make sure the undead were following, but mostly he kept his eyes on the road in front. Zombies moved towards him, their arms raised, ready to claw, their open mouths readying to bite. He ducked, he dodged, he dived. He didn't run. He kept walking, leading the undead away.

That worked for nearly half a mile, until he turned a corner and found two-dozen zombies clustered around an abandoned post-office van. He turned around, and found twice that number following him a few dozen yards behind. That was when he started to run. But on every road there were more and more of the undead. And then he found the road ahead full of so many that he couldn't get past. He turned around, but the road behind was no better. In desperation, he kicked down the nearest door, hastily throwing up a barricade as he looked around. He was in a coffee shop a few days away from being opened. He found his way to the back. Zombies filled the road outside. He was trapped. At least there was food. It wouldn't be long before the creatures dispersed, he thought. He sat down to wait. Minutes turned to hours, then to days.

17th April

For the thousandth time, he peered through the window, eyeing the silent undead outside, measuring his chances if he tried to run through them. Suddenly, one near a side road stood and started to move away. And then another. And another. Soon they were all moving, shoving and pushing and walking into one another as they headed towards... he didn't know what and it didn't matter. They were leaving and that meant he could escape. He could rescue the broken-legged man. For Chester, after days of reflection, that was all that mattered.

He waited a few more hours before leaving. He crept when he could, ran when he couldn't, and finally reached the Crystal Palace transmitter. The car was still where he'd left it. McInery hadn't sent anyone to check on it or him. He got in, and drove down the hill to the house of the broken-legged man. He pulled the car to a halt in the street outside and went into the house.

"Hey! Are you here! Where are you!" he bellowed as he ran from room to room, but the house was empty. The man had gone. Might he have left a note? There wasn't time to check. Through a window from a small room at the top of the house he saw the undead moving down the street towards the car. He ran back downstairs and outside but hesitated before getting back in the car. He'd done everything he could. He'd come back for the man and he'd looked for him, but he was gone. Chester didn't want to leave. He had been certain his future was tied to the man with the broken leg, but the undead were getting closer. There was no more time. He got back in the car and drove away from London.

Part 4: Raft
Isle of Scaragh, North Atlantic

1ˢᵗ July

She was still alive. More than that, she felt well. Fish, crab, and fresh air had done wonders to her physique. Her clothes, which had been tattered after the wreck, were now ragged. They wouldn't survive much longer, but appearances meant little. Whenever she looked in the small mirror, taken from the wrecked lifeboat, she didn't see her own tort skin, but the ravaged face of the Abbot in those last moments before she filled in his grave. She didn't look in the mirror often.

Yes, she was alive. She'd reconciled herself to that, though it had been hard. During those first few weeks, she'd done little more than wait to die, and think of her son. She'd finally allowed herself to mourn. Entire days were spent lost in grief, yet hunger and thirst always brought her out of it. As time had gone by, she found she no longer wanted to die. As more time passed, she found that she wanted to live.

She sat down on the beach, and stared at the waves. She no longer expected the undead to come, nor feared them if they did, but she couldn't stay on the island. While she'd become adept at catching crabs and fish, there were fewer nettles to go with them, and the roots she found were ever smaller. If she wanted to live, she had to escape. And she did want to live. But why?

That question had been troubling her for the last couple of weeks. There was something someone had said or not said, or done or left undone. Between the evacuation and her arrival on the island, every moment had been filled with action, and then despair. It was only now that she had time to think.

She stared at the waves. Then at her hands. Then at her arms. The teeth marks were still visible. Then she knew.

If she was immune, then wouldn't Jay be immune? Wasn't there at least a chance that she'd passed on to him whatever it was that had kept her safe? And with that realisation, she was consumed with angry guilt at her own self-pitying arrogance. The Abbot had been right. Guilt had caused her to pursue revenge when she should have looked for her son.

She had to leave the island. She stood up, and walked down into the waves. She'd waded chest deep before reason returned. She couldn't swim across the sea. She needed a boat. She waded back towards shore, angling towards the lifeboat. She clambered up onto the rocks it was still pinned to. First outside, then inside, she examined the sharp-toothed gash in the hull. She peered out to sea, then at the boat, the shore, the hut, and the island, searching for inspiration in how to seal it. Reluctantly, she admitted what she'd known from that first morning on the island. The boat was a wreck. It would never float again. But she had to go back to the mainland. She had to try. With difficulty, she quelled the nihilistic impulse to try to swim. She would drown. She knew it. That would serve no purpose. There had to be another way. But what? She turned away from the ocean and looked back at the shore, and saw the cairn she'd built over the graves.

She'd suggested a raft to the Abbot, hadn't she? He'd said it took nails and rope and that there were none on the island. But how would he know? He hadn't had time to travel further than between the hut and the graves. She began an inventory of all the materials she could find.

3rd July

At first, it had come to very little. In her mind she saw rafts as she had on the television, made of tree trunks held together by rope. She'd tried sawing through a pine with the serrated edge of the spade. After an hour's effort, she'd barely grazed the bark. As for rope, the Abbot had been correct. There really wasn't any on the island. She'd considered digging up the bodies, stripping the clothing from them, unravelling the thread, and then braiding it together. She only considered it briefly. It was something that would take months of labour. There wasn't the time. Not anymore. Not if Jay might be alive.

She'd subdued her frustration and turned her attention back to her surroundings. There was nothing of use on the island save the jetty, the hut, the wreck of the boat, and the detritus coating the beach.

5th July

She eyed the roof of the hut. It was made of two flat sections that met at an angle of thirty degrees, affixed to the walls.

"Bolted on, it looks like," she murmured. But the walls were twelve feet high. She needed a way of climbing up to examine them properly. It took another hour of staring at the collection of junk on the beach, and wandering around the hut, before she saw what was in front of her eyes. The bunk beds. They were metal framed, and screwed into the floor and walls. It took most of the day to detach the bunks and drag them outside.

She clambered up to examine the roof. There were brackets under the eaves, bolting the roof to the walls. Someone had made a half-hearted effort to seal the bolts in plastic, but salt-water had found its way in. Most of the bolts were rusted into their sockets. Having no wrench she had to hit them loose with a rock. By nightfall, with her hands bloody from where she'd missed, the bolts were finally loose. She collapsed by the fire and slept.

6th July

She was up before dawn, and up on her improvised scaffolding soon after. She had a plan. She'd take the roof off, then take down the walls, and reassemble the hut upside down on the beach. The walls could be trimmed to a height of about five feet with the serrated edge of the collapsible spade. She'd practiced on a section by the doorway and found it was easy to cut. She had no illusions about the boat she was creating, but it only needed it to float for a few hours over a few miles. That wasn't too much to ask. She hoped.

Slowly, she made her way around the roof, removing the bolts, carefully placing them in the now empty first aid kit. She would need them later. In half an hour she was ready. She just had to slide the roof off towards the beach. Gravity would do the rest.

The sea breeze had become familiar to the point where she ignored it. She didn't notice that the wind had picked up until she'd slid the roof out three feet from the wall. A gust came in, entered the gap, and picked up the roof, spinning it over her head. She reached up in a futile attempt to grab it. Unbalanced, she fell. Her improvised scaffolding toppled on top of her. She tasted blood, and something else. A tooth. She spat it out.

For a long minute she lay unmoving, unblinking, doing nothing but breathing slowly through gritted teeth. When she tried to stand, she found she had a long shallow gash on her leg. Dripping blood onto the wooden walkway, she ignored the pain as she limped along to the end of the jetty. The roof did float and was now fifty yards out to sea.

10th July

With a grunt of effort she dragged the hut wall down the beach to the water's edge. She'd had to wait until the cut on her leg had scabbed over - she didn't want to risk an infection and all that would mean. She got an edge of the wall out into the water. No, she realised with relief, *onto* the water. It floated. She pushed it further out until it was bobbing freely up and down on the waves, then she clambered on top. It sank. She had half expected that. It didn't matter. The principal was what counted. The walls would float. She'd be able to cut them into shape and… she wasn't sure. But she could work it out. She would work it out. She rolled off the prefab and into the shallows. She waited, expecting the wall to bob up out of the water. It didn't. She grabbed it, and dragged it back to shore. It was sodden, soaked through. She had assumed it was made of wood, or at least of fibreboard. It wasn't. Sandwiched between thin layers of waterproof laminate was a compressed mixture of cloth and paper. Water had seeped in through the exposed edges turning the interior into nothing firmer than papier-mâché.

15th July

A squall the night before had drenched the now exposed hut. The three remaining walls had soaked up the water and then collapsed shortly after dawn. Nilda sat on the jetty, staring forlornly out to sea. She'd reconciled herself to death, but now that she had the smallest glimmer of hope to grasp, she found her every attempt frustrated. The only things of use in the remains of the hut, like the folding chairs and tables, were made of metal. Metal didn't float. Not easily, and not in any sense that was meaningful to her. Idly, her hand reached out to pluck an errant splinter from the jetty. She held it up. Then she looked down at the wooden jetty and she laughed.

18th July

Pulling out the nails holding the wooden planking of the jetty to their supports had been time consuming. She'd had to wear down a groove next to each nail and then carefully lever it out. In her eagerness, she'd lost two to the sea. But now she had a stack of planks, and a neat pile of nails.

"So what's next?" she asked the empty beach.

21st July

She had nailed the planks together, one layer underneath, the other on top, each layer holding the other in place. It was time for a test. The raft floated, not on the waves, but a few inches below them.

"That's good enough to get out of the bay, isn't it?" she muttered as she dragged the raft back on to the beach. "Yes. Yes. It is. But that's not going to be good enough. No. Not good enough. What's missing? Sides! I need sides!"

She looked about for other materials. She could see none. Biting down her frustration she began another long walk around the island. She followed the cliff edge, peering down to the rocks below in the hope something might have been washed onto them. There was nothing. She went inland and scoured the forest floor, and then she returned to the ruins of the boat, going over it again and again. But she had done that many times, and when night fell, was unsurprised that her search had once again come to naught.

22nd July

She threw another branch onto the fire. It was important to keep the bonfire blazing. There was only a slim chance anyone would see it. Slim chances were all she had. She stared at the raft. There was nothing on the island, nothing to make sides except the wooden jetty itself.

"Then make it smaller," she said. "Use the planks to make the sides."

Slowly, methodically, not allowing herself to give in to anger at herself for not realising the obvious earlier, she took her raft apart.

24th July

Raft Mark-Two was much smaller than the first, but it had sides. She took it out to the shallows. It sank a few inches, but for a moment she stayed dry. Then the water began to seep through the gaps. Wet and miserable, frustrated with yet another setback, she dragged her raft back to shore.

"Tar, that's what the Navy used, wasn't it? Didn't they used to call sailors Jack-Tars? Well that's what I need," she muttered. "But how do you make tar. It's a by-product of oil, right? And that doesn't help me at all. What else could I use? Beeswax? There aren't hives on the island." She had looked.

She growled in anger. She'd tried screaming, but that had done nothing more than leave her throat raw.

"Tar. Oil. Wax. Rubber," she muttered to herself as she slowly turned in a circle, trying to see the obvious that she'd so far missed. Then she saw it.

"Plastic."

There was enough of it on the beach, though less than when they'd run aground. She'd taken to collecting it, and piling it up in the tumbledown house. It had given her something to do.

She grabbed a handful from the beach, sorting through it, finding the pieces she thought large enough. Then she banked up the fire, moved the raft close, and began melting the plastic onto the gaps.

The first piece caught in her hands, burning onto her fingers. She ran down to the sea, plunging the hand into the waves. She had to peel the melted plastic off, and took a layer of skin with it. For some reason, she found that funny.

She tried again, this time laying the plastic in place and holding out a burning branch from the fire close to it. It worked. She felt she'd proved the principal. How long the seal would hold, or how effective it would be, she wouldn't know until she tested it. And she couldn't do that until she'd sealed at least most of the gaps.

25ᵗʰ July

It began to rain. The fire went out.

31ˢᵗ July

She'd had to wait for the rain to stop and the raft to dry out, but she'd sealed about three quarters of the raft. She was impatient. She didn't want to wait. Three quarters was enough, she decided, at least for a test. She took it out to the shallows. It worked. Mostly. When she dragged the raft back to the shore she found a quarter of the plastic had simply washed away. She used up one more of the precious few matches to relight the fire. As she waited for the flames to take, she gathered more plastic from the house. Then she realised that the raft was too wet. Again, she would have wait until the wood had dried.

6ᵗʰ August

She took the raft out. It was completely sealed this time and eighty-percent of the seals held. She took it back to the shore. While she waited for it to dry, and with no cloth for sails, she turned her mind to oars. During the wreck, one had been lost over the side, and the other had landed on the rocks. One oar would not be enough. As she would be taking little food with her, she couldn't risk becoming adrift on the vast ocean. Once more she examined the wreckage of the boat, the hut, and the litter on the beach. The metal uprights from the bunk beds would do as a pole. She had the nuts and bolts to attach it to something flat and with that, the craft could be propelled through the water. That only left finding that flat piece of... what? There wasn't time to carve something from wood, but there was the lifeboat. Using brute force as much as the serrated edge of the spade, she hacked away at the wrecked ship's hull.

9th August

The rains came again, harder and more persistent than before.

30th August

All the seals held. She had taken the raft out, paddling a short way from shore. She had wanted to keep going, but it was getting dark. She would leave first thing in the morning. She sat by the fire, throwing on branch after branch. Whatever happened, whatever the weather, in the morning she would leave. Nothing would keep her on the island. Watching the flames, she fell asleep.

She was woken by a crunching sound. She jumped to her feet. There it was again. She peered out into the night. She thought she could make out a figure. No, figures, two of them, and they were coming up the beach. The undead. They had found her. She bent, scrabbling on the ground for the spade. Let them come, she thought, she was ready.

"I'm ready," she said out loud.

"Are you? What for?" a voice asked.

Nilda froze. Of all the things she'd expected, human beings were not among them.

"Who are you?" she asked.

"Francois Coultard, madam. Sargent-Chef de la Brigade des Forces Spéciales Terre de la République Française." He snapped off a wry salute. "We saw your fire, we thought we'd ask if you would mind sharing it."

"You're French?"

"He is. I'm not," the other person, a woman, said. "Is it just you here?"

The Frenchman stepped closer to the fire. He wasn't in uniform, but more a civilian approximation of it. On his back was a rifle. A pistol was holstered at his belt, next to a knife. On the other side he wore a small axe. She considered the woman's question, and then the man's weapons. They made her cautious, but she could see no purpose in a lie.

"It's just me. The others are dead. We came here on that boat." She pointed towards the shadow of the wrecked lifeboat. "They died. Radiation poisoning. Their graves are over there."

There was a hiss from the Frenchman, and he pulled something out of his pack. By the way he waved it in the air, then at the ground, then at the water lapping against the beach, Nilda guessed it was a Geiger counter.

"Non," he said. "It is fine. Just a little above background. The same as we measured on the ship."

"I'm sorry about your friends," the woman said, as she approached Nilda. Nilda thought she was going to put a comforting arm around her. Instead she draped a long coat over Nilda's shoulders.

"Here," she said, as she pulled on the lapels to close the coat over the tattered remains of Nilda's clothing. And then the woman paused and looked into Nilda's eyes. A long searching moment later, she nodded.

"My name's Kim," she said. There was another pause. Eventually she added, "what's yours?"

"Oh. Yes. Nilda."

"How long have you been here?" Kim asked.

"I don't know. Weeks. No, it's been longer than that. A month. Two? It was a few weeks after the evacuation that we... I left Penrith."

"Then you've been here nearly six months," Kim said, gently.

"Six months?" Nilda shook her head in disbelief.

"You must have found fresh water here," Kim said.

Nilda nodded.

"And food?"

"Fish. Crabs. Dandelions and stinging nettles," Nilda said. "Nothing else. I tried to catch birds. It wasn't as easy as I thought it would be."

"Better than you'd find in most English restaurants before the end," the Frenchman murmured.

"But you say the other people died of radiation poisoning?" Kim asked as she threw a glance at Francois.

"They came from Glasgow. The bombs, you see. They were..." She stopped

169

Kim nodded her understanding. "We'll have to send a team to properly check this island. If it is safe, then we'll be moving some people here. An uncontaminated island on the route to Norway is important." She saw the confusion in Nilda's eyes. "You don't know where you are? You're about thirty miles from Iona. If the wind had been blowing the other way this place would have been coated in radioactive fallout. You were lucky."

"Lucky?"

"Well, okay, maybe not lucky," Kim said. "Look, we're based out of Anglesey. We've got the power plant working again. There's food, and there's as much safety as you'll find anywhere on this planet. As far as we can tell, we're the largest community left in this corner of the Atlantic. You can come with us if you want. But if you want to stay here, I'm sorry, but you will be getting company. We really do need islands like this."

"You can have this place," Nilda said. "Just let me get off it."

"Of course," Kim said softly.

She nodded to the Frenchman and led Nilda down the beach to a small boat.

"Wait," Nilda said, one foot in the dingy.

"What?"

"My raft."

"Your what?" Francois scanned his flashlight across the beach. "You mean that thing?"

"You try to build something better with no rope and no tools," Nilda said defensively.

"Hmm," the Frenchman grunted.

"Can we tow it with us?" Nilda asked. "I want to see if it... well, if it floats."

Francois looked questioningly at Kim.

"Fine," Kim said.

The Frenchman attached a line to the raft and pushed it into the water. Nilda climbed into the dinghy and they were soon heading out towards the waiting ship. The raft stayed afloat until they were out of the bay. A wave, barely noticeable to Nilda, passed under the dinghy then swamped her improvised craft. It sank. Francois let go of the rope with a shrug.

Nilda turned away from the island, looking towards the waiting ship and the future.

31st August

Nilda watched the sun slowly rise above the horizon, turning the ink-black sea into a kaleidoscope of grey. She hadn't tried to sleep. Kim had offered her a bunk in one of the cabins, but there were other people there. Having gone through her story once with Kim, she didn't want to do it again.

Instead, she'd found a quiet spot at the boat's stern, inside an enclosed viewing platform. The walls and ceiling were made of transparent glass, or perhaps crystal, certainly the ship was too luxurious for it to be plastic. She ran her hand along a savage gash that cut deep into the bench's comfortable fabric. She supposed a battle must have been fought on the ship. From what Kim had told her, battles of one sort or another had been fought everywhere on the planet. Her eyes were drawn once more to the ocean, empty of everything but the frothing white caps churned up by the boat's engines. The island had disappeared below the horizon while it was still dark. She'd fought her own battle there, though she wasn't exactly sure who or what her foe had been, nor whether she'd won.

There was a muttered cursing, quickly followed by a quiet rebuke. Two figures trudged out from around the side of the boat, and down to a row of large barrels crammed into a walkway between two sets of sloping solar panels. It was a man and a young girl. She was bundled up in a jacket too big. He wore nothing but a shirt. The sleeves were rolled up almost as if he was displaying the vivid tattoos covering each arm. Taken with his scars, and the gold tooth that glinted when it caught the early morning sun, he had an almost piratical appearance. The slightly sinister impression was dispelled when he gave a soft laugh after the girl dropped a rope he threw to her. With unexpected patience he showed the girl how to tie the barrels to the deck. Judging by her increasingly vocal protest, the girl was not happy at being awake at such an early hour.

The girl, she realised, was around Jay's age. Nilda closed her eyes, expecting to cry, but found she was unable. There was too much life, too much normality around her, yet she felt strangely detached from it all.

The moment Nilda had set foot on board, Kim had hustled her down to a large cabin and nearly pushed her into the shower. Nilda had washed and offered a muted thanks when she was given clothes that were clearly the other woman's spares. She had tried not to sound ungrateful, but being so unexpectedly rescued didn't feel real. No, she corrected herself, it was discovering that there were people still willing and able to rescue others that she found hard to believe.

Kim had explained what had happened. How the virus was an accident which Sir Michael Quigley had taken advantage of to seize power. How the bombs had been part of a nuclear attack of which every government had their part. How there had been a mutiny across the world as military units had baulked at orders that would have destroyed the human race. The end result was a few thousand survivors carving out a life on Anglesey, and chaos everywhere else. Only an occasional and indistinct radio signal hinted that, somewhere, others might have survived.

Nilda weighed the news. Objectively she knew it was bad. But she didn't feel in any way disappointed. Her focus since the outbreak had been on survival, then revenge, then on dying, and then on building the raft. She had given no real thought to what she would do when she made it to land. As she sat in relative comfort, watching the patient man and sullen girl, she realised that she'd never expected to survive the ocean crossing. The raft was nothing more than an elaborate method of suicide.

"Mind if I sit? I brought coffee," Kim's voice cut through her thoughts. Nilda looked up. She hadn't heard the woman approach.

"Thank you," Nilda murmured, moving along the bench.

"Here." Kim held out a thickly sliced sandwich. "The meat's tinned, but the bread's fresh. Or it was fresh when we left. There were a string of grain ships on route from Trois-Riviers to Rotterdam when the outbreak hit. The government in Ottawa recalled them. The ships turned around, but the Royal Navy was sent to hijack them. They turned around again, but turning around a freighter isn't as quick as wishing it. By the time they were set on a course for the UK, the first bombs had fallen. And so we have grain. More than we need and more than enough until we can get the farms working."

Nilda took the sandwich, tried to remember how to smile, took a bite, and found she wasn't hungry.

Kim placed an insulated mug next to Nilda, and took a sip from her own. "You know what I want?" the woman chattered on. "Chocolate. Not powdered cocoa, and not just a bar, but a real luxury assortment. Something with truffles and pralines. The kind you'd get knowing that you'd regret the expense the moment they were gone, yet would enjoy every bite all the more because of it. Since that's not on the cards, I can only offer you coffee."

"Thank you," Nilda said. She knew the younger woman was being kind, offering conversation as an alternative to introspective gloom. The things that people had talked about when the world had been normal, the usual niceties of family and friends and life itself, all now seemed taboo. She looked around, seeking inspiration for some neutral topic. She settled for asking, "is this your boat?"

"Mine? With a name like the Smuggler's Salvation? No, it's Miguel's." Kim nodded towards the man near the boat's stern.

"Ah," Nilda took another look around, taking in the sleek profile, the comfortable though ripped seats, and the solar panels. "Let me guess. He made his money from computer games and named the boat after one of them?"

"Oh no, he renamed the boat when he took control of her. He was an actual smuggler, mostly from El Salvador up into the U.S. He definitely wasn't one of the good guys." She shrugged. "But that was the old world. In our new one that began back in February, all that counts is that he saved lives. When the news started broadcasting the outbreak, he did what pretty much everyone who had a boat did, he headed out to sea in the hope he could wait it out. The difference between him and most other people was that he had food, water, and fuel. He didn't head up to Greenland—"

"Greenland?"

"That's where most people with boats went. It was the one place, other than the UK, that wasn't broadcasting that they'd been overrun. That was only because the few people who lived there had already headed off into the tundra. But Miguel decided to take his boat across the Atlantic. That was how he was caught up in the mutiny. You know, the naval battle I told you about? His ship was sunk and he ended up in the water. Then this boat came drifting along. The crew were dead, but they were still on board. He cleared the ship of the undead, then helped with the rescue. And that's how this boat, like so many others, ended up on Anglesey."

Nilda gripped the cup firmly, holding it in front of her face as a shield against the disconcerting normality of a conversation over tepid coffee. While she tried to think of what, among the million and one things Kim could tell her, she truly wanted to know, she took a sip. She watched Miguel take the partially coiled rope from the girl's hands, shake his head, and tell her to start again.

"And the girl is his daughter?" Nilda asked.

"Annette? No, she's... well, mine I suppose, as much as she's anyone's. Bill and I found her out in the wasteland. But she's why I'm here on the boat. And that's why I can't sleep. I've got the aftermath from all of this to deal with when we get back. I'm hoping that the sight of a very bedraggled and thoroughly exhausted girl will mollify Bill. That's why we've got her on punishment detail."

"Punishment? What did she do?"

"She ran away. Sort of. She was on the ship and refused to get off, but they needed to depart and catch the tide. Since I wasn't going to leave her, and since the mission was important, we both ended up joining the expedition to Svalbard. Not that I thought it would end up the way it did," Kim sighed.

"That's why she's being punished, because she ran away?" Nilda asked, curious and suspicious at the same time.

"Not exactly. She ran off because we had a row, and we had a row because... well, it started with a journal. Bill wrote it when he was trapped in London, then kept writing when he escaped, and kept on writing when he and Sholto, his brother, trekked to Northumberland to kill Quigley. Naturally, Annette was proud of that. Like I said, as odd as we are, we're the only family she's got. So when the power came back on, she copied the journal. And there was no law against that. Oh no. We're a nation of laws, but because there had been no electricity, no one thought to tell anyone not to use up all the toner in the photocopiers. She'd made two hundred copies before anyone realised. Before Bill or I knew, she'd handed those out around the island." She sighed. "Everyone read it. Of course they did. For a culture that grew addicted to twenty-four hour news, this was the closest thing to a patch. But Bill was furious."

"People didn't react well to it?"

"No, it wasn't that. For the most part, people didn't care. By then, everyone knew the story. After all, it's a small community on a small island. The problem was that he'd included a lot of his private thoughts in the journal, and it was those he didn't want everyone to know. There was a time, just after we rescued Annette, when someone did read the journal. To say Bill thought that an invasion of privacy would be a gross understatement, but that doesn't matter. You can read it yourself, if you want. And that, basically, was the problem. Suffice to say that there was a row, and Annette decided she'd had enough. Since there was only one boat leaving the island, she tried to take it. Since I couldn't get her off, and departure couldn't be delayed, here we are."

"You found a family. That's a good thing. Something to hold on to."

"Yes," Kim said. Earlier, Nilda had told her about Jay. "Yes, it is."

The silence stretched.

"Why did you go to Svalbard, then?" Nilda asked, preferring to have the woman talk than sit in uncomfortable silence.

"Oil, that's the next big problem. Thanks to the nuclear power plant we have electricity. Thanks to the island we have safety. More or less. And we have food as long as you don't mind a diet that's mostly fish and bread. We've even got enough space, though probably not for the long term. What we don't have is oil. We hardly have any diesel or petrol left, either. That's not a problem for life on the island, but if we're going to find out what's going on in the rest of the world, if we're going to try to rescue others, then we need to be able to reach them. We can't do that with sailing boats alone."

"You want to rescue them?"

"I want to rescue everyone. Wait, that sounds… I mean, we've got a bona-fide nuclear power station. For maybe ten years we'll have electricity. Nowhere else does, at least not that anyone's been able to find. When the power came back on, they began hacking into the satellite network. They've got control of three now, I think. As far as they can tell, there aren't any lights on anywhere else in the world. If we can gather all the survivors together, we can make a real attempt at rebuilding, so when the power station does have to be shut down, civilisation won't collapse with it. For that we need oil. That's why we went to Svalbard. There's a NATO supply dump there, and it's still got oil, enough to get a fleet down into the southern hemisphere. With that we can recrew some of our larger ships, we can go out and find an offshore rig that's survived, and we can find all those other survivors. I mean, they have to be there. I can't believe that we are all that's left. Take Svalbard. There are people there. Of course, that's now become a problem. They won't just give us the oil. They want to trade it. And there's only one thing they want and… well, we'll sort it out. We have to, and at least trying to deal with bureaucracy makes a change from the undead. Anyway, I reckon that's been nearly half an hour. I think Annette's had enough. Excuse me." Kim stood up and left the viewing room.

Nilda watched as the woman thrust into the role of the mother walked down the deck towards the still protesting girl. She felt a wave of bitter grief sweep over her. She tried to cry, but the tears still wouldn't come.

Part 5: Justice
Anglesey and Cumbria

1st September

As they approached the port, Nilda was shocked by the number of boats. Some operated under sail, but most were small rowing boats. In each, people quietly fished. Or, she realised as they got closer, the people were holding rods, but most were doing nothing more than staring listlessly at the waves. Few bothered to even look up as the Smuggler's Salvation approached. Miguel took to standing in the prow bellowing at them to get out of the way. Whether it was the faded paint, roughly patched sails, or vacant expressions, the impression Nilda had wasn't of industrious life but of a medieval hand-to-mouth existence.

"We're using the old ferry terminal on Holyhead as the main port," Kim explained. She, with an agitated Annette fidgeting next to her, stood with Nilda near the bow.

Nilda looked in the direction the other woman pointed. There were a couple of ferries, though she hadn't immediately recognised them as such. They were festooned with clothes drying on the railings and over the sides. Long cables snaked up from the shore through portholes and into the ships. Nilda guessed those provided them with electricity. On deck were dozens of people. Everyone seemed glued to a screen or fixed on what they could hear through headphones.

"It was like that when we left," Kim said as she followed Nilda's gaze. "You know, because of the power coming back on. I guess people want to pretend the world's back to normal."

Except it wasn't normal. Not when everyone had a weapon stacked nearby. It was far from the idea of civilisation she'd been expecting to find. She turned away from the ferries and saw the ships she should have noticed first.

"What are those?" she asked.

"Which? Oh, those. They're the grain ships," Kim said. "There are more on the main island. Fish can be traded for grain to make bread. That was… well, I think that might have been a mistake. Since everyone came in by boat, they've stayed on those boats, going out to fish when they really should be farming. I know the grain's not going to last forever. And that's the problem. We need to think of the future and… Oh. That's not good."

"What?"

"The Vehement." Kim pointed to a submarine tied up to the dock. Cranes stood nearby, and she saw others being pushed along the road towards it. Cables and tubing ran from pumps on shore into the boat around which there was a hive of frenetic activity.

"It's meant to be in the south Atlantic rescuing a hospital ship that was stranded down there. And if it's back here instead… well, that's going to be a big problem. I suppose I could… no, there's my welcoming committee. No doubt they'll tell me soon enough."

Nilda looked towards the small group waiting on the quay.

"Who are they?" Nilda asked.

"The baby is Daisy, the man holding her like she's about to explode, that's Sholto. And the man with the cane is Bill. Our welcoming committee. So if you'll excuse me, I better get Annette ready for this."

Nilda felt a sudden wave of jealousy that Kim had managed to create a family amidst the chaos. It seemed the mirror opposite to her own life.

A dockhand threw a rope to one of the waiting sailors. The ship was pulled close. Kim jumped across onto the quay, Annette behind. Before her feet had even touched the concrete, the man, Bill, ran over to her and made as if to hug the girl. Whatever row they'd been expecting didn't materialise. Nilda saw Kim smirking. The other man, Sholto, started to laugh, and the baby gurgled along. Annette, her pre-emptive anger turning to confusion, broke away from the man's embrace and ran, crying, up the road.

It was too much for Nilda. She turned away from the scene to find the French soldier Francois, standing by her side.

"Here, come with me," he said. "You'll need to see the doctor. I'll show you the way."

He led Nilda away from the docks and into a town too small for a hospital, but where a GP's surgery had been taken over and converted into a clinic. He left her at the gate, bidding a polite farewell.

"There's nothing really wrong with you," Dr Marcy Knight said, after a few hours of waiting, testing, examining, and waiting some more. "In fact, I'd say you were quite healthy."

"Really?" Nilda asked, surprised.

"Sorry, let me clarify that," the doctor quickly added. "There's nothing immediately wrong with you. And compared to most people who come in here, you are healthy. It's the high protein, low carb, vitamin rich diet you've been on."

"What about the radiation. I got sick."

"Vomiting?"

"Yes."

"Bloody diarrhoea?"

"No."

"Blood in the vomit?"

"No. I was just sick. Feverish."

The doctor nodded. "And how long did it last?"

"A day or two."

"And did it start after you drank rainwater?"

"I think so."

"That's happened to a lot of people," the doctor said. "We don't know exactly what it was, and it's hard to find out since, by the time anyone gets here, they've recovered. It wasn't radiation poisoning, beyond that I can only guess. It could have been something bacteriological resulting from all the dead bodies, or it might have been a weapon someone tried to use on the undead that got caught up in the weather system."

"But not radiation?"

"No. Definitely not that," the doctor said.

"And I won't... turn into a zombie."

179

"No. You're immune. A lot of the survivors are. It's impossible to work out an exact figure, but somewhere between two and ten-percent of the population would have had natural immunity. Among the survivors here, it's a little higher than fifty-percent. As far as we can tell it only offers immunity against the undead. Nothing else. Look, I'll level with you. I'm talking about the short term. Right now you're healthy. Medium to long term, that might be different. I don't know. It's too early to say. So many bombs were dropped that we've all become exposed. I can't even guess at the dose you've received, but on that island, so close to the Scottish mainland, it's far higher than anyone would call safe. You've a significantly increased risk of cancer and other chronic conditions. These days, realistically, chronic is fatal. But whether this is going to be a problem in five years or ten or twenty, I can't say. But then again, I can't predict whether you'll live that long anyway. All I'd say for now, taking in your age, is that I would advise you against having any children. Sorry."

"But what about family. I mean. Children. If I am immune does that mean…" She trailed off as the doctor shook her head.

"No, I'm sorry. Immunity doesn't seem to work that way. We don't have much to go on, but we're certain of that. I'm sorry. Do you have children?"

"I did." One last piece of hope died, and as it did she realised how small that hope had been.

She found she was looking out of the window. A boy of about six was trying to kick a football into a circle chalked on a brick wall. She could see a neat set of scars on his shaved head.

"What happened to him?" she asked.

The doctor turned to look. "That's Philippe. Philippe Umdumwe. We brought him with us out of a refugee camp in Mali on the day of the outbreak."

"Oh." There was a story there, but Nilda found she didn't care. "So what happens now?"

"You should rest. Just for a day or two. Get some food, some clothes, luxuriate in the healing power of light and hot water. Give yourself time to take it in, but not too much time. You don't want to wallow. We're all

180

broken. We've all seen those we love die, and we've each got our own guilt and regrets. That's in the past. We're here, we're alive, and if you choose to stay, there's work to be done. But you're free to leave if you want. There are trips to the mainland for supplies, and you can always catch a ride with one of them. Some people are talking about sailing down to Europe or Africa or even further. And if they can sort out the fuel problem there'll be expeditions to North America. Or you can stay here. What did you do before?"

"Before?" Nilda had to think for a moment before she remembered. "Nothing much. Nothing that would be much use here."

"No? Well, there's fishing, farming, and the militia. Fishing really means gutting and preparing. We've plenty of people who know how to use a boat. Farming means digging. We don't have the fuel to spare for machinery. The militia, that's just what it sounds like, our nascent army. They do the scavenging, setting up the safe houses, and that sort of thing. But like I said, take a couple of days to rest first."

"Where do I do that? I mean, I don't imagine money matters anymore and even if it did, I don't have any."

"We've plenty of room, free electricity, and clothes to spare. You need to go to Trearddur Bay on the other side of the island. It's just a short walk, but we're running the administrative side of the government out of a school there. They can sort out a housing allocation. They'll talk you through your options."

Nilda realised that she was being dismissed.

"Thank you, doctor," she said, standing up.

She went outside and breathed the air. She did it again, and then she looked about. It seemed almost normal. There were no cars on the roads, and no engines purring in the distance, but everything felt alive. She could hear voices, distant and nearby, and none sounded afraid.

She passed a shop window. Inside, a small group were carefully dismantling the shelves and counters. Nails were being pulled and stored in boxes. The countertops were being neatly stacked. She guessed they were to be reused or turned into something far more useful somewhere else.

181

There was a clatter and a curse, followed by good-natured laughter as someone dropped a shelving unit on another's foot. It seemed surreal, all of these people, all here, all alive, and all seemingly oblivious to what had happened in the past few months.

It was the quiet before the storm, she thought, remembering a conversation she'd had once with Sebastian. Or, really, one that Jay had had with him. He'd been studying those months after the Second World War had been declared but before the military had been built up to launch a counter attack. Having people wasn't enough to build an army. You needed to keep it supplied. Nails required raw metal. They required factories. She doubted there were any of those on the island. She moved onto the next shop. It had been stripped. Even the flooring had been taken up.

Whatever those nails were used for, what would happen when they were all used up? Perhaps there were cargo ships filled with raw steel out there, abandoned somewhere on the ocean or now crewed by the undead. Could a foundry be constructed? Probably. But were there enough people to work it? And what would happen when the steel ran out? She doubted that any mine would ever be opened again. How could it be run without machinery? Even forced labour wouldn't work, not when you would need as many guards to keep the undead at bay as you would to keep the labourers working. No, there would have to be expeditions to the mainland. Where do you find nails? Other than hardware stores, she didn't know. And how would it be carried back? Kim and the doctor had both said there was no oil. So all expeditions would rely on bikes and rowing boats. There was no other way. How many people would die on those expeditions just to bring back a packet of nails? What was that line? For want of a nail the kingdom was lost.

Power and tools and the knowledge of how to use them, that's what they had. The tools would wear out, and so too would the power plant. Within a few years, the lights would finally go out. Then what? This place would become some medieval serfdom. The last refuge of humanity, clinging on, desperately refusing to acknowledge that the time for their species had passed.

She started walking again, looking at the buildings in a new light. Some were stripped bare, others being stripped, and a few seemed occupied. She heard music coming from a flat above one shop. It was a cello and very definitely recorded. She didn't know the piece. All classical music sounded the same to her. It sounded like something Sebastian would play, something by Bach or Brahms or Beethoven, or one of those other dead old men whose names always began with a 'B'.

A little further on, the road ended in a stretch of parkland being dug up by a group of survivors clearly less happy than those stripping the shops. They hacked at clods of dirt and carried lumps of turf to a waiting cart. She was relieved to see a couple taking a break. No one yelled at them to get back to work. In fact, as far as she could see, there was no one directing them at all. It wasn't quite serfdom yet, then.

One paused in his digging and met her eyes. She got a hostile glare. The man nudged his neighbour. They shared a muttered comment. From the tone she guessed they were unhappy seeing someone not working as hard as they. She quickened her pace, wanting to get away from those looks. They'd found life here on Anglesey, but the fight for survival wouldn't stop. Electricity would make life easier for now, but not for long, and it still wouldn't be easy, not here or anywhere else, not ever again.

In which case, she decided, there was nothing here for her to stay for. And she realised she'd already made that decision. She had to go back home. She had to find her son. She had to bury him. But first, she would allow herself a day or two of sleep.

She looked up and saw the sea. She'd taken a wrong turn.

"Excuse me," she called out to a bearded man ambling slowly up the other side of the street. The man stopped. Nilda crossed the road to speak to him. He was dressed as a civilian - everyone she'd seen was - yet he carried an assault rifle over his shoulder.

"Wotcha," he said, cheerfully. "What's up?"

"I was looking for Trearddur Bay, but…"

"Let me guess. You're new here and looking for the school, but you've got lost? Yeah, last time I was back here, I told 'em they needed to put up some signs. Don't ask for a sea view."

"I'm sorry?" she asked.

"When they give you a housing assignment, they'll give you a choice. They'll ask if you want a sea view. Say no. I know it sounds nice, but the only view you'll get is of someone gutting fish. That's to say nothing of the smell. You can't get it out of your hair. They're filling up the houses down on the front, you see. It's easier to keep track of the newcomers that way. Your best bet is to have a look at the jobs-board first. Find something you want to do, and volunteer for it. Then you'll get a room with that work detail."

"I, uh, don't know that I'll be staying," she said, though she didn't know why she was confiding in the stranger.

"Totally understand," he said. "I feel the same way. This place is just too weird. It's like an ostrich farm."

Nilda gave him a quizzical look. "An ostrich farm?"

"Smells a bit, and everyone's got their head in the sand," he explained. "Ask them for a place at Wisteria Lodge, and tell them Chester sent you. Don't worry," he added. "It's a hotel, just over there. The Railroad uses it. There's dozens of us, but always more rooms."

"The Railroad?"

"Dumb name, right?" Chester said. "We go out to the mainland, find survivors, bring them back, set up safe houses along the route, that sort of thing. We always need new people, unfortunately. No strings. Just come along, meet us, eat with us, and see what you think. If you think it suits you, you can come back to the mainland with the next expedition. If you don't, you can still catch a ride and go your own way once we hit the shore. It's your choice, and it's better than waking up smelling like rotten fish."

"Maybe," she said.

"Fair enough. The offer stands. Right, the quickest way of getting to the school is to take the side roads. But if you do that, you're likely to get lost again. The longer but simplest way is to follow the road down to the waterfront, take a left down there by that pub, you see? The one with all those people sitting outside. Then follow the road for about…"

But she'd stopped listening. As he'd been talking, she'd followed his gesturing arm. She had looked at the pub. She had seen the people lounging at the tables outside. And she had seen him. She had recognised him instantly. How could she not? Her entire world shrunk. Chester, still giving directions, was forgotten as she began to sleepwalk down the road, her eyes fixed on the not-so-distant figure. How did he get here? How long had he been here? Could it really be him? Was it just a trick of her brain? No. With each step closer, as impossible as it was, certainty grew. He seemed happy and carefree, sitting at a table with a group of others. She quickly glanced from face to face. She didn't recognise any of them. She turned back to him. His face was one she would never forget.

She started to walk more quickly. He looked so different. Not older, not really, but… matured? Something else? She wasn't sure. And then he stood up and picked up the sword. It had been lying on the table. He mimed a thrust, then a swing. She heard laughter from the group. She knew the sword. It was the replica gladius that Sebastian had given her son. It had to be.

She broke into a run. She tried to shout, but it came out as an unintelligible scream. Heads turned. She didn't notice. Her universe consisted of no one but her and the figure with the sword. She covered the distance quickly. The figure turned. He saw her, and froze in place, and she no longer had the breath for anything but running.

She could see his expression, see it turn from bemusement to confusion. And then, when she was only a dozen paces away, to terrified recognition. He brought the sword up in front. She didn't care. She leaped, her hands outstretched, reaching for Rob's throat.

They fell in a tangled mess, the gladius skittering across the road out of the man's hands. She started screaming a bellow of furious rage as her nails dug into his throat. And then there were hands pulling her off. Someone was talking, yelling at her. She couldn't hear the words. She just wanted to kill her betrayer. The arms were strong. They had her in a tight grip, lifting her off Rob and off the ground. She thrashed and kicked. Close to her ear she heard a muffled grunt of pain, but the grip didn't slacken.

At her feet Rob was coughing, his hands clasped around his throat. He crabbed backwards, well out of the reach of her flailing feet. Her berserker rage subsided, replaced by a cold fury. She became aware of the world beyond Rob. She realised she was being held by the man she'd asked for directions.

"Just calm down," Chester said, and she realised he'd been saying the same thing for a few minutes.

"All right," she said, slowly forcing herself to relax. "You can let me go."

"Yeah, I've heard that before," Chester said. He didn't loosen his grip. Nilda kicked out, backwards, but her feet flew through empty air.

"Please," Chester said gently, "don't do that."

"You left me for dead," she screamed at Rob. "You abandoned all of us. Mark, Tracy, Sebastian. You let the children die. They would have lived if you'd helped us."

Rob got to his feet. Nilda saw fear in his eyes. He bent to pick up the sword.

"That's my son's sword," Nilda wailed. "What happened to my son?"

"Leave it there," Chester said, addressing Rob. "I said leave it!" There was a dark menace in his growl, something that even cut through Nilda's own pain.

Rob paused, and glanced at the people with him, and then at the small crowd that had gathered. He looked beyond Nilda, then at the big man holding her. He licked his lips, and bent again to pick up the sword.

"Don't move," the big man hissed. He was addressing Nilda, but she'd started thrashing again.

"All right, what's this then?" another voice asked. The crowd parted. An old man, leaning on a stick, limped into the space between Chester and Nilda, and Rob.

"That sword," Chester explained. "This woman claims it was her son's. Says this guy stole it."

"I see," the old man said.

"And I believe her," Chester added.

"Ah, I see," the old man said again.

186

"It's mine," Rob wheezed.

"Well, we'll see about that," the old man said. He took a step forward. "Leave it on the ground, sonny, and you and your friends go away."

Rob didn't move.

"I said leave it." Where the large man's voice had been full of menace, this older man's words were calm, almost regretful. His hand dropped to a short handled spear strapped to his belt. As he did so, half a dozen others in the crowd stepped forward, hands all going to weapons and tools at their belts. Rob backed away.

"You're new here," the old man said. "So perhaps you haven't learned yet, but there are rules. There are laws, but for a quiet life, the best one to remember is that what I say goes. Right now I'm telling you to clear off. Go on."

"Wait! My son! What happened to Jay?" Nilda pleaded.

Rob looked at her, nothing but scorn in his eyes.

"Like I told you," he said. "He died."

And Nilda remembered the figure in the firefighter's jacket and the scarf waving above the undead crowd. She slumped forward, feeling the total agony of loss once more.

Rob walked away. Some, but not all, of the people he'd been drinking with followed.

"Okay Chester," the old man said once Rob had disappeared. "You can let her go." Chester did.

"My name's George Tull," the old man said. "I'm the power that pushes the throne in these parts. That's a joke," he said, but on seeing her expression added, "but probably not an appropriate one. Think of me as the deputy mayor. Now, this sword, you say that's your son's?"

"Yes. Sebastian gave it to him. Um… an old teacher. A friend of ours. He said it was an antique replica. His retirement plan. He gave it to Jay."

"Jay's your son?"

"Rob was there. He said it was the zombies. But it can't have been. How would he have gotten the sword? He must have killed Jay." The words came out in a staccato babble. "Then we left. And a few hours later we got attacked. I went to help. So did Tracy. Well of course she would.

187

Mark was one of the people at the back. But Rob didn't come to help. They all died. Sebastian, Mark, Tracy. And he's responsible. And if he had the sword then he's just as responsible for Jay's death. Probably he killed him."

"Alright, alright," George murmured. He sounded uncertain.

"You said there are laws here?" she said, as calmly as she could manage. "Then I want him arrested. I want him charged. I want justice."

"No," George said. "You want vengeance. I can see that clearly enough, and the two aren't the same thing." He bent to pick up the sword. He turned it over in his hands, examining it carefully. His eyebrows rose in surprise. "Now there's a thing," he said. "You said it was a replica?"

"And an antique. Sebastian's retirement plan."

"Probably was, as well. Wish I'd thought to collect something like this myself. Still, if I had… Chester, do me a favour. I want you to keep an eye on this woman, sorry, what's your name?"

"Nilda."

"Really?" He looked at the sword again. "Well, that's appropriate. Chester take Nilda down to the King's Arms. Get her some food and—"

"I don't want food," Nilda said, "I want—"

"Justice, yes. And I'll see to that. But first, you could do with a meal."

"So, Nilda, I'm Chester Carson. Nice to meet you," Chester said.

"What? I know that. You already told me," she replied. They were sitting outside a pub about a mile further along the seafront from where she had confronted Rob.

"Yeah, I'm just being polite," Chester said. "It's what people do, isn't it? When they meet. They go through all those formalities like name, history, job, and all the rest."

She turned to look at him. He was smiling.

"You want to make conversation?" she asked.

"Well, as it happens, yes," he said.

"Why?"

"Partly because up until two hours ago, I was on a boat. Before that, and for the last couple of months, I've been wandering around Wales and the Midlands, saving people and watching others die, trying to get them all here. Don't get me wrong. I don't mind doing it, but there's not been much opportunity just to sit and shoot the breeze. And when I did get back here, I'll admit, I wasn't looking forward to it. I was expecting that I'd end up being part of an assault on some place up in Northumberland that's become the last bastion of the British government. Except I get told on the boat that it's all over. The war's won, so to speak. Quigley's dead and we've got electricity on Anglesey. So I was wandering around, planning my day, dreaming of a hot shower, some hot food, and an ice cold drink, and wondering whether I could manage all three at the same time. Then I met you, and now I'm here."

"You could leave," she said. "I'm not stopping you."

"Yeah, right. You heard the old man. He wants me to keep an eye on you, so that's what I'll do. But as I said, that's only partly why I'm curious. The other reason is that Mr Tull expects me to find out your story. We might as well get that part out of the way, and then we can have a go at normal conversation, or just sit in silence. I've had a lot of practice at that." He sounded affable and his tone was light, but there was an edge to him, an alertness as if he was ready to spring at any moment.

"I was on an island," she said. And she told him about the survivors from Glasgow and the Abbot, though not about his past.

"That's rough," Chester said, and seemed to be genuinely sympathetic. "There's nothing quite like the inhumanity of man. What about the sword? Tell me about that."

She did. She started slow, but the words soon came tumbling out, full of self-recrimination and bitterness.

"I'm sorry," he said, and again he sounded as if he meant it.

"There's no way Jay would have given up that sword. Not if he was still alive. Rob must have killed him. Or left him for dead. He lied about that and hid the fact he had the sword."

"Okay, but why? No disrespect, but a sword's just a sword. With the undead, it's no better a weapon than a crowbar. Believe me, I know."

"Why? I don't know. Ask him. Maybe he wanted Tuck's shotgun. Maybe he wanted her. Maybe both. Jay wouldn't stand by and let that happen. Because of that, or afterwards, he'd have had to kill both of them."

"And you're basing that on your knowledge of him?"

"And what he did afterwards." And she told him about their flight from the town.

"For what it's worth," he said when she'd finished, "I believe you. But it's not worth very much. We'll have to see what the old man has to say, but at the very least I reckon Mr Tull will let you keep the sword."

"What about Rob. There needs to be justice. There needs to be a trial."

"Well, that might be a bit tricky," he said.

"Why?"

"Lack of evidence. It's your word against his."

"He left me to die!"

"A lot of people have done that," Chester said. "Self-preservation isn't a crime. Not here. The sins of the past are ignored, if not forgotten. Take me, I wasn't exactly the world's most honest citizen, and now I'm a pillar of the community. To be frank, you'd have done better to wait until there was no one around and dealt with him yourself. And you can't," he added pointedly, "do that now."

She'd thought much the same herself. "He said there were laws," she said. "It doesn't seem like there are. I mean, how did he get to be in charge, then?"

"You mean Mr Tull?"

"Yeah, why isn't it a general or... well, someone younger?"

"Well, he's not in charge. Mary O'Leary is. She's the mayor. And she's older than him. Spends most of her time in a wheelchair."

"And that makes even less sense."

Chester laughed. "Really? You expect sense in a world turned upside down and inside out? Who'd trust a general? Who'd trust a politician? Who do you trust to run the place except the people who don't want the job, but have proven they can do it?"

"I've heard that expression, and I've never believed it," she said. "How *did* they get the job?"

"Well, broadly speaking, you had a lot of different groups arriving here about the same time. You had Mister Mills and the crew of the HMS Vehement. That's a hundred or so submariners who'd just fought a pretty nasty naval battle a few hundred feet beneath the waves. Then you had Sophia Augusto, the captain of a fishing trawler, who'd just rescued a few thousand people out of the ill-fated flotilla that tried to cross the Atlantic. Then there was Leon and Francois and their ragtag military unit made up of the survivors who'd made out of Ireland. Those were the units who'd made it out of the nightmare in Europe and Africa. Then there was Mr Tull, Mrs O'Leary, and Bran, leading this procession of survivors up through England and Wales. They were travelling slowly, and perhaps because of that or perhaps not, they'd had to fight their way across the country. Throughout it all, Mrs O'Leary was the one who'd had the ideas. I guess people looked at her and said to themselves that if she could find the strength to keep going, then so could they. And here's the thing, they all did. The ones who stuck with her, they all lived. But not everyone did stick with her. Quite a few took one look at this very civilian group of the old and young, and headed off on their own. They died, and when you come across someone who's now undead, but who a couple of days ago was going on about how they could make it on their own, that makes it starkly obvious which is the winning team."

"That doesn't explain why she's in charge."

"After they got here you mean? Well, that's pretty obvious really. None of the others wanted to lead, but at the same time someone had to. You just had hundreds of nuclear bombs being dropped. Civilisation had collapsed. Half the world had tried to kill the other half, and no one had a clue whether anyone was going to wake up the next morning. Amidst all that, you had Mrs O'Leary, who comes across as a sweet old grandmother, and like all sweet old grandmothers she's as hard as nails. They set up a council. All the groups are represented on it. Not that there's much by the way of politics going on. Even here it's all about survival."

"That sounds... I don't know. Ramshackle."

"Well, it works. More or less. If you ask him, Mr Tull will give you a history lesson on how all countries were founded that way. Me, I don't think it matters. I don't think we need leaders. Everyone just has to do all they can, eat no more than their fill, and take nothing they don't need. If everyone does that, we might still be sitting here this time next year. That's about as much as anyone can hope for."

"What about these safe houses, what are they?" she asked.

"Pretty much what they sound like. We find a place that has a good escape route, rig up some flags outside, and leave some food and directions to the next one along the road. A lot of people had food for a few weeks, or could find that much in the buildings nearby. They stuck it out as long as they could, but the supplies always ran out. They took to the road with no real notion of where to go or how to survive. Left on their own out there in the wasteland, they'd just fight among themselves. Anyone left standing would be killed by the undead. The safe houses are about giving people another option. Come to Anglesey and get as close to a normal life as you'd get anywhere else."

"Do many come?"

"A few. Not as many as there were. People can feel that winter's coming. There are a few still holed up in castles and stately homes or in the cities. We know about some of them, but there's not much we can do to help. There are some who don't want help and others who don't want to be found." He shrugged. "We do what we can because that's all that we've got left, but it's not going to be enough. Electricity's great, and it makes life easier, but it doesn't make staying alive any easier. But that's not my problem. I just go where I get sent. That's enough for me."

Silence settled. Chester made no further attempts at conversation. He seemed happy enough watching the waves.

An hour later, George returned. He didn't come alone. A boy of about twelve was pushing a wheelchair. In it was an old woman.

"That's the mayor," Chester whispered.

"Seriously?"

"Yeah. Sit tight. I better go and have a word." Chester stood up and walked to meet them. As he approached, the woman spoke to the boy. He wandered off towards the seafront. After a few minutes of quiet conversation, Chester wheeled the mayor, with George walking alongside, to the table at which Nilda sat.

"Nilda, welcome to Anglesey. I'm Mary O'Leary. Elected mayor because no one objected too strongly."

Nilda nodded, waiting for the woman to go on.

"George?" the mayor said.

"Right," the old man took out the sword and handed it to Nilda. "That's yours, I believe."

"And Rob?" Nilda asked. "What's going to happen to him?"

"We don't know. Not yet," the mayor said. "It's your word against his."

"I see," Nilda said.

"I'm sorry," George said, "but all we *know* he did was abandon you to die." He looked at Chester. "And we can't hold that against anyone."

"So you're letting him go?" Nilda asked.

"For now," the mayor said.

"Tell me," Nilda asked, "how many people voted for you?"

"I was elected when our numbers were fewer," she allowed.

"Which isn't what I asked. Was there a real election? Or was it just that you were appointed by others, and everyone else went along with it."

The mayor sighed, but she didn't answer.

"As much as things change," Nilda said, "they always stay the same. That woman, what was her name? Kim. She told me about the outbreak. Said it was all about some small group of politicians wanting power. Seems to me like it's much the same here. You've no justice. No laws. No mandate to govern. But everyone is frightened. They're all scared. They'll do whatever you ask because they've nowhere else in the world to go. No matter how bad life is here, it's better than what they had out there. There's no freedom. This," she waved her hands. "All this, it's just a prison, only one where the inmates don't want to escape."

"Yes. Yes," the mayor said. "That's broadly true and completely wrong at the same time. We have a chance to build something new, something different. Something better than all that went before. That has to start with forgiveness."

"Oh yeah? You're saying that if you had the person responsible, the person who created the zombies, here, right here on this island, you wouldn't just put them up against the wall?"

There was an uncomfortable shuffling of feet.

"What?" Nilda said. "No, wait. You're not... you're telling me you *do* have the person responsible here?"

"He's quite mad," the mayor said. "And quite harmless. He thought he was creating a cure for all the world's—"

"Oh, you've got to be kidding me. What is this place? You have the undead outside, but you've let the monsters inside the walls!"

"It's not quite like—" George began.

"I don't want to hear it. I don't want to hear anything more. You can keep this place. With your electricity and your militia and your gentile tyranny. I want no part of it."

She grabbed the sword and stormed off.

"That," the mayor said, "went as well as could be expected. Chester, you go after her."

"You want me to keep her from going after that man?" Chester asked.

"No, Bartholomew and Thaddeus are watching him."

"Who?"

"That doesn't matter," Mary O'Leary said. "I want to you to follow that woman and keep her safe. I think she's serious. I think she's going to leave. Go with her."

"Back to the mainland?" Chester asked wearily.

"Yes. I suspect she'll head north, back towards where she lived. There's a job we need doing. It'll be on the way."

"Another one? Well, fine. What?"

"There's a wind turbine factory in Hull. George, give him the address."

"Hull? That's nowhere near Cumbria," Chester said, taking a folded map from the old man.

"It's closer than here," George said. "We want you to see if the turbines are still there."

"Turbines? You're talking about the factory they built at the port," Chester said. "I remember reading about that. Why not just send a ship?"

"If we knew the factory was still there, we might," George said. "Hull took a beating. Only conventional weapons—"

"We *think* it was only conventional weapons," the mayor cut in. "You'll need to take a Geiger counter with you."

"I'm liking this less and less," Chester muttered.

"Well, that's the extent of the bad news," George said. "Mister Mills reckons it was just conventional weapons, and I'll take his word for it. What we don't know is whether the factory is still intact. If it is, and if the turbines inside are undamaged, then we want to bring them out."

"What for?" Chester asked.

"Did you hear about Svalbard?" George asked.

"Not really."

"There are survivors there," the mayor said. "And they have oil thanks to a NATO supply dump on the island. It's all refined, and there's enough to get the North Atlantic Fleet all the way down to some haven in the southern hemisphere. They won't give it away because they've been using it to keep the generators running for the seed vault. To describe their stewardship of that place as zealous doesn't even come close. But they are willing to trade. If we can give them another power source, they'll give us the oil. All of it. For now we're having to make do with a few barrels, just enough to take a tender up to the north with a doctor and a dozen chickens. In exchange we'll get…" She shook her head. "That doesn't matter. The important point is that those wind turbines in Hull represent our best chance of trading for all we need."

"If they haven't been blown up," Chester said flatly. "And what'll you do if they have? Send some of us up to Svalbard to take the oil by force?"

"No," the mayor said flatly. "There's been enough killing. You're not the only person we're sending out, but if none of you find anything we can

195

use, we'll give them the Vehement and its nuclear power plant. But I'd rather not do that. Not yet. We still need that submarine."

"Alright, fine. So I'll go to Hull. And if the factory is intact, what then?"

"Now we're on to the second part of the operation and why we can't just send a sailing boat in to have a look from the harbour. We need to know whether there are any survivors in the city. Any signs of life at all."

Chester mulled that over for a minute. "Why?" he finally asked.

"Because the turbines are large," the mayor said. "The only way of getting them out is with some heavy lifting equipment. Right now, the only thing we have that meets that description is helicopters. We were planning on using them to rid Britain of the undead, so we'll combine the two missions. The helicopters will take off from various spots along the west coast, and fly east to converge on Hull. When they get there, we'll use them to load those turbines onto some barges. Following close behind will be the undead. We'll destroy them. Not all of them, we would never get that lucky, but we'll be able to eliminate enough that going out into the mainland turns from downright suicidal into only almost-certain death."

"Wait." Chester suddenly understood. "That's why you want the submarine. You're planning on using the nuclear missiles?"

"Can you think of any other way to get rid of all those zombies?"

"Well, no, but give me time and I would. You can't drop more bombs on the mainland. What about the fallout? You'll be irradiating a whole swathe of the countryside."

"Which," the mayor said, "thanks to the undead, is currently useless to us."

"Look, Chester," George said. "We've been going over this, looking at it from all angles, and I don't mean just me and Mary. We can't get the conventional explosives in there. We don't have the fuel for that. Cruise missiles aren't going to do it, and that leaves the Trident warheads. It's all we've got left."

"It seems… after all the bombs that have been dropped, that we should use more seems… it just seems wrong."

196

"The normal rules stopped applying in February," George said. "So we're waiting on you. Go with this woman. Find out what that factory is like."

"When by?" Chester asked.

"Before the weather changes."

"That's not much help."

The old man took out a bag hanging behind the wheelchair. "It's a sat-phone," he said. "The batteries can be charged with a hand-crank. You call us when you get there, you tell us what it's like, and we'll arrange for you to get picked up when the helicopters come in. Alright?"

Chester took it. "You know, sometimes I wonder why I don't just walk away."

"Well, have a look at this." George handed Chester a bundle of papers. "You'll find your answer there."

"What's this?" Chester asked.

"A journal. Written by Bartholomew. It explains what happened. The conspiracy if you want to call it that, and how it all started."

"Oh? And what's that to me?"

"You're in there," George said.

"I am? Where?" He began to open the book.

"Later," George said, putting a hand on the book and closing it. "You'll have plenty of time for reading out in the wasteland. There's one last thing. Now where is it...? Ah, here."

"A smartphone?"

"No. Well, yes, but not exactly. We've got control of some of the satellites now. One of them's been taking pictures of the mainland. We've got some photos of Hull. The resolution's not too bad, either. Not up to spy-satellite quality, but you can see where a cruise ship rammed into the docks. Those pictures might be of use, and if we can, we'll get you some more. The real reason you want this phone is that we've two other satellites just tracking the hordes. If you plug the smartphone in..." He peered at the sat-phone. "Here, somewhere, you can use it as a screen and get real time data on where the horde is."

"So we can avoid them?"

"I imagine you'd want to. Now, let's see…" The old man glared for a moment at the two devices. "Chuck," he bellowed at the boy throwing shells into the sea. "Come over here and show me how this works, again!"

Nilda prowled the shoreline, sword in hand, staring at the sea. Her first thought had been to commandeer a boat, but they all had their electricity coming from cables snaking across from nearby houses. She doubted there was fuel for any of the engines and she wasn't going to try a sailing boat. She'd been shipwrecked once, and it wasn't an experience she wanted to repeat. That left a rowing boat. There were plenty of those, but even through her fury, she didn't want to steal from people who had so little.

She heard footsteps crunch on the pebbles behind her. She turned and saw Chester.

"You're going to scare people, waving that thing around like that," he said amiably.

"So? What are they going to do about it?"

"Them?" he nodded towards the boats. "Nothing. Or do you mean the mayor? Well, she's likely to send someone like me down to talk to you."

"And how are you going to stop me?" she asked, flexing her grip on the sword.

"Stop you? I didn't say I was going to stop you. I'm going back to the mainland. I thought I'd offer you a ride."

"Why?"

"Because that's where you said you wanted to go," he said.

"They asked you to?"

"They asked me to go back. There's a factory in Hull they want me to look at. You said you were from Cumbria, and I reckon that's where you're heading back to, so since we'll be going in the same direction we might as well travel together."

"Hull is miles away from where I'm going."

"It's still the mainland," he said with a shrug.

"And you're going on your own?"

"No," he said patiently. "I'm taking you with me. Like I said."

"I'm not working for that woman. Or anyone else," she said.

"Alright. Fine. Listen," Chester said. "For good or ill, they keep people safe. They keep this place working. They keep people alive, and maybe they'll do a good enough job that there'll be people still alive a generation from now. Look about you, Nilda. This is it. This is civilisation. It's all that's left. Our species is dying and we're still not safe. I'm not sure I agree with everything they've done, or what they're planning to do, but this is the only chance anyone's got, and we've only one shot at doing it right. So come with me, maybe we can do some good out there."

She gritted and ungritted her teeth, clenched and unclenched her jaw, gripped and regripped her fist around the sword that a friend she'd undervalued had given to a son she had lost. She remembered the words of the Abbot. She closed her eyes, and let her anger go.

"I want to find my son. I want to bury him," she said.

"Then we'll find him."

"It won't be easy. I mean, it could take a long time."

"It'll take as long as it takes." Chester turned to take a long slow look around the island. "Yeah, of all the things I thought might happen, of all the places I thought I might end up, it was never anywhere like here."

"You're a strange man," she said.

"I died and was reborn."

"You're religious?"

"I mean, I was bitten and I'm still alive. I spent a night thinking about all I'd done, and then the next morning I woke up and found myself alive. After that... Have you ever found yourself the victim of events? That no matter what actions you take, you're always reacting to those of other people? Well, I realised that, and I understood that tomorrow I might be dead, but today? Today I'm my own man walking under the sky."

"Very poetic."

"My gear's over at The Lodge. We'll get that. And you'll need more than just a sword. Come on."

He led her along the beach until they reached a large guesthouse overlooking the sea.

"Wisteria Lodge," Chester said. "We keep the fish gutting on the other side of the island."

"I'm not staying here," Nilda insisted. "Not for a single night."

"No, of course not. I mean, who'd want to spend a night in a real bed without having to worry about whether you were going to wake up surrounded by the undead? But we do need supplies."

He led her up the path through a still-manicured garden.

"Hey Bran." Chester nodded to a smartly dressed man who sat on his own outside the main doors. Running from just below his eye down to his lip was a recent scar. Next to him was a chess set. He seemed to be playing against himself. Bran waved a hand in vague acknowledgement, never taking his eyes off the chessboard. Chester shrugged.

"Come on," he said to Nilda. "The storeroom's inside."

The storeroom wasn't what she'd been expecting. There were no metal-framed shelves, just rows of stacked plastic crates.

"This was the dining room?" she asked.

"Probably," he said, walking down an aisle of plastic crates until he found the one he was looking for. He opened it and pulled out a small rucksack.

"Bag," he said, throwing it to Nilda. "Clothes are in the boxes over on that side. Not much selection, I'm afraid. It's all come from a cargo ship that was close enough to be easily looted. Not great quality, either. I think this lot was all destined to be sold in a supermarket."

"Clothes are clothes," she said with a shrug as she opened a crate.

"Yeah, that's nicely stoic," he muttered as he grabbed an already packed bag from a stack on a table. He opened it and checked the contents.

"That'll do," he muttered. "You know how to use that sword, or will you want something else?"

"The sword will do."

"Fine. I'll get you a rifle."

"No," she said. "There's no point. It'd just be extra weight."

"You sure?"

200

She hefted the half-filled bag. "How much ammunition can you carry? Because however much it is, it won't be nearly enough."

"Suit yourself, but personally, I find one bullet at a time is always enough."

Two hours later Nilda found herself standing on the deck of a battered tender, watching Anglesey slowly recede into the distance.

"Get some sleep," Chester said. "It's going to take us a while to get up to Cumbria."

"They could have found a faster boat."

"Can't waste the fuel. Besides, not much point arriving at night. But stay up here if you prefer the company."

Nilda glanced over at the squawking crates of chickens, then followed Chester inside.

2nd September

"Come on, then. We're here."

"Where's here?" she asked, sleepily trying to remember where she was and who was asking the questions.

"Two miles from Whitehaven," Chester said. "This is about as close as we can take the boat. From this point forward, we're on our own."

He helped her into a small inflatable, and with the tide's help, rowed towards the town.

"You know," Chester said as he rowed, "that this was the last place in the UK to ever be invaded. And the only place to be invaded by the Yanks."

"What happened to it?" Nilda asked.

"It was during the War of Independence—"

"No, I mean the town. Was it bombed?"

Chester threw a glance over his shoulder. "Oh. Right. Yes. But only by conventional weapons. Conventional! Ha! Don't know why, but someone out there really didn't like the place."

The buildings were in ruins. All that remained were broken walls, shattered windows, burnt timbers, and collapsed roofs.

"When we get ashore, keep quiet," Chester said. "It's been a while since I came through here. Geography's kept the place reasonably clear of the undead, but that doesn't make it safe. We keep some bikes down near the railway line. We'll get those, then head east through the lakes. There's a safe house we can stay in about ten miles from here."

"I don't want to rest. I want to—"

"Get back and find your son," he cut in. "Yes. You said. But I've been awake now for about thirty hours. So we'll sleep there, then go on tomorrow. Now, shh! We're getting close."

They pulled themselves along the seawall until they reached a rusted ladder. Chester loosely tied the boat to one of the rungs, and then they climbed up onto the quay.

The town was eerily silent. Up close, the devastation was even more apparent. It was like nothing Nilda had seen before. Even in the news footage of war zones or disaster-hit areas, there was life. There were people. Here there was nothing but the sound of an occasionally falling tile or cracking timber.

"This way," Chester said softly, gesturing towards the north.

They picked their way through a litter of melted plastic, broken glass, chipped brick, and broken stone. And then she saw her first body, and the sight brought her to a sudden stop. She had seen the dead and the undead, but not the charred remains of someone whose skin had been seared from bone.

"Come on." Chester grabbed her arm and pulled her away.

They crept along a path that ran parallel to the shore for a few hundred yards until they reached a car park by the railway tracks. At the edge was an abandoned storage container.

"The bikes are in there," Chester said, pointing. And as he stepped forwards a zombie moved out from around behind it.

It was the most pathetic creature that Nilda had ever seen. The right eye dangled from its socket, bouncing against its decaying cheek with each limping step. The flesh on the left side of its face was charred and flaking. The right arm hung limply from a dislocated shoulder, ending in a hand with only one finger that twitched back and forth as it slouched towards them.

"I'll do it," Nilda said, drawing the sword. She hadn't noticed before how well balanced it was. It felt light and somehow right in her hands.

As she approached, the creature became more animated. Its mouth moved up and down, and she saw the teeth had gone. She brought the sword up in front and noticed the outline of a bee etched into the blade. She wondered why someone had done that. Then she dispelled all thoughts and questions and focused her attention on the zombie.

The creature stumbled, tripping on its own feet. With one hand on the grip, the other on the pommel, Nilda plunged the sword forward, twisting the blade as it stabbed through the creature's damaged eye socket and deep into its brain. The zombie collapsed to the ground, unmoving.

It was easy, she thought. Almost too easy. She tested her emotions and found she felt nothing. Bending, she cleaned the blade on the remains of its jacket, then sheathed the sword. She knelt and began searching through the zombie's pockets.

"What are you doing?" Chester asked.

"He was somebody's..." She looked at the remains of the face. "Son, I think. Maybe somebody's father. It's hard to say how old he was when he died." She found a wallet. "This is a human being, Chester. We shouldn't forget it. Someone may be looking for him. They could spend their entire life wandering the countryside, never able to rest until they know." She opened the wallet and pulled out a credit card. She tucked the wallet back inside the man's jacket, but put the card into her inside pocket. Then she stood up.

"Ready now?" Chester asked.

"If you are."

They took two bikes and cycled east. Chester knew of a path that cut through the Lake District. As the sun rose and they left town behind, Nilda became starkly aware of how much the world had changed. There were far fewer birds and even fewer insects. When she spotted a solitary butterfly flitting around the canopy of a spreading willow, she almost wanted to stop. Then she heard the wheeze of the undead slouching towards them. She kept on. The zombies were easily outpaced, and they reached the safe house less than an hour later.

It was massive, with ten bedrooms and two kitchens, three hundred yards up a steep slope overlooking Crummock Water. It was the type of house Nilda had never even bothered to dream of owning. She restlessly paced from room to room, knowing the agitation was caused by the uncertainty of what they would do once they reached Penrith. She tried not to admit it, she tried not to think it, but she knew the chance of finding her son was non-existent. Or she may find him but not recognise him. Or someone else may already have killed him. She would never know, yet she had to try, and she would keep on trying until, ultimately, she too would die.

She wandered back into the living room where Chester had lit the wood stove. On it a kettle slowly boiled. Chester himself was sitting in a chair nearby leafing through a bundle of papers.

"What's that?" she asked.

"It's a journal. Mr Tull gave it to me. Said I should read it," he said, glancing up. "Unless you fancy playing chess or something?"

"No. Not really," she replied, slumping into a chair opposite. Chester nodded and returned to the journal.

"Is it the one that guy…" She tried to remember the man's name. She couldn't. "Kim said something about a journal. It was about the outbreak and all of that."

"Yeah, this is it. Or the conspiracy behind it all."

"Oh." Nilda wasn't interested in that. It was just history and of no use to her future. "So why did the old man give it to you?"

"He said I was in it," Chester said, looking up again. "I haven't found that part yet. There's a lot of wandering around England while not very much happens." He flicked back a few pages. Then a few more, and a few more, and he suddenly stopped. He saw his name about a third of the way from the beginning. He read on, then went back and read the entry from the day before. He laughed.

"What?" Nilda asked.

"I found it. The part the old man was talking about. Listen, 'Chester Carson. A part-time criminal on his way to becoming a full-time fence.' That's me!"

"Really? That's all it says?"

"Yeah, just one line in some letter this guy found. A copper wrote it, left it in a cottage. This guy found the letter, and my name was mentioned in it. I got drafted into a work detail clearing bodies from a supermarket. There'd been a... well, a riot, I suppose. People wanting food. They got shot, and then..." He trailed off.

"Were you?" Nilda asked after a few minutes of silence.

"Was I what?"

"A part-time criminal."

"Oh no. I was very definitely a full-time criminal, but I didn't have anything to do with fencing. No, that was all handled by McInery. Shows the coppers never had a clue."

"You were a crook?" She found she was unsurprised.

"I was. And a good one," he said it with pride.

"House breaking?"

"Oh no. There's no money and too much risk in that line. N'ah, we dealt in data. We had this slick little operation. Or McInery did. We ran pop-up coffee stands all over The City. We'd clone cards. That was our bread and butter. We paid our rent by stealing phones."

"There can't have been that much money in that."

"Not in the handsets, though there was always someone in China or Russia who'd want a model that hadn't been released out in their corner of the world. But that wasn't our line. When I say we stole them to order, I mean that we'd get a name and be asked to steal a specific someone's specific phone. Always the work phone, and always to copy the data and make sure that the mark got it back without ever knowing it had been stolen. Bankers mostly, sometimes people in insurance. Now, there was a lot of money in that. And politicians, of course..." And he trailed off again, lost once more in his own memories.

"But you got caught?" she asked.

"Inevitably. That's the risk. Of course, McInery was known to the police you see. She was one of the few employers who'd offer a second chance to criminals like me. That was a brilliant cover for her. A thoroughly respectable philanthropist, and the old bill never had a clue what she was up to."

"But how did you get caught?" Nilda asked, intrigued despite herself.

"Usually the marks had more than one phone. One for family and friends, one for work. In the mornings, they'd be using their personal phone, eeking out just a few more minutes of social media and music before the daily grind began. They wouldn't notice the work phone was gone until they got up to the office, and then they'd come looking for it. And wouldn't one of the nice chaps running the little pop up coffee stall have seen it and chased after them, and handed it in at the reception to their building? That's how we usually did it. A banker in Liverpool Street wasn't to know an insurer in Bishopsgate had had the same thing happen to them the week before. It wasn't like anyone was about to admit to dropping their phone with its oh-so-proprietary data on it. The problem was with the people who only had one phone. That's how I got caught. Red-handed, literally. With one hand in this woman's jacket pocket."

"Ah."

"Quite. No doubt about my guilt whatsoever. So I copped to the theft and to a few dozen others. That's why I was in the cells when the outbreak hit."

"And that's what you did? Picked pockets. Forgive me, but you look a little large for that part."

"Oh you know what they say, size isn't everything. But I did a bit more than that."

"You were a leg breaker?"

He just shrugged. "I did... what I had to."

"Did you kill anyone?"

He paused before answering. "What I did and what I didn't do is all in the past. It doesn't matter. I might have been a bad man, by society's definition, and yours, but I wasn't evil. I've seen evil. I've seen... but that's in the past too. For the last six months I've been getting people to safety. Helping strangers survive. And that's what counts."

Nilda grunted. She didn't have an opinion on Chester. He was useful to her for now, and she had no plans for later. She leaned back in the chair and closed her eyes.

Chester stared at the stove, remembering the time after the outbreak. He shook his head, trying to dispel the images, trying to forget it all. It was long ago. It didn't matter. Yet there were some things he couldn't forget.

He opened the journal again at his name. He didn't think that this was the reference Mr Tull had wanted him to see. Idly, he flicked forward a few pages until he came to another name that he recognised. Cannock. His shoulders slumped as he read on. He threw a glance towards Nilda, but the woman seemed to be asleep. He read on, then he went back and read those few pages again. Cannock was dead. He felt relief at that. It was good to know he wouldn't meet the man somewhere out in the wilderness. Was that the part Mr Tull wanted him to read? Did he, in some way, blame Chester for the horror's Cannock had committed? No. He couldn't. Chester thought back to those conversations he'd had with the old man, but he'd never mentioned Cannock once. No one knew about their past. And really, what did it matter? Cannock was dead.

He turned to the front of the book and read it from the beginning. He stopped when he came to the house in Sydenham, and the man with the broken leg.

He read the words over and over again, and then he read on until he reached the end. Then he started from the beginning, reading far more slowly. He'd thought his life was tied to that of the broken-legged man. He was right. They *were* linked, and more closely than he'd realised. It was more than coincidence. It was something else. And what was he going to do about it? Should he do anything?

He glanced again at Nilda, then stood up, and put the journal into the stove. He watched the flames lick at the pages until only ashes were left.

"All sins are forgiven," he murmured to himself. "Except the ones that can't be."

3rd September

"There's the train line," Nilda whispered.

"Where your friends died?"

Nilda stiffened.

"Sorry," Chester said. "But look, we can't get any closer. There's just too many of them."

Nilda hated to agree, but there were well over fifty of the undead. Some on the tracks, others on the embankment. All were squatting silently. One of them wore the jacket of a firefighter.

"What are they doing?" she asked, turning away from the pack.

"Who knows? They get like that. Unless there's some noise, they'll stay, silent, unmoving, until there's some other threat. We'll have to leave them."

She took a breath. "Give me those binoculars."

"You recognise one of them?"

"I don't know. We took a bunch of jackets from the fire station."

Chester nodded and opened his pack. "I'll do it, he said, as she reached out a hand to take them. He raised the binoculars to his eyes. "Man. I'd say in his early fifties. Grey stubble, greying hair—"

She snatched the binoculars from him. "Sebastian!" she hissed, gritting her teeth to stop it turn into an anguished wail.

"Right. Is there anyone else?" He waited. Nilda didn't move. Her eyes were fixed on her old friend. "Nilda, do you recognise anyone else?" Chester insisted.

"What? Oh. Right." She sighed and slowly tracked across the crowd. "The woman, two feet to the left, missing her…" She swallowed. "Missing half her face. That's Tracy."

"Okay. Anyone else?"

"No. I don't think so. No."

"Fine," Chester grunted, unslinging his rifle. "Get ready to run. We'll go east, then south. We'll head to your old place, stock up on food, and work out a plan from there. The suppressor on this isn't great. They're going to wake up, and they're going to come after us. When they do—"

"I should do it," Nilda said. "They were my friends."

"Well, that's nicely romantic, but in the real world I'm the one who knows how to use the gun."

"We could leave them and just go," she said. "You don't have to risk yourself like this."

"I know I don't, but it's the right thing to do." He raised the rifle. "Ready?" he asked.

She looked down the road at the figures there. He pulled the trigger. The rifle cracked a soft shallow report. Sebastian, or the zombie who had once been Sebastian, collapsed.

Nilda stiffened, but before she could say anything Chester fired again, and Tracy collapsed. Nilda's soul screamed, but before it could reach her lips, Chester had grabbed her arm and was dragging her away.

They ran, hid, skulked through the streets and hid again, taking eight hours to cover the few miles to her old house. When they arrived, it wasn't like she remembered. Rain had soaked through the broken door. At some point a falling branch had smashed a window. When she went inside, she found an unfamiliar musty odour of neglect, tinged with the beginnings of rot. She stood in the hallway for a moment and half wished she hadn't come back.

"You said the food's under the floorboards in the bedroom?" Chester reminded her. "Let's get enough for a couple of meals and then get out."

She nodded and followed him upstairs. The door to the bedroom was closed. She thought she'd left it open. She reached out a hand to the doorknob. Chester gently stopped her and motioned for her to move to one side. He opened the door. Her old bedroom was empty. In fact, it was tidy.

"That's not right," she said.

"What?"

"I broke the door and smashed the crockery. I emptied out the drawers. I wanted the place to appear looted so no one would think to look under the floor."

"Smart. Except someone's come in and cleared up."

She bent down and ripped up the carpet. It came away easily. The tacks had been removed.

"Here. Help me," she said as she levered at one of the floorboards, then found she didn't need his help. The nails were loose.

"The food's still here, then," Chester said, looking at the array of cans.

"Not all of it," she said, as she knelt down. "There was more. A lot more. This is about half. Here, help me get up some more of the—" She stopped. She'd noticed an empty plastic bottle lying in the gap where one of the tins of ham had been. She'd remembered placing the ham there, remembered thinking that they'd keep it for Jay's birthday. The tin was gone. Instead there was a bottle, and as she leaned forward to pick it up she saw it wasn't empty. Inside was a piece of paper. Her hands shaking, she fumbled with the cap until she had the bottle open. She took out the note. She read it. She collapsed.

Chester caught her. He lowered her to the floor. He saw she was breathing, and then he saw the note in her hand. He took it, carefully and read:

"Hi Mum. I know you'll find this. I know you'll come looking for me. We can't stay here any longer. There's no water left. Me and Tuck went back to the school, and then we went to the bus depot, but you'd gone. I don't know where you went. So we came back here and waited, but the water's running out, and each day there's more of the undead. We've got to go. Tuck thinks the cities are going to be safer because of the evacuation. We'll find somewhere safe. You remember that place, the one where you first met Dad. We'll leave a note there. Maybe you won't ever read this, but if you do, then that's where we've gone. I'll see you soon. I love you. Jay."

Underneath was written another, though briefer, note.

"I will keep him safe. Don't worry. Tuck."

It was half an hour before Nilda woke up, and another hour after that before she was calm enough to talk.

"Alright," Chester said. "So where's this place he was talking about?"

"London," she said.

"Right. And who's Tuck?"

"She's a soldier. Former soldier. I didn't get her story, not properly."

"A soldier. That's good. Your lad's in good hands then. Well, come on. There's at least four hours of daylight left. We should get going."

"This, uh... Should we take some of the food?"

"No. The MREs are lighter, and we don't want any extra weight if we're going to cross the country. Now, I reckon we should cut down to Hull first. While you were... resting, I was on the sat-phone. I called Anglesey. They got some satellite images of Hull and I—"

"No. I'm going straight to London."

"Yes, so am I, but my way'll be quicker," he said. "Look at how long it's taken us to get from Whitehaven to here. We go to Hull, then find a boat and follow the coast and come in up the Thames Estuary."

She looked at him sceptically, but then nodded her agreement. They left the house, and headed south.

Epilogue: Silent Companions
M25, North of London

18th July

"OK, so that's the sign for 'attack'. And this is the sign for 'retreat', right?" Jay asked.

Tuck rolled her eyes, shook her head, and with as much patience as she could, showed him again.

"Yeah. OK. I'm getting it. I was never good at languages," he muttered.

She didn't reply. Taking out a knife, she knelt by the body of the dead zombie and cut out the crossbow bolt from its eye. Then she began working on the two bolts in its chest. She still wasn't convinced that the bow was much use, but she preferred the familiar comfort of a long distance weapon. Only when she was finished did she join Jay at the edge of the bridge overlooking the motorway.

"If we follow this road," Jay said, "we'll be in central London by nightfall."

Gritting her teeth in frustration, and as gently as she could considering it was for the thousandth time since they'd left Cumbria, she gripped his shoulder and turned him to face her.

"Sorry," he said. "I was thinking, if we follow this road, we can get to Westminster by nightfall."

"No. We'll go around," she signed slowly, mouthing the words clearly in the hope it might help him learn. "Find the river. Find a boat. Follow it into London. That's safer."

"Safer?" he signed back.

She nodded, restraining herself from clapping sarcastically. It had been a long journey down from Cumbria.

"And then where?" he asked. "I mean where in London do you think will be safe?"

"I'm not sure," she signed. "But I knew a Major who owned a house in Richmond. There were fruit bushes in the back garden."

"Richmond? Where's that?"

"On the Thames." She tried to think of landmarks he might be familiar with "Near Kew."

"Kew?"

She sighed. "Kew is where the botanical gardens are," she laboriously explained. "And there must be some fruit trees and vegetables growing there."

"Must there?" he asked.

In truth she didn't know. She had only visited the house once, but they had taken a walk down to Kew. It wasn't long after she had been released from hospital. They hadn't spent long in the gardens. Despite what the Major said to the contrary, she was sure everyone was staring at her scars.

"Yes. There must," she signed. "At the very least it's worth looking. You can't tell me you don't want some fresh fruit. I'm getting sick of all this dog food. Anyway, you know what they say, nothing ventured, nothing gained. Then we can follow the river to Westminster. That should be far safer than wandering through the streets."

He stared at her, clearly not understanding at all.

She sighed, took out a pen, and wrote it down.

"Okay. Cool. Kew first, and then we go to Westminster. And then…"
He didn't finish. He didn't know what would happen then. All he knew was that if his mother was alive, she would be looking for him, and since she hadn't been at home, he couldn't think of anywhere else in the world she might be.

"And then we'll see," Tuck finished, kindly. "Today we're alive. In a century we'll be dead, so let's let tomorrow take care of itself."

She looked at his blank expression, sighed and, once again, took out the notepad and pen.

To be continued…

Made in the USA
Columbia, SC
16 March 2019